HUMANITY REMADE

PROJECT OLYMPUS

MICHAEL W. LANE

To Aunt Debbie,
Thanks for all of the support!
Lots of love,
Michael Lane

ISBN: 978-1-7370300-0-3

This book is dedicated to the only things in life that truly matter; faith, family and friends.

CONTENTS

ONE
BRIEFING

A FEELING of dread rushed over him, overwhelming his senses. He could feel his heart racing, the deafening heartbeat seemed as though someone was pounding directly on his ear drum. Every muscle in his body felt as though it was made of stone, freezing him in a sort of personal concrete prison. His eyes darted wildly as though he expected to spot imminent danger. He was oblivious to the smell of dust but not its taste. The feeling of the surface that he laid on was cool and gritty, the rough texture noticeable with every slight movement. The steady rapid drum beat that enveloped him began to give way to a woman's cry. The cry grew in intensity as he became more aware of his surroundings. As his eyes adjusted to the dark, he began to make out objects from his narrow field of vision.

From under the bed, the small space between the floor and the bottom of the frame had become his only window to what was happening. A faint light from under the bedroom door barely illuminated the very basic surroundings, the concrete floors and walls, the metal frame of the bed, and the small wooden legs of the nightstand. The door slowly began to open as unintelligible conversation occurred between sobbing. He seemed upset with himself that he couldn't make out the conversation, it was just too muddled to understand. Six people entered the room, distinguishable only by sets of shoes. One of the pairs of shoes seemed familiar but he couldn't quite place how he knew them. Four others wearing what looked like military boots, more than likely male but hard to tell from his vantage point, moved to surround the bed. The boots landed on the ground with a dense thud, kicking up enough of the dust for him to notice that he has been holding his breath since they walked in. He took a small breath and held it once again. Almost as soon as he did, he felt a building cough. The stress of holding in the cough caused sweat to bead on his forehead like dew gathered on an early spring morning. He managed to work through the cough, trying very hard not to focus on it.

Garbled voices spoke unrecognizable words while the intent reignited his feeling of dread, they'd come to take him away. The sounds of arguing escalated as the feeling of dread turned to panic. He tried his best to subdue the rapid escalation of adrenaline coursing through his veins but was only somewhat successful. The voices grew louder, but it seemed no matter how loud they got, he still couldn't seem to make out what they were saying. A sharp scream, with a pitch that would surely shatter even the thickest glass, cut through the voices as a hand reached under the bed toward him. He tried to fight it, but it was no use, whoever was pulling him out from under the bed was impossibly strong. As he was being pulled out from under the bed, the light from the open door became blinding and obscured their faces.

Harden jolted awake just before he was able to see their faces, he grasped for air as though he had been underwater the whole time. A feeling of calm gradually overtook his panic as he realized it was just a dream. It was the same dream, a nightmare really, that had become an almost inescapable inevitability. There were slight variations from night to night, but the same paralyzing fear persisted. He knew now that he was back in his room. He looked around, seeing the familiar sight of his desk, his gear, his closet door. He breathed a sigh of relief as he looked down at himself, noticing he was drenched in sweat. He moved himself to the edge of his bed and sat up, placing his bare feet on the cold floor. He looked down at them as his attention turned to the disc-shaped devices attached to his ankles. He ran his hands up the thin metal bar that led to the next disc on the side of his knee. He couldn't remember a time when he didn't have the exoskeleton, now it was a part of him, like any other body part. It provided some comfort to know he was the same person as before he went to sleep, a 19-year-old soldier in the UNIC, but not just any soldier, a TITAN. He stood up and the lights brightened, revealing the scant detail of his room. The room was devoid of any decor, cold and sterile, serving only the most basic of functions. His room was not unlike every other soldier's room; four metal walls, a bed sitting on a metal frame, a small metal desk with a rigid-looking metal chair, and three doors. One door led to the bathroom, the other door was for his closet which had a large mirror hanging next to it, while the third door led to the hallway. As he moved to a door that led to the bathroom, he removed his clothes and stepped into the bathroom. There was no distinguishable shower in the room, simply a large showerhead protruding from the ceiling and a small drain underneath. As he stepped under the showerhead, the water began to flow. He lingered under the water, holding his hands against the wall as the torrent of water collided against his head, splashing and cascading down his body, while the remnants of his dream continued to haunt him.

Harden finished his shower, unable to escape the feeling that somehow, everything was off, that something just wasn't right. This wasn't the first time he had these feelings, he had felt this way for most of his life. Once he was finished, he grabbed a towel off of an unassuming shelf and moved to the sink. The metal sink almost blended into the wall, as if the wall had grown the sink as an appendage. He brushed his teeth and moved from the bathroom to his closet door, as he walked by the mirror next to the closet door, he paused to glance at himself. This wasn't done from a place of vanity but out of the desperate hope that a revelation may stare back at him. He looked himself up and down for a moment. His hair was a dark brown and faded on the sides to a short and manageable length on top. His green eyes seemed to almost swirl as he tried to look deeply into the window to himself. He stood tall around seven feet, toned and muscular, seemingly a perfect human specimen. He was after all, a TITAN, an enhanced human infused with nanites.

Nanites were nanometer-sized robots injected into humans to augment and enhance their physical characteristics. The nanites worked on a molecular level to help a human grow to be stronger, faster, and healthier. He shook off the disappointment when no revelation struck him and opened the closet door to reveal a meticulously organized closet. Black long sleeve shirts hung in a tightly condensed group, next to it were his pants, and finally jackets. Below the shirts and pants were three drawers attached to the back of the closet itself. He opened one of the drawers to grab a pair of boxer briefs and put them on. He then took one of the pairs of pants off a hanger and put them on as well. The holes in the pants seemed tailor-made for his body, fitting precisely over his discs which allowed them to protrude through the holes in the fabric. He pulled a shirt from a hangar and stretched it over his torso, it had the same fit, allowing the discs to protrude through the holes. He opened the top drawer and grabbed a pair of socks from a stack that looked like someone had just opened a brand new pack and placed them there. Under the drawers were four pairs of black sneakers, all exactly the same. He looked into the mirror once again after closing the closet, moving close to the mirror, causing it to fog slightly from his breath. He tried once again to search for an answer where none existed. He felt the same familiar disappointment that always followed his futile attempts for answers, bringing himself back to reality before opening his door to leave the room.

He made his way through the barren hallways of the compound, turning down hallway after hallway before arriving at an elevator. He waited for only a moment before the doors opened, the sensors recognized that someone was waiting to use the elevator. He pressed a button as it began to move, bringing him to the common level of the facility. The doors opened as Harden moved toward the mess hall, seeing that some of his team was already in line. They were earlier than they typically would be, but Harden knew why, it was the last day of their deployment, after today, they would be going back home.

Harden grabbed a tray, glancing down only briefly at the unappetizing mix of blobs and goops that were slopped onto it, and headed toward the table. Toa and Coughlin were already sitting down as Harden approached. Toa always looked out of place sitting at any table, he was built like a tank, even compared to other TITANs. His dark tan skin, shaved head, and homemade tattoos rounded out his unique appearance. It was almost like he was designed to be the team's heavy weapon expert, but his personality often clashed with the perception his physical appearance demanded, a lighthearted jokester who cared more about making others laugh and enjoying life than following the rules. Coughlin sat next to him, her proportioned but athletic build, jet black shoulder-length hair, and lighter skin contrasted against Toa's dominating appearance. While she might have been overshadowed by Toa physically, she had more than enough grit and attitude to be his equal or better.

"So, finally ready to get off this rock?" Toa asked as Harden sat down on the opposite side of the table.

"You know he is," Coughlin replied for him.

"I'm sure he can't wait to see her," Coughlin continued in a jokingly mocking tone, making kissing gestures toward Toa.

Toa played along with Coughlin, making the smooching sounds while looking at her with his best puppy dog-eyed impression. Harden shot them both a glare before smiling and looking down at his tray. They knew him all too well, all of the TITANs had grown up together but being on the same team afforded little in the way of privacy.

"Yeah yeah, can we just finish eating so we can wrap this up and get back?" Harden asked while devouring his assortment of slop.

"Well, we're still waiting on Zhou and Jossen so no rush," he replied. Toa was cut off as Zhou approached, sliding next to Toa but not budging him an inch.

"Don't wait on my account, this food is almost not worth the effort," Zhou said as he stirred one of the piles on his tray with a spoon.

Zhou was the brains of the team, tall and lean with a scruffy head of black hair. His energy was unmistakable as he seemed to constantly be moving, his leg bouncing almost rhythmically under the table. He would always be looking around, multi-tasking between the current situation and the million thoughts running through his head.

"You guys almost done?" a voice demanded more than asked.

Jossen appeared at the table, seeming to have eaten most of his food before even putting his tray down. Jossen was distinct among the group, every aspect of his appearance and demeanor screamed military, from his crew cut to his posture, to his need to control the situation.

"Yep," Harden responded, as everyone else kind of just nodded.

"We have like five minutes left. We need to report in," Jossen reminded everyone.

"Dude, it's Friday...relax!" Toa said as he leaned forward onto the table and finished his food.

Jossen took pride in his leadership role, connecting this duty directly to his own self-worth. He often came across as an overbearing parental figure, keeping tabs on what everyone was up to and making sure no one got in trouble, he took this responsibility very seriously. Even the tone of his voice demonstrated his commitment to the role, only breaking character on the rare occasion they weren't on deployment or operating in their official capacity.

"That's my point, let's wrap this up so we can get back to the Forge. You can relax there," Jossen reminded Toa.

The UNSS Forge was one of 5 starships in the United Nations Interstellar Corps. These 5 starships were enormous, housing populations rivaling that of any major colonies. They had capabilities of faster than light travel and could mobilize the largest military force humanity has ever known, they provided the UNIC a near-universal presence.

The team made their way out of the mess hall and into the elevator, heading up toward the ground floor. They exited the elevator and moved down the corridor toward the hangar. As the doors opened, natural light flooded their vision, overpowering the artificial light that in comparison seemed dull.

"Almost late," a UNIC officer said as he approached the team.

"Almost," Toa responded, as he could feel the disapproval beaming from Jossen.

"Last patrol around here for a while. I would be lying if I said I didn't mind you leaving. I always feel better with some TITAN boots on the ground," the officer said.

"Yeah," Jossen replied, trying his best to hide the disdain he had for the necessary but mundane patrols.

While Jossen knew the importance of patrols and reassuring the public that the TITAN program was there to protect them, he always felt it to be a waste of time. He preferred the satisfaction of an assigned mission, completing an objective always renewed his feeling of self-worth.

"Well, let's get to it," Jossen said as the team made their way toward the opening of the hangar.

As the team made their way out of the hangar, the nanites that were contained in the discs began to stream out in a frenzy. The mesmerizing swarm enveloped each TITAN's body in a suit of armor, appearing alive and crawling at speed to completely cover, solidifying once finding their place. As Jossen stepped foot onto the dirt in front of the hangar, his metallic armored black boot left an impression, compressing the dirt under his exaggerated weight. The rest of the team followed suit with almost identical armor, the only exception being slight variances in protrusions. The armor made each TITAN look even larger, bulkier, and ultimately more intimidating than their normal TITAN selves.

"We'll head down to the market and split up from there,"

Jossen said as he started moving down the dirt road and toward the colony.

It didn't take the team long to reach Taat, the colony that was established 15 years prior on the planet of Akimi. This planet was not that different than humanity's home world, Earth. It had a breathable atmosphere, similar gravity, and some local vegetation, but there were several distinctions when comparing the planets. The most obvious being the two moons that hung in the brilliant daytime sky, looming large like the watchful eyes of a being too vast to imagine. Another less obvious distinction would be the areas of the planet that were less hospitable to life forms. These were areas where gases on the planet were escaping, creating swaths of toxic fumes and preventing the existence of almost any life.

The market bustled with activity as the TITANs approached the market. They looked around to see merchants selling local and exotic livestock, fruits, vegetables, tools, handmade goods too numerous to count. Out of the sea of people not one of them seemed to even acknowledge the presence of the TITANs, they instead kept to their routine. While it was not an everyday occurrence, TITAN patrols were merely seen as a dog and pony show by the UNIC to show the resistance that they had these tools and were willing to use them.

"Ok, let's split up. Toa and Zhou, you're with me," Jossen said as he started down one of the bustling side roads.

Coughlin and Harden started off in the opposite direction. They passed by large buildings at least six stories high, very basic in design as they were designed to serve the most basic of functions. It was a monotonous sight, these large buildings crowded both sides of the streets with narrow alleys carving a thin distinction between them.

"I'm so glad this is our last day here," Coughlin said to Harden as they continued down the road.

"Yeah, it's nice to get off the Forge every once and a while but a month here is more than enough," Harden replied as a mother and her child caught his eye.

The mother seemed desperate to avoid eye contact with the TITANs while grabbing the child's arm and hurrying into one of the buildings. This was not a unique reaction, many citizens harbored skeptical feelings toward the government as a whole but in particular the TITANs. Some viewed them as an unstoppable tool of the government, one that can be turned on the people with a push of a button. Harden turned his gaze back toward the street. He knew there was bound to be resistance among the people here, but he also knew that no matter what they might try, the TITANs were equipped to handle anything.

"Tell me about it. I think a week is more than enough. The resistance knows the one sure way to destroy a TITAN... bore them to death by hiding," Coughlin said as she continuously scanned the surroundings.

The two stopped in their tracks as several large vehicles made their way toward them. They looked at each other before stepping to opposite sides of the road, allowing enough space to see both sides of the vehicles but not enough to allow them to pass. The vehicles slowed as they approached the two TITANs.

"Hey there!" the driver of the lead vehicle exclaimed.

"Hello," Harden replied in a stoic voice.

"Have to say, it's been a welcome sight to see you TITANs way out here," the driver continued.

"Where are you headed?" Harden asked.

"Just hauling this tritium over to the base," the driver responded.

Harden made his way around to the back of the truck. He wrapped his hand two times on the back door, signaling to the driver, he would like him to open it. The door hatch began to lift, revealing the cargo, piles of raw tritium from the mines. Tritium was dense, weighing too much for anything to be smuggled under a pile that size. Harden made his way back to the driver.

"Clear," Harden said as he motioned for them to continue.

"Thanks!" the driver said as he pushed the button to close the hatch back up.

The team finished up the remainder of their patrols and met back at the market. The sun still clung to the sky as the team looked up to see a falcon transport ship coming through the atmosphere and head toward the base.

"Well, it looks like our ride is here," Jossen said as the team continued toward the base.

The falcon had landed just outside of the base. From the outside, the base looked like nothing more than a large garage. The pilot of the falcon was walking back to the falcon from the hangar as the team approached him.

"Ready to go?" the pilot asked as he continued walking.

"I was ready to go three weeks ago," Toa responded quickly.

The pilot chuckled. "Just let the duty officer know you're heading out and I'll prep for takeoff," the pilot replied.

The team walked into the hangar and quickly found the duty officer.

"Well you're probably happy, but I always hate when TITANs leave," the duty officer said as he tapped on a tablet he was holding.

"You're all set. Enjoy the break Delta team," he said as he motioned to the falcon with his head.

"Thank you sir," Jossen said.

The team approached the falcon, the workhorse of the UNIC. They were used to transport troops, run supply drops, and provide air support in combat situations. They made their way to the back-loading ramp and boarded the cargo area. The cargo area was large enough to fit about 30 troops in bench-style seats that lined each side. The center of the cargo area was large enough to fit two small land-based vehicles. As the team settled into the seats, they heard the voice of the pilot in their helmets.

"Ok guys and girls, what do you say we get back to the Forge?" the pilot asked as the craft began to lift off.

"We're more than ready," Jossen replied as he leaned back slightly in his seat.

The falcon rumbled slightly as it left the atmosphere. The pilot entered the coordinates for the Forge and came across the comms once again to inform the team.

"Engaging the SD drive in 3...2...1," the pilot said as the subtle queasy feeling when entering a space distortion set in.

The falcon used the SD drive to distort space around the craft, allowing for faster than light travel. The ship disappeared from the space above Akimi and reappeared in the space around the Forge. The Forge loomed as large as a planet compared to the falcon. Smaller craft buzzed around it, like an enormous beehive with hundreds of worker bees coming and going. The falcon began its approach, bringing the scale of the Forge into focus. The falcon navigated the steady flow of ships and entered one of the dozens of hangar bays toward the aft of the starboard side and set down gently.

"Well here we are, home sweet home," the pilot said as he powered down the engines.

The falcon's ramp lowered as the team disembarked. As they stepped foot onto the hangar bay, they were approached by another team of TITANs who had just arrived as well. Epsilon team had just finished their deployment as well and were eager to see their fellow TITANs.

"Hey Jossen!" Rossi called out.

"Rossi, I hope you had a more interesting deployment than we did," Jossen responded.

"The only reason I didn't die from boredom was Coughlin here," Toa interjected while nudging Coughlin.

"Not even a rumor of the resistance on Virvel. It's like they went completely silent," Rossi responded.

"Well, I'm hoping that we actually get assigned a mission on the next go, these show of force deployments are the worst," Wu, another member of Epsilon team, said.

"Yeah, I think we're due. How many of these deployments have we done now?" Zhou asked Jossen.

"This one makes fifteen," Jossen said, taking a moment to count in his head.

"Oh well, at least this deployment is done. Time to get back to normal for a little bit anyway," Wu said.

Both teams made their way through the hangar bay to the freight elevators and headed for the lower levels, making small talk as they did. The lower levels of the Forge were designated for TITANs as the structure of the levels and rooms were designed with their unique proportions in mind. All of the lower levels had noticeably higher ceilings, wider doorways, and larger rooms. This wasn't the only reason they were confined to the lower levels though, the director of the TITAN program did not want TITANs mingled with ordinary military personnel. While there were several reasons for this, the prospect of distraction and influence were on the top of the list.

The teams exited the elevator on level 3, entering a long but spacious and brightly lit corridor. The corridors branched out to various parts of the level, a seemingly endless maze of hallways and doors, but the TITANs had been roaming these halls since they were toddlers. Every turn they made was subconscious, using instinct to navigate while they continued their banter. After several lefts and rights, various TITANs began to go in different directions, they headed to their rooms or to the social areas.

"Hey guys, I'll catch up with you later," Harden remarked as he broke from the group and headed for his room.

"We need to give that new sim a shot. How about we meet up in an hour," Toa told Harden.

"Sounds good to me," Harden replied.

Not a moment later, he arrived at his door, he stood there for a moment as a small circular orb embedded in the door turned green. The doors opened, revealing a room that was exactly the same as the one from the base on Akimi. TITAN quarters were established on every UNIC base and utilized the same design, there was a psychological reasoning behind it, but not one of the TITANs seemed to mind. He walked over to his desk and sat down, his mind focusing on only one thing since they landed on the Forge. He tapped on his desk and a screen projected above it, recognizing his biometrics the computer logged him in. He began scrolling through messages and looking around on the UNIC system before he realized he was supposed to be at the simulator. He couldn't believe an hour had flown by but headed out to meet Toa.

Toa was already waiting at the door to the simulator room with a line of other TITANs forming behind him when Harden approached. The line was populated by TITANs in groups of two, the simulator was made up of several rooms, but each training module could only handle two TITANs at once.

"I was beginning to think you stood me up," Toa said with a smile.

"Sorry, got sidetracked," Harden responded as he took his spot next to Toa

"The good kind of sidetracked I hope," Toa said, nudging him.

Just then, the door opened, Toa and Harden walked in as the door closed behind them. Three hours later, the two exited the room, visibly exhausted but celebrating as though they had just won the big game. They went back and forth, rehashing moments from the simulated battle they had just fought, laughing and talking about blowing this up and taking that shot as they moved back toward their rooms.

"That sniper shot though, man! That was crucial!" Toa said excitedly.

"Thanks, but if you didn't take out that tank, we would've been done in stage 6. That was insane, not sure whére you came up with that move," Harden said as he hit Toa on his shoulder.

"Well, I'm done for. I think that's the new workout though," Harden said as they approached his hallway."

"Definitely, we owned that sim. Anyway, I'll catch ya in the morning," Toa said as he nodded his head slightly.

Harden and Toa went their separate ways. Harden went back to his room, after a long boring day, that simulator was a nice distraction. He took off his clothes and headed for the shower where he lingered as usual. After the shower, he laid in his bed with a hesitant anticipation of the nightly ritual. Eventually, he resigned himself to the inevitable.

He woke up as he did most days, jolted from his sleep, although this time not drenched in sweat. He got up and put his clothes on. It was Saturday and their team was on leave, one of the only times when the TITANs were able to do as they pleased. Once he was dressed, he headed out into the Forge.

He made his way down the brightly lit corridors, not even the slightest bit aware of his surroundings. The evenly spaced lights in the solid white ceiling and the stunningly plain grey walls were as common as breathing. As Harden continued down the hallway, a door began to open just up ahead. Another TITAN stepped out from his room, wearing the same black shirt and pants that he had on. He had the same black sneakers, the same discs, in fact, the only way to tell them apart from behind would be by their hair. While Harden had short brown hair; the other male had a medium length, shaggy, dirty blonde head of hair. As Harden continued walking, the other male looked back.

"Another day, huh Harden?" Jones said as he waited for a moment for Harden to catch up.

"Yeah," Harden responded with a sigh.

They continued walking to the elevator as more TITANs began coming into the hall.

All of the TITANs would only be heading to one place this early in the morning. The mess hall on the Forge was far better than the slop they were served while deployed, and this mess hall was exclusively for TITANs. It gave them a space to develop a sense of community, as they all shared the same objectives and experiences.

"Hey! Hold the elevator!" a female's voice yelled from down the hall.

Harden immediately knew it was Taylor, he would recognize her voice anywhere. She was raised in the same phase as Harden, a group that has been together since they were six years old. As Harden and Jones walked into the elevator, the doors remained opened while four more TITANs entered. They were all dressed the same way as well, varying in height but all between seven and seven and a half feet tall. Even though Harden couldn't see Taylor clearly through the four people who had just entered the elevator, he didn't need to. He pictured her in his mind; she was on the taller side at seven and a half feet, her shoulder-length dark brown hair highlighted by blonde streaks, pulled back in a ponytail, her deep piercing green eyes, her small nose wrinkling slightly as she smiled. The thought of her smile led him to smile.

"Thanks," Taylor said as she got on the elevator just before the door closed.

"Hey, you made it," Harden said.

He always found himself speaking awkwardly around her, wanting to say something smooth but never getting it right. Taylor moved around some of the people to get closer to Harden. By this point, Taylor knew it was his way of trying to flirt, but she wasn't going to make it easy on him.

"Yup," she said as she was next to him now.

"What did you end up doing yesterday?" she asked, making small talk just before the elevator reached its floor.

"Toa and I tried the new training simulator on level 6, we were able to get to stage 8, not too bad," he said as people began getting off the elevator.

"Yeah, next time you give it a shot, let me know. I've been wanting to try it out, maybe a change in partners could help," Taylor suggested.

"Sounds like a plan," Harden said clumsily while searching his thoughts for a more charming response.

As they stepped off of the elevator, they arrived where the entire group had been headed, the dining hall. It was enormous, built specifically to service the 7,500 TITANs assigned to the ship. The mess hall was one of the few areas where every TITAN could socialize, providing enough space for all of them to eat together. There were 500 long thick metal tables with attached benches resembling reinforced picnic tables arranged in rows. While the mess hall rarely held all of the TITANs, as some were on deployments, the background noise was loud enough to drown out most people's own thoughts. Harden and Taylor grabbed their trays, got their food, and found a seat.

Harden enjoyed spending time with Taylor even though he was silent most of the time. Although they had grown up together and the feelings between them would be obvious to any person not socially challenged, they never acted on them. As they ate, Harden tried to think of something to say.

"Hey! You two love birds have room for one more?" a voice broke the silence, saving Harden from a potentially embarrassing moment.

"Hey Toa," Taylor said as she looked up from her tray.

"Hey," Harden said as he looked up and saw Coughlin behind Toa.

"Oh man, I heard Toa and Harden had some trouble in stage 8 was it?" Coughlin asked Toa as she sat down.

"Yeah yeah, say what you want Coughlin, maybe next time you and me give it a go," Toa responded, smiling and winking at Coughlin.

"I would but honestly you can't send a man to do a woman's job. I think Taylor and I would wreck that program," she responded smiling back.

Toa saw himself as a ladies' man, but truth be known, he was only one lady's man, and Coughlin knew it. Although the UNIC would not allow them to engage in relations, that didn't stop the TITANs from bringing it to the very edge, keenly aware not to push too hard. Every aspect of the TITANs life in this place was monitored; every conversation, every movement, and certainly any physical contact with anything intimate requiring immediate intervention by the administration. Toa was constantly being reprimanded for violating regulations, whether it was the deliberate innuendos or the tattoos or the constant advances toward Coughlin, but Coughlin loved it. She had as much of a thing for Toa as he had for her. They would go back and forth with insults and innuendos, seeing who could make the other blush or be left speechless. It wouldn't be hard to see why Toa would be crazy about her. She played off of him as though they were made for each other. When he wasn't looking, you could catch her twirling her hair while she stared at him.

By this time, the mess hall was lively with activity as TITANs were eating and talking, moving from table to table to catch up with others who were getting back from their deployments as well. Some of them discussed what they saw from the resistance while others anticipated what action they might see once they were deployed. Jossen moved through the crowd with purpose as always, making a straight line for Toa, Harden, Coughlin, and Taylor.

"So, I don't get an invite for the sim?" Jossen asked as he took a seat.

There was an awkward pause before a response.

"It seems as though these two love birds were the first of us to try it," Coughlin answered as she leaned into Toa's shoulder.

"I was actually able to get a spot with Jones for this afternoon," Jossen said.

"It's definitely a workout, that's for sure. Stage 8 seemed like a global war with all guns aimed at you," Harden chimed in.

Everyone finished eating, making small talk, as one by one, the group headed their own ways. As Harden and Taylor got up, she heard a voice call out from across the room.

"Taylor, what was that lady's name we ran into on

Chaac?" Cohen asked, motioning for her to come over to their table.

"I'll catch up with you in a bit," she told Harden and headed to the table.

Harden made his way to the elevator. His thoughts remained on Taylor as the elevator doors opened. He entered and moved to the side of another TITAN that was in the elevator.

"Harden, what are you up to on this fine Saturday?" Parson asked.

"Wanted to get an early start, the DEC is always packed on Saturday," he responded.

The Digital Environment Creation rooms were a place where anyone on the ship could immerse themselves in any environment they chose. It was a great way to relax and get away from the monotony of the daily life on the Forge.

"That's where you're headed?" Parson asked.

"Yeah, I plan on relaxing for a while, you?" Harden replied.

"I'm headed to the game, I've got a score to defend," Parson responded.

"I heard about that, all that practice starting to pay off huh?" Harden continued.

"Finally, right? Gibbons held the title for way too long. You can only stay on top for so long though, can't be number one forever, but I'll try to hold on as long as I can," Parson responded as they both came to the elevator.

Harden pushed the button and the doors opened immediately. They both entered and Parson pressed the buttons for both level 15 and level 24. The elevator moved quickly to level 15.

"Good luck," Harden said as Parson exited.

"Luck has nothing to do with it. Have fun on the deck," he responded as he turned the corner.

The elevator doors closed, and Harden was quickly brought to his floor. He stepped off the elevator when it reached level 24. Stepping off the elevator on level 24 was like stepping into a different world. It had the feel of a spa, light neutral colors stretched down the hallway while the floors appeared to be a light grey distressed wood. He made his way down several hallways and past several doors. Some of the doors led to physical therapy areas while others led to physiatrists' offices. He arrived at a set of double glass doors with the words *The Deck*, the nickname for the DEC, engraved above the door tracks. He stepped forward and the door opened. There was a woman behind a desk, she appeared to be in her fifties and had her face buried in her screen. She did not have the same discs that the others had, and she had the average height of a normal human. The screen in front of her was being projected from the desk, hovering in the position a typical screen would be mounted. Harden stood there for a moment, waiting for the woman to acknowledge his presence. She continued to type on her desk while paying absolutely no attention to him. Finally, Harden cleared his throat, hoping to get her attention. Indeed it worked, the woman motioned her hand to swipe the screen away and it disappeared. The woman had dark short hair with black-rimmed glasses. She turned her head slightly to the side and smiled.

"How can I help?" she asked Harden.

"I'd like some time if it's not booked up," he said politely.

"Let's see," she responded as she motioned her hand upwards, and the screen reappeared.

"I think we can do that, looks like bay 11 is open. I just need your ID please," she said as she typed a bit more.

Harden put his hand on a discolored circle that was embedded in the desk. It only took a moment for the discolored circle to light up and read his file, pulling up his public information. Of course, most of his information was classified. Being a TITAN and being in the Operator program meant classifying his actual name, any of his UNIC records, and most other information. The Operator program was one of three programs that the TITANs were assigned to. The other Guardian and Brute programs were just as classified but served other purposes. The purpose of the Operator program was to create an elite military team.

"Excellent, 201 you're all set," the woman said.

Harden moved toward bay 11. *201,* Harden thought to himself as he made his way past bay 8, he hated that they had to be referred to by numbers outside of their own kind or if they were on mission. While they were told it was for their protection, Harden just didn't see the point. He arrived in front of bay 11, walked through the door, and entered the room. The room itself was completely empty, a large empty space with square panels from floor to ceiling. The panels on the ceiling provided light as they glowed softly. He turned to the area just to the left of the door.

"The cliffs," he said as he walked toward the middle of the room.

The room began to go dark. Once all of the light was out, the walls and ceiling began to light up in sections. Once all of the panels were lit, the illusion was complete. Harden found himself on the edge of a cliff looking over an expansive ocean below. The sound of waves crashing against the rocks and the wind blowing gently made the illusion so realistic. Harden sat down at what appeared to be the cliff's edge. He stared out into the ocean, as the sun rose on the horizon. He took a couple of deep breaths and tried his best to relax. As he let himself become immersed in the moment, he felt the buried anxiety from his almost constant nightmares melt away. All of the sudden, he heard a familiar voice.

"The cliffs again?!" a female voice said.

"Taylor, what are you doing?" Harden asked as he jumped to his feet, startled and feeling a bit embarrassed.

"You know this thing can give you the illusion that you're anywhere, a gorgeous bungalow on the beach, a beautiful waterfall in the rainforest, a white sand beach," she said, looking around at the view.

"Well aware, sounds like you're kind of stuck on beaches though. Were you looking for me or just going around seeing what everyone's up to in their bays?" Harden asked, looking to change her focus.

"Yeah, our weekend just got cut short. Director Barnes wants to see us in the briefing room in thirty," she said as she turned toward the door.

"The beach," she said with a slight smile as she spoke into the same panel Harden did when he activated the cliff illusion. The room went dark again, and a white sand beach scene appeared panel by panel stretched as far as the eye could see.

"Maybe we can have a beach day together some time, it does get kind of boring sitting on the beach by yourself. The tan is worth it though," she said.

She left the room as Harden followed. They proceeded back through the reception area and to the elevator.

"Any idea what the director's got in store for us this time?" Harden asked, trying to make conversation.

"Nope, just got the message and was told to come get you," she replied.

They faced forward as the elevator headed for level 3, each of them nervously looking at each other when the other wasn't. The doors opened as they arrived at level 3 and Harden waited.

"Ladies first," he said, motioning for Taylor to disembark first.

Taylor rolled her eyes while smiling slightly and stepped out. They made their way to the briefing room where their teammates and two other teams were already waiting.

"Took you long enough," Jossen said to Harden as soon as he walked through the door.

"Well I for one am pissed, we couldn't get deployment cut short for this? Always cutting into my free time," Toa remarked

"Free time? What exactly do you do with your free time? Sit in your room with the latest sim? what a waste," Coughlin asked rhetorically.

"I would spend it with you, but you're just mean," Toa said jokingly as they both smiled at each other.

"Enough," Jossen said sternly, feeling embarrassed that his team members were the last to arrive.

Jossen could feel the arrogant smirk from Rossi, Epsilon's team leader. It was always competitive among the teams, between the squads and divisions, and within the commands. Every team wanted to be the best, turning something as boring as a briefing into a competition. Who will be assembled first, which team will be assigned the higher priority task, and it went on and on. Jossen always wanted to push his team to be the best but juggling the various personalities was the hardest part of the job. Knowing when to push and when to give was an art in itself.

Harden took a seat next to Zhou as Taylor had found a seat among the Sigma team. Not a moment later footsteps were heard approaching, two very distinct and familiar sounds. The echoing clack of the director's heeled shoes and the steady thud of the Admiral's boots. Director Barnes was older, the team couldn't quite place her age but figured she was somewhere in her late sixties. She once had black hair but most of it had gone gray at this point. There were a few streaks of darker hair visible through the gray as it was pulled back into a very tight bun. She wore thin black rim glasses that seemed permanently fixed in position. She wore a long white lab coat over a pair of white pants and a white button-down shirt. She provided a stark contrast to Admiral Vincere. Although they were both older, appearing to be around the same age, the Admiral wore a black military uniform. It consisted of black pants, a black button-down, and a black jacket that was folded over itself in the front, fixed with buttons. The metals on his chest indicated he had seen numerous battles and emerged victorious each time. He was stern, his face weathered and serious. He stood straight and proud, projecting his metals and weathered face as trophies of dedication. While the TITANs would dorf both the director and the Admiral physically, the two stood as tall as mountains with their positions and influence.

"F1 Alpha 3," Director Barnes greeted them by their squad designation.

"We have just received intelligence regarding the resistance commander's location. It is our understanding that he will be at the following coordinates for the next 3 days," she said as she lifted her hand upward.

A 3D projection of a planet with a pulsing circle seemingly identifying where on the planet he was located appeared before her.

Admiral Vincere stepped forward. "Your objective will be to infiltrate the base, retrieve the commander, and return him here."

"Is that all?" Toa asked, making light of the serious tone.

"You may have jokes 312 but I can assure you, this is anything but routine," the Admiral responded, glaring at Toa.

"The fact that the last two missions against the commander of the resistance resulted in the loss of 10 operators should tell you something. Both Bravo and Echo team tried to take out the commander, both failed," the Admiral said, attempting to cut through the nonsense and instill the seriousness of this mission.

"This will be a difficult mission, we suspect that you all may not make it back," Director Barnes said, trying to re-enforce the Admiral's point.

"You kidding? With this squad, we've got this, " Toa couldn't help himself, he had to try to lighten it up.

"While I appreciate your enthusiasm 312, you need to understand what you're getting into," Director Barnes said.

Though Harden didn't like being referred to as a number, he especially hated it when Barnes did it. She had insisted on it from the very beginning, refusing to call any of the TITANs by name, using only number designations. The standing explanation was that it may have been a coping mechanism for Barnes, having to play mother to all of the children in the TITAN program.

"Why don't we just dust the place?" Jossen suggested.

"103, our intelligence suggests that he is secured in a hardened bunker. We've attempted dusting sites before, we can't risk his escape again. Each failed attempt on the commander has resulted in operator losses and increased the resistances' resolve. It's extremely difficult to get intelligence on his whereabouts and we cannot accept failure this time. Each failure puts more citizens, more infrastructure, and the UNGA itself at risk," Admiral Vincere replied.

"Ok, so how are we deploying?" Jossen asked.

"The squad will perform an orbital drop. Once on the

ground, each team will approach the various rally points indicated here," the Admiral said as the 3D projection rotated and enlarged.

The enlarged projection showed a vast compound with a variety of buildings, bunkers, and hangars. There were numerous turret locations as well as anti-aircraft weaponry. The projection then began to zoom in again, showing even more detail as the Admiral spoke again.

"You will need to enter the heavily fortified compound here, here, and here," he said as he pointed to the projection.

"Intelligence suggests they have multiple assault vehicles on site so exercise caution. We don't know which building is actually housing the commander, so once inside, you'll need to identify which building he is in," Admiral Vincere said.

"Extraction?" Jossen asked.

"Once you have the target, you will need to make your way to these coordinates. A falcon will be perched, ready to pick you up shortly after you signal," the Admiral said and handed each team leader a small clear panel the size of a business card.

"Although others would prefer we bring the commander of the resistance back alive, I will consider the mission a success as long as he is off the field," the director said.

All three team leaders nodded and acknowledged the orders.

"Good. I know you won't let us down. F1 Alpha 3 head to the armory and load up, the Condor lifts off at 0800. You are dismissed," Director Barnes said as Harden felt her stare linger on him.

She immediately turned to the Admiral and they both left the room. All fifteen operators stood up and headed for the door.

"Seems a little odd doesn't it?" Taylor asked anyone who would listen.

"What seems odd?" Rossi replied.

"A kinetic weapon deployed from orbit would have enough impact to destroy almost any bunker. As for him escaping, you would think they would send a fleet...I mean it is the commander of the resistance, not some mid-level officer. If they think they can end the resistance by bringing him in, why not send everyone?" Taylor said.

"You heard them, 408. They need the best on this mission, if they were to send a whole fleet the commander might be able to escape in the confusion. I agree that a precise strike with the right team would be the best option...and what better team than us," Jossen answered with a typical Jossen response.

Of course Jossen believed the mission began as soon as the briefing ended, choosing to call each member by their numbers. The team leaders knew better than to allow teammates to question the orders coming from the top. Once the doubts start to set in, it could be difficult to manage.

Outside the briefing room, the Admiral stopped the director after they stepped into a small room.

"Do you really think this is a good idea?" Admiral Vincere asked.

"What better mission could a team ask for before retirement?" she asked right back.

"Sending a team on a mission like this then retiring them afterward seems like it could pose a problem. If they somehow bring the commander back alive," he said as he was leading Barnes.

"If they bring back the commander, then I will have another difficult decision to make, but for now we stick to the plan," she said sternly.

"Let's just hope they take out the commander and make it to the falcon. We can't have another team end up like Bravo team, which by the way you still haven't resolved," the Admiral said.

"I am well aware Admiral, this mission will go as planned. As for the next team, they are being prepped," Barnes said.

"Good, we need to keep things moving, there's no room for error. They have us under a microscope, watching our every move. You know what they'll do if they find out," he said as he began to turn away.

"Again, well aware Admiral, thank you," she said snidely.

As they departed down separate hallways, the director approached a door. The door opened to a dark room as she spoke softly into the darkness without entering.

"Everything is proceeding according to plan," she said as she immediately turned and continued down the hallway.

Meanwhile, the team made their way to the armory and then the hangar. As they approached the hangar, they spotted their ride. Director Barnes was standing next to a Condor. The Condor was a massive cargo drop ship, used to transport heavy weaponry and large crews. As the team approached, Dir. Barnes began to speak.

"I don't believe I was able to articulate myself well enough in the briefing. This mission is of critical importance. We have the opportunity to bring the war against the resistance to an end. I am relying on Delta, Epsilon, and Sigma to succeed where many others have failed. The resistance commander is a seasoned veteran, in the past, we used to fight on the same side. He was a good man and a great soldier. Please do not underestimate him," the director said as she motioned for them to enter the Condor.

The teams entered the Condor in single file, still in the

clothes they started the day with. Once they boarded the ship, Jossen gave the order.

"Ok, team, let's suit up," Jossen said as Rossi and Cohen gave similar orders.

The discs on their exoskeletons appeared to move though it wasn't the discs that moved, rather the armor pouring out of them, it seemed to move like a living liquid around their bodies. It wrapped them from head to toe in a black suit of armor. The Condor's door closed, and the ship took off. The director watched with a calculated look as the ship left the hangar.

"It starts, the beginning of the end, no matter the outcome," Barnes said to herself as she stood alone in the hangar.

In an undisclosed location lightyears away from the Forge, A woman stood in front of a desk in a dim office room. She stared at the back of a chair, unable to see the person sitting in it. The desk had very little on it other than some dust. The walls of the room were covered with maps of ambiguous terrain with circles and lines drawn on them. Behind the desk and chair, a window looked down to what appeared to be an assembly area. A large underground cavernous room four stories high bustled with activity.

"You asked to see me sir?" the woman asked.

"Yes, what is the status of the teams?" a male's voice asked.

"They've deployed," she said.

"Have all of the preparations been made for their arrival?" the man's voice asked.

"Yes, although I'm not sure about them making it down here. You're putting a lot of faith in them and not much in our soldiers. Our teams might take them out before they make it," the woman said.

"I put a lot of faith in them because they're supposedly the best. They are well trained, disciplined, and ultimately, they don't have a choice, they have to succeed," the man responded.

"And if they're too good?" she asked.

"They won't make it past the rings no matter how good they are, again, they have no choice. I want one team posted at the east bunker with the hellfire. I want four teams posted at the choke point. Everyone else is to go to the west bunker and make their way to the hangar and prepare to evacuate. When all of this is over, they're going to dust the whole place," he responded.

"Are you sure about that sir? We'd be leaving a lot of valuable resources behind," the woman said.

"We don't have a choice lieutenant, we have to make it look believable," the man said.

"Understood sir," the woman confirmed as she made a salute and left the room.

"Indeed, the beginning of the end is here," the man said softly.

Back on the Condor, the squad made its way into space, the teams heard a voice over their comms. "We will be engaging the SDD in thirty seconds."

The space distortion drive creates a distortion in space and allows for a type of faster than light travel, effectively bending and folding space. Each member of the team knew the basics of how the drive worked but when it came to specifics, and really anything related to technology, the engineers were the brains specializing in technology. Each team member specialized in something. Team leaders specialized in tactics and strategy, Guards specialized in heavy weapons and vehicles, Mechanics specialized in engineering and explosives, and Scouts specialized in marksmanship and recon.

"Ok, we ready to do this or what?" Jossen asked as he made the rounds.

He took a look at everyone, each step he took made a loud hollow bang. When in their armor, the weight of each footstep on the metal flooring of the ship sounded thunderous.

"Oh yeah," Toa said as he patted the large package that was strapped to his back.

Jossen made his way over to Coughlin. "505?" he asked.

"Yes sir," she said in a very sarcastic way. She knew he was just trying to get everyone excited, but she preferred just getting the job done, she didn't need or want a pep talk.

"406?" he moved in front of Zhou.

"Yes sir," he said excitedly, although he always wanted to be polite and make Jossen feel like he was doing a good job.

"201?" he asked as he approached the side of Harden.

"Ready," he remarked.

"SDD engaging in 5, 4, 3, 2, 1," the voice was heard over the comms again.

The space in front of the ship began to warp, distorting by appearing to fold and twist. The ship then advanced into the distortion. Its lights dimmed to almost total darkness. The ship emerged through another distortion as a voice was heard in the ship once again, "SDD disengaged. We will reach the drop point in five minutes. Preparing for orbital drop."

"This is it, everyone in positions," Jossen said.

The teams prepared themselves by getting into formation in the cargo bay of the falcon. Orbital drops were an essential tool for the UNIC, allowing teams the element of surprise by dropping on or behind the enemy in a short amount of time. Orbital drops weren't without risks though, falling from space was a risk but a fairly common practice for TITANs.

Back in the underground resistance complex, the lieutenant made her way through a maze of corridors. She arrived at a plain-looking solid grey door. She stood for a moment and took a breath before entering the room.

"Sir, we've just detected space distortion above sector 7," she said.

"Understood, sound the alert. We've been preparing for this. Let's show these operators and the UNIC what the resistance can do," the man said.

"Yes Sir!" the lieutenant said enthusiastically. She exited the office and made her way straight to the command center.

"Ok everyone, you know what needs to be done. Let's teach these operators a little something about the resistance," she commanded as a group of officers scrambled to implement her orders.

"Let's see if these operators can live up to the hype," the lieutenant said to herself in a soft snarky tone.

TWO
THE MISSION

FIFTEEN OPERATORS STOOD in the deafening silence, the kind of silence that was so noticeable, it left all who witnessed it in awe. A strobing red glow illuminated the space with a faint repetitious reminder of where they were. They stared forward at the cold metal door, it almost seemed routine. Each operator motionless as they awaited the signal. Standing side by side in three rows of five, it would be almost impossible for anyone to tell them apart. The dull matte black finishes of their helmet, each one almost identical to the next with only the slightest of differences. Slight differences in their collar guards alluded to differing physical characteristics of the person inside. The shoulder plates displayed one of three emblems, the Greek symbol for their teams, as though it was etched into the armor itself.

There was a loud echoing bang that always preceded a deployment like this, it smashed its way through the silence as the sound was multiplied by each soldier in the squad. The sound of the mag-grav component equipped within their armor, more specifically their boots, firmly attaching them to the metal surface they stood upon. They all remained perfectly still, stoic, as though they existed in a photograph. The moment was interrupted by a soft but inherently robotic female voice that seemed to have a slight British accent.

"Deployment in T minus sixty," the voice said.

It was almost soothing for the briefest of moments until the door they were standing in front of began to open. A rush of air immediately slammed them, like a hurricane slamming into a forest of redwoods. The operators remained still as the rush of air subsided almost as soon as it began. As the door slowly opened, it was as though the universe itself was finally revealing all of its secrets. At first, a black nothingness that would make the most religious person question their meaning, until the shimmer of light as if heaven itself had requested their presence. The light would have undoubtedly been blinding to the naked eye, but as the light moved past, a brilliant blue hue was visible. The colors became more vibrant with each passing second, mixing blue and green hues, as the object exuding these colors became more apparent. Then, as the door continued to open for what seemed like an eternity, the planet below exposed more and more of itself as the door finally settled in its fully open position. The squad looked down at the surface, a seemingly peaceful place when viewed from this far, the history and the future nonexistent, as only the present was visible. Gentle rolling clouds were visible as they moved at a geological pace, much like an optical illusion that gave the impression of movement so slight it may not be real. It would be easy for one to be lulled into a false sense of calm. The beauty of what they were witnessing wasn't shared by everyone, in fact, only a select few among humanity would be able to take part in this. The squad moved closer to the opening, coming to the edge of the opened door. With each step closer, nothing but silence. The sound of the boots adhering to the metal surface no longer striking the same tone it previously did. The only thing between the platform door and this planet was a stretch of nothingness, a black void that would unapologetically devour anyone or anything that didn't respect its power.

"T minus ten," the voice said, resounding in their helmets and instilling a sense of reality in the moment. Each squad member began to brace themselves as they appeared ready to jump.

"Deploy," the voice instructed without emotion but with a tone that seemed engineered to instill a sense of duty.

Each squad leapt into the abyss of space in the direction of the planet. At first, it seemed as though they were motionless, floating into the void as it beckoned them. They moved forward at what seemed like a snail's pace, but as they began to fall into the gravity of the planet, they picked up speed.

A soft fiery glow began to envelop them as they descended through the Planet's atmosphere. The soft glow evolved into a violent display as if the planet was warning them that entering this place may cost them their lives. Although this defense was usually successful against more typical planetary threats, the team was prepared. As they made their way through the atmosphere, they began to group in formation. The formation was tight, a relentlessly rehearsed and painstakingly executed maneuver. They adjusted their bodies to achieve the desired direction, every slight movement having an enhanced impact on formation and landing. With everyone in position, they began to move faster, tucking their arms and angling downward. The ground below came into focus with more vivid detail as each second passed; grassy hills painted a green across the landscape, the deep blue of the water as it twisted and turned through the hills provided sharp contrast, and the patches of brown appeared like an invader against the landscape. As they continued their rapid descent, structures and compounds came into focus as well. What appeared to be dots quickly scurrying around, like a colony of ants rushing to avoid impending destruction, provided a glimpse of what they could expect when they landed.

As the surface approached rapidly, even more of the landscape below came into focus; the large concrete buildings tucked into berms of land, what appeared to be anti-aircraft weapons posted strategically throughout the compound, and guard towers positioned around the perimeter. All of the defenses detailed in the briefing and then some. All three teams spotted twin rhino tanks standing guard at various entrances. These hulking tanks featured triple jointed treads, reinforced armor plating, four large ZPE cores, and two large, mounted weapons on a rotating turret. The tanks were equipped with a jolt railgun and a direct energy laser weapon or DELaW. The zero point energy cores stuck out of the back of the unit between the treads, glowing blue as they produced the energy needed to power a vehicle of that size. A dozen or so badgers came into view, scattered throughout the complex. The badgers were typical ground transportation for any military units. The badgers were designed to carry a small crew rapidly over difficult terrain. The vehicle had an open frame design with no roof, roll bars were the only safety feature on board. A driver's seat, a passenger seat, and two platforms above the back wheels provided accommodations for personnel as well as a place to man the mounted machine guns. As the wind steadily rushed past them, they spotted the vehicle they were hoping to see. A falcon sitting on the launch pad in front of a smaller bunker. They looked just past where the tail met the body of the craft, a round bulge indicated this falcon was equipped with its own SDD. While it had become increasingly rare to find a falcon without this upgrade, it was a good indicator that the commander was close by.

When the teams came within about 200 feet of the ground, each team leader gave the command to "Deploy RT." The command was heard across every team member's comms and was displayed on their heads-up display. At that moment, the suit began to move and change as if it was alive. The retro thruster program within the suit initiated. The panels began to move and created flaps that rose up to catch the wind and slow the descent. Small thrusters then emerged from under the flaps as they approached the ground. The team leader landed first with a thud, crouching and putting his hands out to balance and absorb some of the impact. The impact kicked up dust and debris, leaving a crater around him. The other team members landed behind him, one after the other, only milli-seconds apart. Each operator created the same scene as they landed, the thick cloud of dust and debris wafted in the air. The team leaders rose to their feet and the suits began to move again. The thrusters moved into the suit and the suit seemed to reform around them. The panels that appeared to slow the descent seem to break down and retreat back into the suit like a pile of tiny bugs. Jossen removed the AAR-10, an advanced assault rifle, from his back and the team did the same, each equipping themselves with their qualified weapon. He issued hand signals to his team, but it was unnecessary, as each member knew what they were there to do. Epsilon and Sigma teams broke off from the group as Delta team moved straight ahead. The operators moved with precision, all of their training and experience evident in every movement. Delta team was to move through the front gate at the SSE while Epsilon and Sigma were to enter from the ENE and NNW entrances.

"I have contact on the northeast side," Rossi's voice was heard over comms.

"Same here," Cohen chimed in.

Delta arrived at the front gate. The 30-foot-high solid metal blast doors loomed large as Coughlin began to stick devices to various points on the door. The rest of Delta team stood to the sides of the door while Coughlin worked. It only took moments as she found her place to the side of the doors.

"Sigma, Epsilon, in positions?" Jossen asked.

"Affirmative," Rossi responded.

"Affirmative," Cohen responded a second later.

Delta team took two steps back as Coughlin activated the devices. The devices began to glow as a loud hiss began emanating from each device. The metal doors that stood as a deterrent began to moan as the devices melted through the thick metal. Within minutes, the doors succumbed to gravity as the 4-foot-thick doors slammed to the ground. They landed with thunderous noise as the dust was forced out in every direction from underneath. Without flinching, the team rushed through the smoke and debris and entered the compound.

"We're in," Jossen said.

As Delta team began to move through the front of the compound, resistance soldiers filtered out from several buildings, scurrying to mounted guns and vehicles. The rhino tanks that had remained motionless suddenly came to life. The team split up as the jolt railguns began to fire.

"Take cover!" Toa yelled as the team took cover behind a building.

The two rhinos fired continuously on Delta team to keep them pinned behind cover. The impacts from the rounds sent dust and debris into the air, creating a smokey curtain that seemed to dance in the wind, while pieces of concrete rained down on them.

"Hey, want to try that tank maneuver again?" Toa asked Harden.

"Depends, think you can do it again?" Harden replied.

"You know it!" Toa said enthusiastically.

Harden positioned himself at the damaged corner of the building as the blasts kept coming, slowly wearing away at their cover. Toa moved around the other side of the building, preparing for the assault. Harden was timing the blasts and sprinted from cover to draw the rhino's fire. As the railguns repositioned to follow Harden, Toa moved toward the back of the tank. The rest of Delta team moved to the corner of the building and started taking shots at the rhinos. They knew that it would not damage them but were just looking to distract. Toa finally got to the back of one of the rhinos, planting a detonation charge on one of the ZPE cores. He took cover as soon as he could.

The resulting explosion brought ordinary soldiers to their feet, the shock wave equivalent to an earthquake. Some of the smaller buildings suffered moderate damage as the rhino was completely destroyed, leaving a smoldering pile of twisted metal in a blackened crater. The other rhino that was approximately 20 yards from the destroyed rhino suffered damage as well. Without the jolt railgun, the resistance soldiers inside were sitting ducks. They exited the rhino with everything they had, but with the heavy weaponry, they were no match for the operators.

Delta team continued to move through the compound, clearing buildings as they went. The resistance soldiers tried their best, but it was a losing battle. Even the lucky shots that did hit the operators were deflected by their armor, having little to no impact. The nanites within their armor reacted to the kinetic energy from the standard munitions as soon as they hit, this reaction deflected the bullets while repairing the armor itself. The resistance soldiers were not as lucky. The operators hit their targets as if they were on a training course with cardboard cutouts. Resistance soldiers dropped by the dozens as the team moved from one building to the next.

Explosions could be heard and felt as Epsilon and Sigma teams continued their push. They encountered the same defenses and achieved the same results. The three teams eventually met toward the center of the compound, leaving just a few buildings that could be hiding the commander. As they converged on the largest of them, they discussed moving in to find the commander. It was then when two smaller bunker doors on both sides of the building began to open.

"Check those doors," Cohen said.

"What is that?" Rossi asked as the door had opened wide enough to reveal something new.

In each of the bunkers, several turrets with four large rectangle boxes mounted on independent arms began to take aim and fire. While the operator's armor could deflect standard munitions, these turrets were anything but standard. Each arm moved independently, tracking multiple targets with ease while firing rounds with relentless ferocity. The armor that had protected the operators thus far couldn't stand up to the barrage they now faced.

"Move!" Jossen yelled as they attempted to take cover.

All three teams scattered as the turrets continued to track them. Harden instinctively ran in the direction of Taylor while the rest of Delta team ran in the opposite direction. Harden shoved Taylor to the ground behind what remained of a concrete wall. He took only a moment to look back and he saw five operators down. In that brief moment of inaction, he was hit several times in the arm and leg. As he fell to the ground, Taylor grabbed Harden and pulled him behind the wall.

"We need to take those out!" Jossen yelled from behind cover as the sound of the projectiles impacting against the concrete drowned him out.

"No shit!" Toa responded.

"Frags!" Rossi yelled as what was left of his team threw their grenades.

Three explosions rocked the inside of the bunker but only managed to disable two of the arms on one turret. At that moment, Toa sprinted out of sight. Jossen was shook up as Zhou lay motionless in the dirt along with four other operators.

"312, what are you doing?" Coughlin both asked and demanded as the turret's relentless assault continued.

"Just hold them off for a minute and don't get killed," Toa replied.

"406! Say something!" Jossen exclaimed.

There was no response from Zhou. There was frantic chatter across the team's comms as the other team leaders sounded a roll call. Only two operators from Epsilon and three from Sigma cleared the field in time. The remaining operators were shocked, a TITAN hadn't been lost in a mission against the resistance since Bravo and Echo team.

Cohen and Jossen ordered their teams to release frags. Several frags made it into the second bunker, disabling several pods on two turrets. A whistling streak in the sky just above the team's heads preceded an explosion, disabling all of the turrets on one side. Not a moment later, a second explosion rocked the other bunker. The operators looked for the origin of the rockets that seemed to come from nowhere. They saw Toa standing on top of one of the smaller buildings behind them. While the turrets were focused on the targets in front of them, he was able to find a launcher.

"Nice work 312," Jossen said as he immediately moved to Zhou.

Rossi, Cohen, Jossen, Coughlin, and Toa made their way to the downed operators. They saw the devastation this weapon caused, ripping holes in their armor as though it was nothing but tin. The areas around the hole seemed to be like charcoal.

"What could cause this?" Rossi asked as if someone had an answer.

Wu, an engineer on Epsilon team, was standing in the doorway of one of the bunkers.

"Not sure what clues we can dig out of this mess," he said as he looked around at the twisted and charred metal.

"Ok, we need a game plan. It's obvious they knew we were coming and I'm sure this isn't their only surprise," Jossen said as he looked around the compound.

"103," Taylor called his attention to Harden.

"201, what happened?" Jossen asked as he ran to check on Harden.

"Hesitated," Harden responded calmly.

Jossen leaned in to inspect the damage. The holes in his armor were similar to the ones in the rest of the operators. He could see down to where the bullet struck his flesh. The wound was bleeding but surprisingly not gushing. The nanites were beginning to repair the damage to the armor but not nearly at the speed they were used to.

"505, go see if you can find a quick shot. At least that will stop the bleeding until we get you fixed up," Jossen commanded.

"Ok, we need to focus, we still have a job to do," Jossen said as he formulated a plan.

"408, you're the only tech operator left. I need you to get those blast doors open," Jossen motioned to the set of blast doors between the two bunkers.

"The commander has to be in there. 107, we'll need someone out here to watch our backs when we go in. 102, we have to bring these operators back, we need them prepped and ready for departure. 415, you're the only scout operator who isn't down or out, we'll need you to come with us as well," Jossen said.

Rossi and Cohen both agreed with Jossen. Knowing that the mission came before the team and before the individual, there was no arguing about who would do what.

"103, I'm ok, I can go in," Harden said as he got to his feet.

"No way 201, you're going to stay put," Jossen insisted.

Harden wasn't about to let his injuries allow Taylor to go without him. He stood up defiantly and dusted himself off. As he did, something fell to the ground. It seemed to be a piece of metal, he quickly moved his boot to cover it in dirt.

"I'm fine. Just a flesh wound," he looked over at Coughlin who had arrived with the quick shot.

"Uh 103, I thought you said he needed a quick shot?" Coughlin asked.

"What do you mean, just give him the quick shot to stop the bleeding," Jossen said, puzzled as to why she would ask.

"There's nothing here but a graze," she said as she looked into the hole in Harden's armor.

"It seemed like more than a graze to me," Jossen insisted.

"I told you, I'm fine. Just a flesh wound," Harden repeated.

Jossen was confused, as he believed the wound he saw looked deep but accepted the situation for what it was. He would rather have Harden than Masse on Delta team anyway, not that Masse wasn't good at what he did.

"Walk it off then 201 and let's go," Jossen said as he moved toward the blast doors.

Taylor looked over at Harden. She knew what she saw but wasn't as quick to dismiss it as Jossen. She paused for a moment and Harden nodded slightly. She had to table this discussion as the Delta team moved to the door.

Taylor lifted her left arm in front of the door control panel. The security features were activated when the teams landed, and a hardened case protected the panel. She began typing on the keypad attached to her arm and the protective case lifted. She started pressing buttons on both the panel and her keypad. After a moment, she stepped back and the doors slowly opened.

What was left of Epsilon and Sigma team had cleared the area. They removed the downed operators and were preparing to set up a perimeter. Delta team stood in front of the blast doors, prepared for a full-on assault. As the doors continued their sluggish pace, more and more of the space inside became visible. With every inch, the team prepared to return fire but as each inch opened, they saw nothing. The doors finally slammed into the open position, revealing a large empty space.

"Everyone, stay alert. There were far more troops scurrying around here when we dropped than we've run into so far, they had to go somewhere," Jossen said sternly.

"It'll be like fish in a barrel," replied Toa.

"The question is, who's the fish?" Taylor quipped as they began to slowly walk into the room.

"Eyes up," Jossen said as he took point.

Harden and Coughlin covered opposite sides while Taylor and Toa covered the rear facing behind them. Moving as a unit, they entered the compound, scanning the room as they continued inward. The dark cavernous room produced an echo with each footstep, each step played over again to anyone who might be listening. Although there wasn't much light, the team was able to identify the features within. There were crates and boxes, supplies that would be essential when sustaining and defending a place like this. A badger in the corner, one that appeared to have been put through its paces. The chipped paint, scattered holes surrounded by char marks, and a cracked windshield painted a picture of the action this vehicle had been in. The team spotted a cage surrounding a lift, this was the only way in or out of the underground complex below.

"Gotta be honest, don't have a great feeling about this," Harden said as the eerie quiet set in.

"201, 505, cover the door. 408, get this lift operational," Jossen commanded while moving toward the lift.

Taylor moved to the control panel for the lift. She again lifted her left arm and began her work. Several swipes and taps of her screen caused the machine to let out a groan, a long deep noise that sounded like a monster had just been rudely awakened from its slumber. The echo magnified the groaning, and would no doubt be a beacon for anyone that would look to stop them.

"312, 505, on me," Jossen said as he steadied his weapon on the safety gate of the lift. The lift finally came to a halt with a slam, putting to rest any notion of having the element of surprise. Jossen opened the safety gate as he readied himself and the team for what was to come.

"201, cover the exit," Jossen commanded as he instructed the rest of the team to enter the lift. "Let's get this done."

Harden wanted to go with them, not knowing what would be waiting for them, more specifically Taylor, drove him insane. He also knew that there wasn't much he could say about it. Someone had to make sure they could get back up and he was the only *injured* team member. Harden backed up to the wall on the side of the lift and activated his armor's recon mode. With the same bug-like motion of the nanites, the suit began to direct light around it, appearing to blend in with the surroundings. While this feature was useful, it required a lot of energy. It could last for a little while but would eventually need to charge. He had to remain still as any extensive movement would create rendering anomalies and give him away. The lift descended into the darkness below while he watched.

"It looked like there were thousands of troops at this compound. If you ask me, it was a little too easy getting in here," Coughlin said as she turned to Jossen.

"Too easy? You call losing six operators easy? That's cold girl," Toa asked.

"That's not what I mean you ass. We took out what, maybe a couple hundred soldiers? Why not have more of them guarding the entrance?" Coughlin wondered.

"I'm sure the commander will be heavily guarded. The rest are down here somewhere without a doubt. We need to stay focused and retrieve the target. It doesn't matter if there are two thousand of them down there, we have a job to do and we don't fail," Jossen replied.

"Not a bit of hesitation there huh 103? Sir, I will follow you down a dark elevator shaft to certain doom any day!" Toa quipped, mixing sarcasm with a slightly demeaning tone.

"Enough. There may only be five of us, but we have these guys outgunned and outclassed. Resistance fighters–please, these guys are parading terrorism as a righteous crusade. Well today, we end the resistance, and we end this war," Jossen said.

"Sir, approaching the level," Taylor interjected. Everyone perked up, weapons at the ready.

"Oh, what have we here? Another long dark hallway, fun," Toa joked.

"Keep it tight," Jossen said as they disembarked the lift and proceeded down the hallway.

At the end of the hallway, they came to a four-way intersection. Each direction had locked blast doors only a few feet from the intersection. The team wasn't sure which way to go and knew splitting up probably wasn't the best idea down here.

"Ok 408, see if..." Jossen said as his gaze darted between each door before he was interrupted.

"On it," replied Taylor before Jossen could finish his question, already tapping and swiping on her keypad.

"Looks like door number 2 is equipment storage and door number 1 is barracks, so door number 3 should be..." she started but was abruptly cut short by a beeping sound.

The red light indicating the door had been locked suddenly changed from red to green on all three doors. The doors began to open. The gravity of the situation became clear as all three doors revealed hundreds of soldiers packed in like sardines, all with weapons drawn.

"Drop your weapons," a soldier demanded.

"Welp, at least it isn't just another empty hallway," Toa said with a resignation in his voice.

Jossen held his AAR-10 up as if to show that he was complying. As he moved slowly to place it on the ground, Toa grabbed the ETS-10, the enhanced tactical shotgun that was on Jossen's back, and opened fire. Taylor closed the gap between her and the ocean of soldiers in front of her, bullets flew but the reaction time of these soldiers was not enough to gain the upper hand. Bullets grazed her armor as she moved, creating visible ripples in her armor but not damaging it. As she engaged in close-quarters combat, Coughlin was dealing with her own problems. Staring down the hallway, she threw her AAR-10 at the lead soldier. The soldier was caught off guard, he attempted to catch it, but Coughlin was already inches from his face by the time the gun hit him. She grabbed it and lifted, slamming this helmet upward with deadly force. The resistance soldiers quickly find their odds were greatly diminished in such close quarters. As Coughlin and Taylor devastated their opponents with speed and force, the moaning of the downed men started to sound like one low-toned hum, the sound only occasionally broken by the smashing of a helmet or the shot of a pistol. Taylor and Coughlin turn toward each other after dropping the last of their enemies.

"What took you so long?" Coughlin asked as the floor was covered by men who lay dead or wounded around her.

"You know you missed one," Taylor responded as she motioned toward Coughlin.

A loud gunshot rang out as the soldier behind Coughlin fired a round point-blank at the back of her head. Coughlin's head jerked forward with the impact, leaving a gouge in her armor, as the impact was absorbed and distributed throughout the armor. She quickly lifted her head and turned to face the soldier who just shot her. As she did, it appeared as though the armor was working to repair the damage done by the shot. She slightly cocked her head to the side as she grabbed the pistol out of his hands. The soldier was shocked, frozen with disbelief as she smashed the gun in his face, knocking him unconscious.

"What took *me* so long?" Taylor asked in a mocking tone.

Coughlin shot her a glance as they moved closer to where Jossen and Toa stood.

"Well, I don't think they were prepared for that," Jossen said confidently.

"If it wasn't for those turrets, they could've sent the UNAF for this," Toa remarked.

At one time the UNAF had been a fearsome military force, consisting of ground, air, and sea forces. They were created in the wake of the formation of the UNGA. Once space travel had become common place, the development of the UNIC had rendered the UNAF obsolete. Back on Earth, the United Nations Armed Forces had become a militarized police force, in charge of handling small-scale disputes and putting down protests.

"I'm pretty sure we'll be up against more than this," Jossen replied. "This target is important enough to warrant sending us. Let's not jinx it now."

"We can go through the lab, it looks like there are more rooms through there. I'm guessing that's where the target is hiding," Taylor said after looking at her forearm screen again.

"Right, through the labs it is," Jossen confirms.

The team entered a room full of scientific equipment. The distinct difference between the labs at AIDA (Advanced Intelligence and Defense Agency) and a resistance lab were glaring. AIDA utilized the most sophisticated equipment and heavily regulated environmental protocols, the resistance labs were pieced together like something out of a Frankenstein book. A mix of scrapped medical and scientific equipment existing in a series of rooms that seemed more like a garage than a lab. The dirt on the floor indicated that this was a heavily trafficked area, something the security protocols at AIDA would never allow. Even with the condition of this lab, the specimens and experiments that were available for anyone to see were far more advanced than the team would have believed.

"Look at this stuff," Coughlin said somewhat excitedly.

"Don't touch anything. We have no idea what they're working on down here. Just focus on the mission," Jossen said as he looked around. "201, how are things topside?" he asked.

"So far, so quiet. Wishing I was down there with you guys," Harden responded with a whispered voice.

"Yeah, well the day isn't over yet," Toa chimed in.

As the team moved through the lab to a door that seemed to lead further into the maze of rooms, Taylor paused at one of the stations. A chunk of black, porous, ragged mineral sat on a steel table. A monitor next to it showing bar graphs, percentages, line charts, and spectrometer readings. The analysis still seemed to be running, indicating the technicians and scientists in charge of this research were just here.

"Um guys, may want to take a look at this," Taylor said, expressing more concern than usual.

"We don't have time, we need to move," Jossen insisted.

"No, you all need to take a look at this right now," Taylor's insistence revealed a hint of panic. The team moved to the station where Taylor was standing.

"Ok, so what is it that we're looking at?" Toa asked.

"This is nanite, but there's something wrong with it. This looks like the nanites on 201's armor when it got hit with that round. It looks dead or deactivated, almost like it's diseased," Taylor replied in a concerned tone.

She moved to pick up a piece and as she gently grabbed it, the nanite crumbled in her hands. She examined it closer as the rest of the team seemed hesitant, their fear of what it could be or what it could mean held them back. The dust in her hand created an effect that both mesmerized and horrified, giving the appearance that her armor was shedding itself. She brushed her hands off as the rest of the team cringed.

"This is not good," Toa said.

"Ok everyone, let's move, that's an order," Jossen said.

The team walked away from the station, each with a growing pit in their stomachs, as they moved toward the door. Jossen led the way as Taylor seemed to linger just a little longer than the rest. The image of the dust on her hand weighed heavily on her mind. The thing that TITANs relied so much on, reduced to dust in nothing more than a basement lab.

"Maybe that's why they want the commander so badly now. Maybe Barnes and Vincere knew they were developing this type of technology. Imagine if the resistance could disable or destroy nanite? The people would panic, the resistance would definitely be emboldened, and these battles would be way more costly," Taylor noted as she moved away from the station and joined back up with the team.

"Maybe. Maybe the UNGA just had enough of the resistance slaughtering innocents, destroying homes, and bringing misery to millions. Maybe it doesn't matter why the UNGA wants him dead. All I know is we have a job to do, and I intend to do it no matter what. Through here?" Jossen asked Taylor as he pointed down a hallway.

"Yeah, should be down the hall, pass the scientists' quarters and lab storage," Taylor responded.

"I want a full sweep. Each office, each room. I'll take point," Jossen said. "Stay close, call your clears."

The team moved through each office and each room. Each time they entered a room with an expectation of confrontation, they were both disappointed and relieved. With every room or office that was cleared, *cleared* was heard across the comms. The rooms seemed to exist within their own time and space, holding the memories of the people they once housed, showing no distinct evidence of recent use. Beds were made neatly while pictures sat on desks.

"This is it," Taylor said as they approached the last door.

"Let's do this thing," Toa said as the door began to open.

The door opened to reveal an expansive room. A massive dark grey metal table loomed in the middle, large enough to seat at least one hundred people, each with their own chair and station. The chairs around the table were smaller than the one at the head of the table and each seat had a station that connected to the large circular device located at the center. Various paintings hung from the walls and sculptures sat atop pillars that lined the sides of the room. Circular designs embedded on the walls, ceilings, and floors seemed to create the illusion that they were moving. At the head of the table, a large chair was facing a digital panoramic screen showing a lifelike scene of what the Earth used to look like: green grass flowed like fabric in the wind, an ocean laid beyond the grass, a deep blue that made the green all the more vibrant. The scene popped against the monochrome color scheme of the otherwise sterile room they stood in. As the chair spun around toward the team, a man dressed in a suit sat comfortably. He was an older man that appeared to have seen his share of action. His face betrayed his demeanor, he wore his experience for all to see. His face made it apparent that the stress of both victory and heartbreak had become too much for him to hide. He conveyed strength and empathy in his gaze. Even though he sat in the chair, it was obvious that this stature was comparable to the TITANs.

The team made their way into the room while the commander sat calmly. The team kept their weapons trained on him, not knowing what to expect. They continually glanced around the room, fully expecting the room to fill with soldiers at any minute. As they approached the edge of the table, the commander spoke.

"I'm impressed," the commander said in a monotone voice.

"Then I'm honestly disappointed," Toa responded.

"You must have no idea who we are," Jossen said as he smiled behind his helmet.

"Oh but I know exactly who you are, more so than you know yourselves. When I say I'm impressed, I mean with your complete disregard for your own lives," he said. He paused before continuing. "Willing to throw away your lives for the greater cause, that's the motto isn't it? Sacrifice for the greater good," the commander continued. He paused again. "You have no idea what sacrifice is, or for that matter, what the greater good is. You children have no idea who or what you're fighting for. So quick to throw your lives away."

The team was tense while allowing the man to speak. Weapons were concentrated on him from across the table with the intensity and discipline their training demanded. Even though he was unarmed, they knew enough not to underestimate any opponent. The words the man spoke meant nothing to the team.

"Enough," Jossen interjected. "You're coming with us." Toa and Taylor began to move around one side of the table while Jossen and Coughlin moved around the other.

"If only you knew the truth," he said in a genuinely disappointed tone.

"That's far enough," the commander said as he stood up.

The team stopped, frozen in their tracks. The circles embedded throughout the room began to emit a very slight hissing noise. The noise rapidly grew in intensity while the team found it harder and harder to move. A twinge of fear hit Jossen as he realized he had just led the team into a trap. The commander's words echoed in Jossen with each passing second.

"The circles?" Jossen murmured.

"Yes, but they're much more than just aesthetically pleasing," the commander said as he pressed a button on a remote.

"Uh, what's happening here guys?" Coughlin asked in panic as she looked at the rest of the team.

The nanite armor began to retreat into the discs, slowly deconstructing as if it was trying to fight it. Although it wasn't the same effect they saw topside or in the lab, the team couldn't help but think back to the crumbled piece of nanite. As the nanites returned completely to the housing, it revealed the soldiers for who they really were. At that moment, resistance soldiers came pouring through the door, filled the room, and surrounded the team.

"Kids?" one of the soldiers asked, completely puzzled at the operators who stood in front of them.

"These are the operators? These kids?" his tone grew angrier.

"Calm down. These *children* are probably as confused as you are right now. Totally exposed. Wondering how this could be happening," the commander said as he moved toward the team.

Jossen stood there, completely exposed, but showed no sign of weakness as the commander came within inches. Jossen's arms were shaking while he tried with every muscle in his enhanced body to reach for the commander. The commander smirked at him, admiring his tenacity while understanding the undeniable fact. These TITANs had come to kill him. The rest of the team tried as hard as they could, straining with determination to break free from the invisible constraints. Upon seeing the man standing face to face, eye to eye with Jossen, another undeniable reality set in. The commander had to be a TITAN.

"We have been studying nanites for longer than you've been alive. You and the ones that sent you here rely on them so blindly. They forget everything we worked for. All of the sacrifices that brought us to where we are," he paused, looking slightly confused when staring into Jossen's eyes.

"You have that look in your eye...like you've still got a card to play," he said to Jossen.

Jossen simply smiled at the man, knowing that Harden and the rest of the operators were still topside keeping guard, assuming they had been listening to the comms and would come down to provide an assist. He hoped that while this man thought he had the advantage, Harden and the others would have the element of surprise.

"That smirk says it all but I'm sure that your optimism is misplaced. We'll get to that in a while, but first, I'm going to need you to answer some questions," the commander said.

"We're not telling you shit," Coughlin interrupted.

"I didn't expect that you would just tell me, and I certainly wouldn't trust you if you did. The question and answer phase will start soon enough. Take them," he commanded as the soldiers moved toward the team and injected each of them with a substance.

"This should help keep you calm for the ride. If you value your teammates' lives, I suggest you relax and cooperate," the commander said.

The hissing noise that had become a constant whining, seized and the magnets released. The TITANs dropped to the floor weakened, beyond the ability to stand, by whatever the soldiers had injected them with. The soldiers then pulled the operators' arms behind their backs and attached restraints. They stood them up and began to escort them out of the room while the reapers became noticeably weaker with each passing second.

"And as for your friend topside, he'll be joining you shortly," the commander said just as the team was being led out the door.

While all of this was happening below, Harden remained next to the lift. The blast doors that had remained open began to close. The remaining operators outside were now stuck outside. Harden heard the last transmission from Jossen.

"Circles? What circles? What the hell are you guys talking about?" Harden asked frantically.

"Guys? 103? 408?" he continued, with no response.

Harden stepped forward slowly, moving toward the lift controls when he heard a sound coming from his side. He turned quickly, his recon mode glitched slightly due to the movement but saw nothing. Harden continued back to the lift controls when he felt a force at his back, an applied pressure that stopped his forward movement. As he turned to confront it, the blur of distorted light flashed in front of him. The realization hit him like a ton of bricks but a moment too late. The device at the floor began to hiss and emit a powerful magnetic field, holding Harden in place while the armor began to retreat into the housing. The soldier standing in front of Harden, still cloaked, jabbed him in the arm with an injection.

"What the f..." Harden wasn't able to complete the sentence before being struck with the butt of a rifle and rendered unconscious.

"The boss wants him loaded with the others," the cloaked soldier said while twenty-five other soldiers came rushing through the door and surrounded the unconscious Harden.

"All that for these kids? I don't get it," one soldier exclaimed.

"It's not for you to get," another soldier responded as he lifted Harden and carried him to the lift. The soldiers met up with the commander at the bottom of the lift.

"Put the proper restraints on and load him with the others. We need to leave immediately," the commander said as he moved closer to the unconscious Harden.

The commander grabbed Harden's face by the cheeks and gave him a once over, as if he was expecting to find something out of the ordinary. The youthful appearance reminded him of himself and he began thinking back to his own past. The commander knew that this is it, the moment he has been preparing for. He released his face and turned away

"Be sure the restraints are properly secured," the commander reiterated.

"Sir, are all of these precautions really necessary? They may be operators ,but they're only kids?" a soldier asked.

"If you knew what these *kids* were capable of, you would kill them here and now. Just make sure they're all secured," he commanded as he continued to walk away. "And begin the evacuation, destroy the lab. They'll take care of the rest for us."

Meanwhile, back on the Forge, Director Barnes sat in her office, staring out the window. The office, meticulously organized and clean, was decorated with only degrees, awards, and honors. It was a window into her obsession with science and knowledge, homage to a focused and singular career. The window she stared at appeared to show the compound that the team just infiltrated in the distance. Smoke was rising up from the compound although it was difficult to determine the status of the mission.

"A disaster!" Admiral Vincere exclaimed with both disappointment and anger, although anger seemed to prevail in his tone.

"Not ideal Admiral, but far from a disaster," Barnes said calmly.

"How is this not a disaster?! The target hasn't been retrieved and most of the team is offline. You have no idea where they're going and the threat still remains," the Admiral said.

"I shouldn't have to remind you what's at stake here. If this gets out, I promise you I will not take the fall. I will make sure the responsibility falls squarely on your shoulders," the Admiral paused.

He looked at the window that Barnes was so intently focused on before looking around the room. He had witnessed some of the achievements displayed in her office. Although there were no personal photos or any indication that she had a life beyond science, he knew better. He knew the personal sacrifices that she had made for the good of the UNGA, for the good of all humanity, but still felt as though she had her own objectives.

"Every milestone we've achieved, every breakthrough, every success now hinges on what happens next. How you let him get the better of you I'll never understand," he continued.

"Just take care of it Barnes or they'll have no choice but to shut you down," the Admiral said and began to walk toward the door.

Director Barnes turned her chair to face the Admiral as he also turned back. Her face projected the image of a strong woman, older but extremely capable. Her discipline and determination were enough to intimidate any man, one of the many reasons she was chosen for this position. She looked him in the eye while placing both of her hands gently on the desk and leaning in.

"While it may not seem it to you right now, I've planned for this. We've been through a lot, we've changed this world in ways no one will understand. You know what we're doing this for–who we're doing this for–all of this, I wouldn't want them to know that after all of this time, you're losing your resolve," she said as she narrowed her gaze.

"No one will question my devotion, only your failures. You're playing with fire Barnes, I've seen what happens to people who think they can control the uncontrollable. Just finish it so we can move on," the Admiral finished as he closed the door behind him.

Barnes contemplated the encounter for a moment then turned her chair back towards the window. A flash of light and the compound was hit with a high velocity, ultra-dense kinetic projectile. The plume of debris reached hundreds of feet in the air as only a crater of smoldering ruins remained. The window went dark as the words *Transmission Ended* appeared on the glass of the window. Barnes turned back to her desk, opened a drawer on the top left, and took out an olive green paper folder. The folder was thick, with inches of paperwork inside. The outside cover is stamped UNIC AIDA TOP SECRET. She opened the folder and stared at it intently.

"I can only hope you forgive me," she said to herself in a whisper as she touched the photo paper-clipped to the corner of the file. There was no name under the photo, just the characters A101.

THREE
HISTORY LESSON

BY THE TIME the resistance base was dusted, all personnel had evacuated. The commander seemed to always be one step ahead of the UNIC. They had made their way through an elaborate underground tunnel to a hangar miles away from the base, launching at the exact moment the projectile hit covering their retreat.

As the commander and the captured operators sat aboard the falcon, the commander studied each of them from top to bottom, committing every detail to memory. The team was secured in their seats across from the commander. Unconscious, they only slouched slightly as the metal exoskeleton kept them more or less rigid. He studied the look of the new exoskeletons. The larger circular discs were located on the chest, hips, and thighs. The smaller discs were at the elbows, knees, and ankles. The soft cool glow they emitted contrasted against the harsher red lighting emanating from the lights above. The ship jostled slightly as they broke through the atmosphere.

"Sir, we've just detected an SDD signature above the compound. The UNIC Condor has left the area," the pilot's voice came over the speaker.

"Understood, maintain course," the commander replied.

He turned his attention back to the team, then looked down at his own hands. He rolled his sleeve back to reveal a small disc attached just above his wrist. He seemed to be entranced by it for a brief moment before pulling his sleeve back down to cover it up. He shook his head slightly as if he could shake his memories off that easily.

"Activating the SDD sir," the voice proclaimed.

The queasy feeling that always accompanied the jump when using the space distortion drive set in. Although it was very low intensity it was noticeable, nonetheless. The commander leaned back in his seat, knowing that when they arrived at their destination, he would have his work cut out for him, but for now, he could relax. After the brief journey through the distortion, a voice once again came over the speaker.

"Disengaging the SDD," the pilot said.

The queasy feeling once again surfaced but only momentarily. The craft jostled once again as the ship entered another atmosphere. Shortly after, the ship began to slow and prepare for landing.

"Touchdown sir," the pilot sounded confidently relieved.

The cargo door opened, and the natural light poured into the falcon. The commander stood up as eight soldiers approached from the other side of the cargo door to transport the team. The soldiers walked up the ramp created by the cargo door and began to release the harnesses of the team members. The TITANs were heavier than the soldiers expected, requiring them to exert a visible amount of effort to support them.

"Bring them to holding, make sure when they wake you let me know immediately," the commander instructed the soldiers.

"Yes sir," the lead soldier replied.

The man proceeds down the cargo door ramp and continues down a path leading to the entrance of a facility, passing ten soldiers on either side of the path standing at attention. The doors open as he approaches and continues into the dark. The soldiers transporting the team follow with only a moment's delay, giving the commander some space. The commander wastes no time getting to work. He makes his way to the command room, a room bustling with activity. There are teams of workers shouting orders, questions, and confirmations while a multitude of screens display ever-changing operational information. The lieutenant approached the commander with intense purpose. While her physical appearance wasn't enough to intimidate many of the male soldiers in the room, it was her fierce confidence that commanded attention. She was tall with soft tan skin, not giving the slightest hint of her battlefield experience. She wore her undercut pixie hair emblazoned with light purple streaks proudly, often celebrating the fact it took her no time to do her hair. Everyone had heard the stories, the rumors, knowing there had to be some truth to them. After all, she had earned her place in the resistance, her place at the commander's side as lieutenant.

"Sir, that went as well as we could've hoped. The evacuation was successful. All ships have landed, and troops have been assigned. We've confirmed that the facility has been completely destroyed, even the remaining operators that were stuck outside the base," she said as she paused for a moment. "Here is today's briefing," she continued as she handed him a thin piece of what looked like glass.

The glass-like material was the size of a thin magazine, although it was very unlikely that anyone in this compound would remember what a magazine was. It had an electronic display that would appear when authenticated by the commander. The display had all of the relevant information the commander would need to bring him up to speed on all of the latest resistance intelligence. The lieutenant always made sure to keep the commander up to date, providing overviews and detailed reports on every aspect of the resistance operations.

"I've also sent all of the intel on the team to your office. The newly updated fleet movements have been uploaded for your review. Several strike teams have been requesting additional support, supplies, and munitions. Take a look at the operational data on this outpost, we will be expanding the R&D sectors based on the influx of personnel. I also have additional supplies being brought in tomorrow morning," she continued. She paused to take a breath as her fast speaking excited nature seemed to have got the better of her.

"Lieutenant," the commander interrupted her with a smile. "Thank you. I will take a look at this in a moment, but I need to speak with you in my office first," he said as he motioned for her to follow him.

She smiled back and followed him as he walked through the command room doors and down the long dreary corridor. He opened the door to his office, and she followed. The door closed behind them as he moved towards his desk. The lieutenant remained just inside the office.

"Any word?" he asked.

"Nothing yet sir," she responded.

"The operators we brought back, they were definitely about to be *retired*. They may seem like kids, but they are older than you think and definitely near the end of their cycles. I don't think they have any idea what awaits them at the end. Just thinking about it really pisses me off. To know that they would destroy lives just to keep a degree of control," he said and fell exhaustedly into his chair.

"They would destroy every person in existence, their own family, if it gave them even the slightest bit more power. You don't think destroying their own property would be a no-brainer?" she asked rhetorically.

"Yeah, but to send these teams, knowing they could be killed is one thing, knowing they could be captured is something else. I feel like something is off, like they meant for us to capture them...we need to be very careful. One mistake and everything we have worked for, that we've built, could come crashing down around us," he replied. He put his face in his hands while he moaned and rubbed his forehead with his fingers.

He was clearly exhausted, not by the physical demands of his position but by the mental. Fighting came naturally for the commander, an effortless reflex that was embedded within him since he was a child. The incredible burden that the resistance placed on him drove his exhaustion, the responsibility of millions of lives. It was not a responsibility he took lightly or one that he did not want. He knew that the only way to break humanity out of its own self-imposed prison was through revolution, which was through the downfall of the UNGA. The hardest part for him was trying to stay one step ahead of the people who built their empire on that very same principle.

"Unless..." the lieutenant spoke but paused to wait for acknowledgement.

The man pulled his face from his hands and looked at

her. The intrigue yanked him out of the self-questioning doubt that had briefly overtaken him. He had found early on that the lieutenant was a great person to bounce ideas off of and the only person he trusted to keep their conversations private.

"Unless there *is* an advantage for the team being captured. Think about it; the team was not properly equipped, nor informed, for the mission. The chances of their success were slim to none...unless AIDA's objective was for them to fail without realizing it," she concluded. She paused again, still trying to wrap her head around her own thoughts, and continued, "AIDA needed them to fail but didn't want them to realize it."

"But what does AIDA gain by sending them here to be captured?" the commander asked.

"Run a complete analysis on each of them and their nanites. Destroy any equipment that isn't attached to them," he instructed the lieutenant.

"Yes sir!" she said confidently as she moved swiftly through the door.

The lieutenant always gained a boost of morale when helping the commander work through a tough spot. He may have been a TITAN, but he was still human after all. She wasted no time ordering the top researchers to perform a full analysis on the team. The resistance, while without the resources the UNGA possessed, had recruited some of the most brilliant minds humanity had to offer. They were the ones that had found the operator's weaknesses and how the resistance could fight back against these enhanced soldiers.

"Barnes...what are you up to?" the commander asked himself as he looked at the briefing the lieutenant provided.

Some time later, in another part of the resistance outpost, Harden experienced flashes of his dreams while unconscious.

Images of him running to his room, hiding under the bed, seeing people's feet approaching, the hand reaching to retrieve him, and him sliding out to see what looked like soldiers flickered in succession to muffled noises in the background. Just as he was about to see the faces of the soldiers and the other two people in the room, he jolted awake in the same way he usually did. This time he felt that he was somehow closer than ever to revealing the identity of the people coming for him. He woke to find himself in a dull gray room. The room was basic, concrete walls and floors with not so much as a window or table. It was large enough to accommodate five large cots laid out on the perimeter. While there wasn't much room in between the cots, there was some empty space in the middle of the room and in front of the door. Harden looked around and saw that the rest of his team was still unconscious. He stood up, moving to check on each member of the team. He was relieved to find that they were still alive and seemed to be ok. He sat back down on his cot. There didn't seem to be any cameras, no guards, almost as though they were thrown in a storage room to be kept out of the way. Harden waited for some time before his teammates finally began to regain consciousness.

"What the hell was that?" Jossen asked, still working on getting himself upright.

"Hey, lower your voice," Harden said in a whisper as he leaned in toward Jossen. "We don't know if anyone's listening."

Jossen tried to stand up quickly but was not able to move as he normally would have. His movements slowed somehow, a sluggish version of his normal self. His anger was temporarily obscured by confusion and the feeling of defeat as he looked around at the team. He quickly pushed those emotions down, allowing the anger to return.

"What the hell is going on here?" he asked loudly, hoping someone could hear him.

"Hey, get over here," Harden said as he grabbed at Jossen with his hand.

"I need to talk to you...to everyone," Harden said in a tone barely louder than a whisper.

He looked around the room seeing that everyone was now regaining consciousness. He waited for a moment as they got their bearings. He paid special attention to Taylor, watching to ensure she was alright.

"You all need to hear this, there was an operator working with the resistance," he began. "I saw one using the stealth mod right before they got me."

"And they must have injected us with something that's inhibiting or disabling our nanites," Taylor chimed in, mimicking Harden's tone.

"Yeah, like it forced our armor to deactivate. I don't think it was just the armor either because I feel different. I think it's affecting us as well," Toa concurred.

"Different how?" Harden asked.

Harden wasn't sure what he meant by different. Harden's confusion became apparent in his expression. He didn't feel any different. *What did Toa mean by affecting us as well,* he asked himself.

"Like I'm not 100 percent," Toa responded.

"I feel it too, like my entire body is heavier than normal," Coughlin agreed.

"I think that whatever they injected us with is suppressing the nanites in our bodies as well," Taylor suggested.

Harden didn't press the issue. He wanted to tell them he didn't feel any different but held it in. He wasn't sure what this meant, and in his mind, it probably meant nothing. He figured it wasn't a bad thing if he still felt fine, at least he might be in a better position to help if needed.

"We need to be smart about this. This isn't a *shoot our way out* scenario here. We need a plan," Jossen said. "But first, we need to figure out what is going on. It's obvious that some details about the resistance were left out during our mission briefing."

"Some details? Ya think?" Toa asked sarcastically.

Jossen looked over at Coughlin who had been fairly quiet so far. "You ok?" he asked, expressing genuine concern.

She sat there, her head hung as she looked down at her hands. The confidence that normally coursed through her veins, fueling her sense of empowerment, had drained from her. A multitude of emotions flooded her thoughts, clouding her normally precise judgement.

"Yeah, I'll be alright," she replied as she clenched her fist, watching her knuckles go white while the muscles in her arm flexed. "I just can't believe the resistance was so prepared for our arrival. If there was even a hint that the resistance found a way to deactivate nanites, it seems like we should have at least been warned so we could be prepared," she said.

"It's hard to believe that AIDA and Director Barnes wouldn't have factored some kind of failsafe into the design," Taylor said, seemingly confused by the situation.

"Well, if we can't get out of here and let AIDA and the UNIC know then every operator out there is vulnerable to the same tactic," Jossen said as he began to lay out his plan.

"Ok, first things first, we need to find out what we can about where we are, and we need to determine if we're still in the compound or somewhere else, but we can't give any hints about what we're doing. We need to scout this room for any weak points, anything we can use to escape, or anything else that will tell us where we are. We have to do it without drawing attention," he said.

The team nodded slightly and tried their best to mimic someone who was lounging around as they attempted to survey their surroundings. Although they tried their best, it came off as forced. They didn't need to keep it up long, as the door opened only a moment later. The lieutenant walked through the door with a commanding presence.

"I trust you are all ok?" she asked, maintaining a very dry and to-the-point approach.

"OK?! No, we are not ok," Coughlin was the first to respond.

"Your people injected us with God knows what and brought us to God knows where...really, where are we?" Coughlin tried a more direct approach to find out where they were.

"Let's not confuse the situation here. Your team attacked us. Your team was attempting a kidnapping at best and at worst an assassination. We lost good men today and for what? To play host to some second-rate operators," the lieutenant said.

The lieutenant often harnessed the past to fuel her passion. She knew what this team had done in the past, what they were sent to do, and had they succeeded...what would have happened. She took a moment to cool down before continuing, knowing that she had to keep her emotions in check.

"We are not the aggressors in this. We don't send children to fight our battles. Unfortunately, you and your team were never told the truth. You, AIDA, the UNIC, and the UNGA are on the wrong side of this conflict...the wrong side of history," the lieutenant finished.

"The wrong side of history?!?" Jossen said as if the statement was the most absurd thing he had ever heard.

He stood up and took a step towards the lieutenant, towering over her as he leaned down to meet eye to eye. The lieutenant didn't flinch or so much as blink. In fact, she leaned into him. She never backed down from a challenge and to her, this confrontation was no different.

"Anyone who runs around killing innocent people, bombing civilians, and torturing prisoners without any regard for human decency will never be on the right side of history. We will always stand up to people like that," Jossen said, maintaining eye contact inches from the lieutenant's face.

She looked him up and down, took one measured step backward, then one measured step to the left.

"If that's how you truly feel..." the commander said as he appeared from behind the lieutenant as she moved. "Then you are in serious need of a history lesson."

He smiled as he stepped forward. He stood face to face with Jossen. Jossen had to look up just slightly to meet him eye to eye.

"You think you know what side of history you're on? How?" the commander asked. "Because someone told you?"

"It's because we are on the side that is trying to stop murderous terrorists like you!" Jossen shouted angrily.

The commander chuckled. "Murderous terrorists?" he asked as he looked over at the lieutenant with a smile. "I'm sorry, maybe I missed something, but who came to kill who?"

"We came to stop you, to stop the violence that the resistance is responsible for," Jossen replied.

"The violence that the resistance is responsible for?" the commander asked as his demeanor turned from one of kindness to anger. "You child, you know nothing of violence."

Jossen began to move closer to the commander, apparently to attack him. The commander turned to Jossen and with effortless ease, pushed the palm of his hand against Jossen's chest. Jossen, thrown off balance, stumbled back. The combination of being off balance and the weight of the exoskeleton proved too much, he fell into a seated position onto the cot.

"You have no idea who we are or what you are for that matter," the commander remarked.

"You and your team have been force fed a false narrative your whole lives. Tell me, how often have you ventured off of the Forge?" he asked, softening his tone slightly.

"I'm sure you've been allowed off of the Forge for a mission here or deployment there but how often have you left the ship to see what it's like in the real world? How often have you visited a colony? How many times have you been to a party? A funeral?" he questioned. He paused, looking at each of their faces. "And Director Barnes...I'm sure she is the closest thing you have to a mother...but she didn't birth you. Can you even remember your parents? Can you remember anything from your childhood?"

The questions hit the team hard. Each of them taken aback by the questions, not expecting the commander to get that personnel. It hit Harden especially hard, instantly bringing the thoughts of his dreams to the front of his mind. He thought about saying something but Jossen jumped in. He seemed unfazed by the commander's line of questioning.

"It's obvious you are a part of the TITAN program...or at least used to be. So what, you got left behind or something and decided to go rogue? And what, we're supposed to believe that you and your people aren't terrorists?" Jossen asked, continuing with the rhetorical questions. "That everything we have been taught, everything we believe is a lie? All because you know about the TITAN program...because you are, wait sorry, were an operator?" Jossen stopped, waiting for a reaction.

"Fair enough," the commander said as he smiled again. "You don't have to believe me. How about I show you?"

The team looked at each other slightly confused. The commander turned around and moved to the door followed closely by the lieutenant.

"This way," he said as he began walking before he stopped. "I guess now is as good a time as any to formally introduce ourselves. I'm Commander Hanlon and this is Lieutenant Rimerez."

"I'm 103 and this is 312," Jossen remarked as he motioned to Toa.

"I'm going to cut you off right there," Hanlon said, "I get the numerical identifications, but your mission is over, I think we can move past the UNIC formalities. I know you have names. I'm not going to have our people calling out numbers when they talk to you."

"Our mission isn't over until we've taken you out," Jossen asserted.

"I'm Harden," Harden introduced and stepped forward slightly.

The rest of the team followed suit except Jossen. He was upset and a little disappointed with the team and himself. He felt as though all of this was his fault anyway but still clung to the notion that it wasn't over, that they could still somehow complete their mission and return home victorious.

"And this lovable gentleman here is Jossen," Toa commented as they began to follow the commander out.

They began to walk the hallways as the commander led the way. Lieutenant Rimerez followed behind the team. While they were not restrained in any way, she wanted to make sure none of them wandered off.

"So, I assume you are all familiar with how the TITAN program functions?" the commander asked as they continued down the hall.

The team continuously scanned and scouted the area as they walked, focused on figuring out exactly where they were and how they could escape. Armed soldiers were posted in pairs at every door. While the resistance soldiers were not TITANs, the team would have trouble overwhelming this force without their nanites or armor. Even if they were able to take out the guards, they still had no idea where they were or how to get out.

"Yeah..." Toa said, "but why do I have a feeling you're about to tell us something completely different?"

"Not completely different, but I want to give you a little perspective," the commander said as he moved toward a door. "Why don't we sit in here?"

He opened the door as the lieutenant walked in first. Jossen hesitated before entering the room. As they did, the lights brightened to illuminate the space. It was nothing impressive, a room that looked to be a repurposed space where a large conference-type table was placed. There were enough chairs to sit ten people at the table and another three against the wall.

"Please sit," the commander requested as he moved to the head of the table.

At each seat, there was a built-in touch screen. In the center of the table, there was a large oval device, which began to glow around the edges. Each team member took a seat around the table as the lieutenant sat away from the table near the door.

"Why would you let us just walk around without restraints?" Jossen waited at the door for a response.

"Think about it...your nanites have been neutralized, the

last time you had to fight without them was, when, never? We train without the aid of nanites on a regular basis, we are armed, and whether you believe me or not, there really is no way out of here...not without the proper clearance," the commander said as he gestured with his hand for the team to enter.

"So you all think you know who you really are? What you really are? I thought I knew too, but I was wrong. I had to find out the truth for myself. The operators, a subset of the TITAN program was created as a military branch of the program. There are other subsets of the TITAN program as well. You are familiar with these I assume?" the commander asked the group.

"You mean the guardians and the engineers," Jossen replied with just a hint of uncertainty.

"Yes, the guardians provide security for the highest level officials in the UNGA, and the engineers provide manual labor for the most dangerous jobs. So while there are differing subsets now, there used to be only one kind of TITAN. These original TITANs created in the first phase of the program were designed to provide the service that the operators and guardians provide. It was only after phase 3 was complete and they moved to phase 4 that they added the subset of engineers to provide labor after the accident on ASX90871," the commander explained.

"That was the hexa-triton mining accident that killed over 150,000 on that asteroid," Jossen chimed in.

"That's right. That accident fueled a demand by the people to find a better way to mine the precious resource. The UNGA responded with engineers. This meant that the government-owned mining companies could get even more profit by not having to provide safer working conditions and increasing their productivity. They sold out members of the

TITAN program as manual labor," the commander continued to explain.

"That's not true, the engineers provide a valuable service for all of humanity, just as every other TITAN does," Jossen interjected, justifying the use of the engineers with the same reasoning instilled by the UNGA.

"You really don't get it, do you?" the commander asked. "The engineers took away a lot of the jobs that regular working people had. This led to unemployment and increased poverty for the most vulnerable while the government pocketed the profit. They force the engineers to perform manual labor...they see them as tools, completely ignoring the fact that they are still humans...however augmented they may be," the commander began to get angry, feeling the need to pause while he composed himself.

"So if you felt this way, why wouldn't you work to resolve these problems instead of murdering innocent people? Why continue to attack the UNGA and its forces, killing civilians in the process? Why not try to find another way?" Harden asked, thinking there had to be a way to address these issues without the violence.

"Again, I have to remember who I am talking to," the commander said. "You have no idea what the UNGA is capable of, what atrocities they have committed in the name of humanity. Your sheltered existence has shielded you from the truths that exist outside of the Forge. When the world was on fire, it was the UNGA, the council that supposedly saved it. What you won't learn about was how the world was set on fire in the first place."

"We did learn how the world was set on fire. You can't blame resource depletion, war, and natural disasters on the council," Jossen jumped in.

The commander stopped for a moment, reaching down to

tap a couple of times on the table. A projection of the Earth appeared above the projector as the commander began to speak again.

"The UNGA is the brainchild of the five ministers: Halin, Gantley, Yamato, Guerrero, and Sarpong. In their day, they were the wealthiest members of humanity, not the most popular, as they seemed to stay out of the spotlight as much as possible. These people have played the long, long game. They were the ones who put the leaders of the world into power, the leaders that would be responsible for the isolationist policies that set the world on a path of destruction. Once they had their pieces in position, they fanned the flames of war while pushing policies that would do nothing to address the climate crisis they helped fuel. They created the perfect scenario for them to become the heroes. After the great war and climate crisis devastated the global economy, not to mention the countless human toll, they held all of the chips. They used their almost limitless resources to establish the UNGA, a global authority that would be able to address all of the world's issues as a cohesive body. They already had the leaders in their pockets, it wasn't a question that they would sign the treaties giving control to the UNGA," the commander explained. The commander paused for a moment.

As the projection of the Earth at the center of the table showed the various countries that existed before the UNGA, the globe then spun as it showed the Earth split into four quarters, a view of how the Earth was divided after the creation of the UNGA.

"So the territories were split, and each minister received a territory to manage. The territory that Minister Gantley was responsible for was space. He was the one who was instrumental in the hiring of Director Barnes to head AIDA. He was the one who had been the leader in this group, a group that has manipulated the human race from the beginning," the commander said.

The projection moved through images from the great war, the climate crisis, the countless headlines of resistance attacks from the UNGA news sites.

"These so-called resistance attacks are nothing more than propaganda," the commander continued as a headline scrolled, "*Resistance kidnaps children, recruits child soldiers.*"

"It would be funny if it wasn't completely appalling. They claim that we forced children to fight for us when it was the UNGA that used children, innocent children to further their ambitions," the commander said, getting angrier as he spoke.

"We've seen the videos from the attacks, the resistance using child soldiers to initiate attacks on convoys. You can honestly sit here and blame the UNGA? We've seen evidence of the resistance launching attack after attack, the carnage left behind, and have fought off some of these same attacks. There's nothing you can say that will make us believe that it was anything other than a terrorist organization launching attacks against humanity as a whole," Coughlin chimed in.

"I'm not asking you to believe me. I'm asking you to listen and see what I have to share, then make up your own mind. Now what do you know about the first subjects, phase 1 of the TITAN program?" the commander asked the group.

"Well, the first phase of the TITAN program saw volunteers undergo Director Barnes' nanite infusion process while being the first test subjects able to wear the nanite armor," Taylor said excitedly.

"The volunteers you're talking about were children. Children that were lied to, manipulated. AIDA deceived them into believing that they were abandoned by their parents, left in an orphanage, that no one wanted them. Director Barnes found them, made us feel special...she said the children were chosen, designed by God, given the perfect DNA and that they were destined to become the greatest of humanity," the commander replied and began to choke up a bit at the end.

He looked up at the ceiling, everyone in the room recognized that this was something that was very personal to him. It was strange for the team to see a TITAN this way, far more emotional than they would have ever believed possible. While Jossen saw it as a weakness, something that he might be able to exploit, the others questioned what could make a TITAN so emotional.

The commander continued. "After the children had undergone the nanite infusion process, a painful and traumatizing experience, their bodies would either accept them or reject them, the child would either become a TITAN or not. The ones who did not survive the infusion process were discarded–nothing more than failed experiments for the AIDA. The ones who did survive were put through the most intense training, designed to develop the most advanced war machine known to man. The nanites wouldn't only enhance their physical characteristics, they would also destroy any connection with the past. The nanites would, for the lack of a better term, rewire their brain. The synaptic connections remade for efficiency with the unintended but welcomed side effect. Truly a soldier engineered for battle in every way possible."

The team was clearly having a hard time digesting this. Each of them tried to think back to their earliest memory, not one involving anything before the TITAN program. Harden seemed to be having more difficulty processing this than the others. He did remember something from before the TITAN program, or was that a false memory as a result of the synaptic reprogramming? He remained silent as the commander continued.

"The TITANs from phase 1 found out later that it was all a lie, everything from who they were to why they were created. The children that had been rescued from a life of loneliness and destitution, were not rescued at all. The children that were the seeds for the TITAN program were stolen from their families, ripped from their lives and their childhood, leaving their families to grieve while the UNGA blamed the resistance. The resistance was the perfect scapegoat," the commander said.

He showed videos of the families pleading for the resistance to return their children while displaying images of children before the infusion process began. They were match after match, all of the missing children appearing in photos apparently taken at UNIC AIDA labs. The team leaned back in their seats. None of them was prepared to hear and see what they did. They all looked blank, each of them trying to find a hole in the commander's story, something they could point to that would discredit what he had been saying.

"I'm not going to lie, this is a lot," Toa said as he sat back in his chair, breaking the brief awkward silence.

"I know it is and there's more. You're all being caught up on decades of information. Information that had to be collected and pieced together. Information that was learned over time, now being crammed into a study session," the commander remarked.

He leaned in and brought up a video showing footage that seemed to be from UNIC AIDA archives. It depicted short clips of young TITANs strapped into chairs while doctors surrounded them. Other clips showed scientists around computer screens displaying programming of some kind. The commander began to speak again.

"It seemed that while the subliminal controls put in place during training and education are effective, they do tend to wear off. The first phase of the TITAN program did not have proper protocols in place to deal with this loss of control. When AIDA and the UNGA found out that the effectiveness of the controls faded with time, they called for the immediate destruction of all phase one TITANs. The UNGA would not risk losing control of their weapons. They devised a plan to dispose of the TITANs by creating a non-existent mission to crush the resistance, all of the TITANs would be deployed but none of them would even survive the journey. While they were obviously unaware of the plot against them, the TITANs were excited that the UNGA finally authorized the complete destruction of the resistance," he paused.

He began tapping on his screen again, bringing up a flight path in three dimensions. The path originated from the Forge, located in Earth orbit, then continued to a point just beyond where a marker pulsated. Another area being displayed showed another marker pulsating while the path continued to a planet.

"Several ships were to take them from Earth orbit to this planet, XRC112. The ships would drop the TITANs to raid the base and crush the resistance. The TITANs boarded the ships and began their journey. The ships would need to reach a safe minimum distance before engaging the SDD. As the ships journeyed to reach that distance, several TITANs noticed peculiar deficiencies in the navigational data as well as the armaments for the mission. After a couple of TITANs reviewed the navigational systems, it seemed that they had been tampered with, causing any destination input to result in a set coordinate value. This meant that the ship, no matter what coordinates were entered, would go to a very specific set of coordinates," he said as he showed the alter flight path of the ship.

"You're talking about the Starhopper incident," Harden said as he noticed the flight path brought the ship right into the black hole at the center of the milky way.

"Yes. The UNGA and AIDA believed that the TITANs would eventually turn on the very people who created them. They are the ones who rigged the navigation systems on those ships. They are the ones who were responsible for the deaths of thousands of TITANs," he continued to explain. "But they soon found out how resilient we can be."

He pulled up the schematics of an SDD on the projection. It animated the breakdown of the drive. It had a solid hexa-triton orb in the center, surrounded by a smooth round metal housing populated with dimples. The housing was contained within a special collar, this collar held the housing and orb in place via a magnetic field.

"There must have been someone within the UNIC that believed the TITANs didn't deserve what was about to happen. As we assessed what our options were, we found that someone had loaded a falcon in the cargo bay...a falcon that should not have been there. Thinking fast, some of the TITANs were able to swap the navigational units from the Starhopper and the falcon. They also swapped the transponder from the Starhopper and the falcon, only to find out that the falcon did not have a transponder, so the UNGA would believe that the falcon was the Starhopper and effectively making the Starhopper not exist. One TITAN would have to fly with the falcon into the black hole, sacrificing themselves to save the rest," he recounted. The commander seemed to look back on the moment in his mind.

"While any TITAN on board would've gladly performed

that honor, it fell to one and that TITAN made the ultimate sacrifice for us all," he said as he pulled up a photo of a TITAN.

"Ruiz made that sacrifice so some of us could survive. Several other Starhopper ships were not as lucky as ours. Once the falcon deployed, the Starhopper set a course for a little known planet on the outer rim of the mapped universe. When we arrived on that planet, each TITAN made a decision. We could go live out our lives forever hidden from the UNGA or we could do what we could to fight the UNGA: join the resistance. I made my decision that day, a decision I will never regret," he said.

The team seemed like they were on the edge of their seats, all except Jossen. He maintained a straight face as if this was a UNIC test, a test to see how loyal they would be. He knew that the others may not see through this, so he continued to replay justification after justification in his head.

The UNGA did what they had to for humanity's sake. They told us what they needed to tell us to protect us. The ultimate goal was peace and if they needed to get a little messy to accomplish that goal then the means justified the end, he thought to himself.

"So that's the story of phase 1. Then what exactly is phase 2, other than a new batch of TITANs?" Toa asked.

It seemed like Toa wanted to push the commander past the difficulties of his memories. As much as he was their enemy, Toa didn't do so well with emotions like this. It was not something that any of them was used to. The team was taught to keep emotions other than anger buried, hidden, or suppressed. Anger was the only useful emotion on the battlefield, anything else was a distraction.

"Phase 2...this phase is when they started to incorporate

retirement into the program for TITANs," the commander replied.

"Retirement?" asked Coughlin.

"Who is the oldest operator team on your station?" the commander asked.

The team had to think about it for a moment. Looking at each other for the answer. It took a second before Jossen spoke.

"I'm pretty sure it's us at this point..." Jossen looked at his team for confirmation.

"Yeah, it would've been Charlie team, but they didn't make it back after taking out that resistance outpost on Ulin," Harden replied.

"Let me guess, they succeeded in their mission though?" the commander asked.

"You know they did Commander, it was a resistance outpost," Jossen said, annoyed by the suggestion that they might have failed.

"Retirement...as the controls put in place become less effective, you're given one last assignment to complete, then you rendezvous with an extraction ship and away you go... never to be seen again...more than likely into the same black hole as Ruiz," the commander said.

"And for the record, the outpost on Ulin was dusted. The UNIC never sent any operators. We lost countless soldiers and civilians, whole families destroyed in the blink of an eye, all because those TITANs were getting too old. Do you still think the UNGA is..." the commander continued before he was interrupted.

The door burst open. A slender man wearing a resistance officer uniform leaned toward the lieutenant, whispered something in her ear, and abruptly left the room, closing the door behind him.

"Sir, you're needed immediately in the comms room. We're receiving a transmission," the lieutenant said.

She quickly moved to open the door for him. He got up and moved toward the door. The team looked around, thinking for the briefest of moments that he might leave them in this room. Their momentary internal celebration came to a halt as the commander spoke.

"The lieutenant will escort you to the mess hall. Grab something to eat and we can continue our conversation later," he said just before exiting the door.

"This way," the lieutenant said while gesturing toward the door.

The team got up, somewhat lazily as they continued to process the information they had just been presented. They followed the lieutenant to the mess hall where as many as forty soldiers were talking and laughing as they ate. The room fell silent as the group entered. They moved in a single file line to get some food. All of the soldiers seemed to be frozen in time, they gawked at the team before turning to each other and whispering.

"Oh my, you must all be bored and full," the lieutenant said as she turned towards the men.

"If you don't have anything better to do than gawk at some TITANs then I'm sure I can find something for you to do," she took a step out of line toward the men.

The whole room immediately turned back to their meal and began eating.

"Let's get some food," she said to the team as they continued through the line.

The cook slopped food on their trays in the most disdainful way he could, slamming the spoons loudly against the tray as he served. Once the team made it through the line, they followed the lieutenant to an empty table.

"Don't mind them," the lieutenant said. "They don't care for operators much."

"How is it that they follow an operator then?" Jossen asked.

"They don't," she replied proudly. "They follow a TITAN. There is a difference you know."

"Oh yeah, what difference? operator, TITAN, it makes no difference. We're all enhanced soldiers designed for one thing: war," Harden remarked.

"Not true," the lieutenant replied. "The TITANs were originally created to bring peace to humanity. They were designed for battle without a doubt, but the original TITAN program saw TITANs and soldiers mixed together—an augmented force—coexisting with the people. The operators were designed for war and purposely segregated from populations to correct the perceived mistakes of the TITAN program, but they weren't mistakes," she said.

"The UNGA thinks of TITANs as tools, nothing more than pieces of equipment to achieve their goals. I wouldn't expect you to understand though because it's all you've known," the lieutenant finished speaking and began to eat.

The team began to eat as each of them thought hard about everything that's been said. The lieutenant's words weighed heavily on them, hitting Taylor and Harden especially hard. Jossen couldn't help but continue the conversation, not accepting the lieutenant's comments as fact.

"You and the commander talk a lot about the UNGA being this terrible plague on humanity and positioning the resistance as fighting for humanity, but all we have seen from the resistance is bloodshed. Innocent people dead as a result of their attacks. While I may not agree with all of the UNGAs methods, there's got to be another way. I've seen the reports, witnessed the bloodshed, destruction, and for what, to take down the council, the UNGA?" Jossen asked.

He continued before the lieutenant could answer. "The same government that enabled humanity to exist beyond the climate crisis, beyond pandemics, beyond world-ending cataclysmic events. All because you think your freedom is somehow diminished? Because of stories you've been told by the commander? Because you've seen some photos and videos that could just as well be fakes?"

Jossen was good at firing off rhetorical questions in rapid succession. The lieutenant stopped eating mid bite. She slowly put her fork down on the tray and stared forward with a glazed look. Jossen's questions ringing in her head, *"because of stories you've been told by the commander?"*

"Not just stories...my experiences. My experiences guide my beliefs. I witnessed firsthand what UNGA is capable of," she replied. The events of that day forever etched in her mind, every moment seared into her memory with vivid detail.

She had just finished a tour with the UNIC as a private at the time; she had just come home on leave. She was from colony 2110, a small colony that had just been established. The colony was basic, similar to one of the old cities on Earth, Boston or New York. There wasn't much opportunity, as many in the colony relied on the mining companies for work. Her father and two brothers worked for the United Nations Mining Federation, a collection of private mining companies managed by government regulators. The conditions were similar to other colonies; the workers would slave away, mining for precious metals. Making the heads of the companies wealthy while paying meager wages and providing less than safe working conditions. As she arrived home that day, she went straight to her family's home, a small unit on the 11th floor of a cookie-cutter housing complex. She paused before knocking on the door, the smell of dinner cooking permeated from just beyond the door. She knocked gently to greet her family and as her mother opened the door, screams of excitement poured out into the hallway.

"Alecia! Alecia's here!" her mother screamed as tears streamed down her face.

She embraced Alecia as though she would never let her go again. Her father and brother came into the room as her mother pulled her into the unit.

"Alecia," her father said as he moved to give her a hug.

"Dad," she responded with a large smile.

She looked around while hugging her father, everything looked exactly the same as it did before she had left. It was both comforting and concerning at the same time, making it feel like she had only been gone for a moment. It took her more time than it should have to notice that her brother was using crutches as he leaned against the doorway to his room.

"Mario, what happened?" she asked as she moved past her father to get a better look at him.

"Alecia," Mario said with a smile.

As Alecia came around the kitchen table, she saw why he was on crutches. She was so unprepared for what she saw that she paid no attention to her own reaction.

"Oh my God..." she said as she cupped her hands over her mouth.

She saw her brother missing a part of his leg from the knee down, she instantly began to cry. Her brother moved over to her using the crutches and gave her a hug, trying to calm her down. He dreaded her return for just this reason. He was not looking for anyone else to feel sorry for him. He found it to be a natural reaction from most, but an unwelcome one.

"It was an accident," he said as he rested on the crutches and grabbed her face with his hands. "I'm ok though."

"What happened?" she asked, not wanting to bring it up but feeling like she had to ask.

"We were in the mine, using the mole," he said, referencing the PDU-9908, a precision driving unit. "When we hit a spot of hexatiton, it jammed the mole and it happened to be my turn to fix it," he said as his eyes began to water, his own memory getting the best of him.

"Anyway, it happened, I'm ok now though, so I'll get through it," he said, trying to shake himself out of it.

"Where's Diago?" Alecia asked, looking around the rooms.

"He's still at work but he should be home soon," her mother said.

"Well, at least you made it home for dinner," her father began. "Your mother's making..." he was interrupted by a large explosion that sounded close.

"Alecia!" her mother yelled.

Alecia's training kicked in, she ran out the door, looking for the source of the explosion. She didn't get halfway down the hallway before a sudden force sent her hurling toward the wall. As she lifted her head up, a loud ringing in her ears left her deaf to the screams that were coming from all directions. It took her a moment to get up, bruised but not badly injured, she got to her feet. The hallway was now a gaping hole in the side of the building, giving her a line of sight to the ground outside. She ran back toward her family's unit, opening the door to find most of the unit missing. Her mother lay just inside the door on a piece of the remaining floor next to the door, badly injured. While the unit had been completely destroyed, Alecia's mother called out desperately for her husband, her sons, and her daughter.

"I'm here mom," Alecia said, tears streaming down her

face as she watched her mother gasp for breath. "I'm here," she kept reassuring her, knowing she didn't have long based on her injuries.

"Tell Mario and Diago I love them. Tell your father I love him," she said as she began to struggle harder for breath. "And I love you too my beautiful Alecia," she said as she took her last breath.

"Mom!" Alecia screamed as though it would bring her back. "Mommy!" she screamed again.

Alecia broke down crying over her mother while another emotion grew like a wildfire inside of her. She angrily got up and ran to the stairs. She made her way to the ground floor and out into the street. She saw soldiers in resistance uniforms running down an alley. She followed them, ready to beat them to a literal death with her bare hands if she had to. As she approached them, she noticed that they were wearing UNIC uniforms.

"Where did the resistance soldiers go?" she asked as she continued moving toward the men.

"We got them," one soldier responded.

"We're clear here, go back home ma'am," another said.

"I'm UNIC, I want to see the resistance soldiers responsible for this," she said, determined to see the bodies of the men.

"Turn around ma'am," the soldier insisted.

"Just show me the body," she demanded as one of the soldiers pulled his gun on her.

"Whoa, I'm UNIC. I'm on your side," she said, not understanding why he would do that.

"I told you to go home!" the soldier yelled as he pointed his gun, hoping she would leave.

She continued moving forward, seeing what looked like a piece of resistance uniform jacket under the soldier's UNIC jacket. She asked herself, were they trying to escape disguised as UNIC?

"What the hell..." Alecia asked as the soldier opened fire.

She flinched, turning her body and covering her head with her arms, expecting to feel the searing pain of a gunshot, instead, nothing. As she turned to look, there was a large soldier standing in front of her, shielding her. It was a TITAN and he had been deployed to help fend off the resistance attack. He dispatched the two soldiers within seconds. He moved over to their unconscious bodies and lifted up their jackets, revealing a resistance uniform underneath. He then lifted one of the helmets to see the soldier's face.

"The resistance was trying to escape by disguising themselves as UNIC?" Alecia asked.

"I'm not so sure," the titan said. "We need to move."

As they made their way through the streets, there was intermittent gunfire and explosions. Rubble, debris, and dust filled the air. Smoke rose from several buildings as civilians wandered around bloodied and in shock.

"Alecia?" a voice yelled from a distance.

"Diago!" Alecia yelled back, recognizing the voice instantly.

As they ran to meet each other in the street, a badger came racing toward them. While neither of them noticed, the TITAN ran towards the path of the badger. The soldiers on the badger opened fire with the machine gun. As the titan tried to block as much of the gunfire as possible, Diago was hit. The badger swerved as the TITAN remained steadfast in his position. The badger flipped as both Alecia and the TITAN ran to dispatch the occupants. The two gunners thrown from the back of the badger quickly got to their feet, but by then, the TITAN was already upon them. One hit from the TITAN was enough to knock the men unconscious, even with the UNIC helmet on.

Alecia had made her way to the passenger, grabbing his gun, and shot him dead. She had to use the passenger as a temporary shield as the driver attempted to shoot her. Before she could return fire, the TITAN grabbed him from the driver's seat, lifting the soldier two feet off the ground. The titan held him there for a moment, trying to figure out whether he should kill the soldier before ultimately deciding to toss him against a concrete wall, rendering him unconscious. Alecia ran back to her brother who lay dying in the street.

"Diago, hang on, we'll get help," she said as she looked around at the chaotic scene. She looked at the TITAN who was again approaching.

"We need to move, now," the TITAN said.

"I can't leave him here like this," she cried as tears once again streamed down her face.

"You don't understand. If you stay here, you'll be dead too," he said in a matter-of-fact way.

"Go Alecia," Diago said as he held his wound. "This is what you were always meant to do."

Diago began to run out of breath. "You need to protect Mom and Dad," he continued to try to speak. "And..."

"Just rest," Alecia said.

He took one last breath and died in her arms. The TITAN put his hand on her shoulder, trying to show compassion for her as well as get her to follow him. She took another second and then stood up. She wiped the tears from her eyes.

"I want to come with you. I want the resistance to pay," she said angrily as she ran back to the badger, grabbing an AAR-10 from one of the unconscious soldiers. She made her way back to him.

"So where to? There must be more of them," she said.

"I'm absolutely certain there are but you can't follow me," he said.

"What do you mean?" she asked, getting upset about the notion of walking away.

"There's something not right about this. I know those men in resistance gear. They're stationed on the Forge, Admiral Vincere's ship. They're not resistance," he said, keeping his head on a swivel.

Alecia was confused, she took a step back.

"I need to get back and find out what's going on," he said as he turned to walk away. "What's your name private?" he asked, pausing after he turned.

"Private Alecia Rimerez sir," she responded as he began to walk off.

"Sir," Alecia stopped him with her words as he looked back. "Thank you."

He nodded and said, "Good luck private."

With that, he ran off. For the next couple of months, Alecia had to deal with the death of her family, the fact that the resistance may not be what she thought they were, and that the people she worked for may have been the reason her family died.

The lieutenant found herself back in the mess hall, she seemed to drift back after escaping the memory. When she tried to speak again, it came out softly.

"Because I watched my family die as a result of a UNGA attack," she said, getting to the answer to Jossen's question. "Because I watched as the UNGA blamed the attack on the resistance. Because a TITAN rescued me and because people need to know the truth," she finally responded. She grabbed her tray and went to dispose of it.

Jossen was left without a retort, without a rhetorical follow-up.. The team sat there, forced to think about every mission they had ever been on, reviewing the details in their minds from a new perspective. The lieutenant walked behind them to wait for them to finish eating, she spoke softly but firmly.

"I don't expect you to listen to me or anyone else. You need to come to your own conclusions. No person or group of people can tell you who you are or what to believe...that is yours and yours alone."

FOUR
REVELATIONS

DR. BARNES slowly pulled back her white fluffy comforter as gently playing music signaled that 0500 had come. She waved her hand in a dismissive motion and the music was silenced. The glass panels designed to simulate windows slowly brightened to a scene of a forest at dawn. She slid to the edge of the bed where she sat up. She began her morning ritual as she had done every day, delighting in the precise order of her day. She started in the bathroom, a meticulously organized and simplistically designed room. The most basic of amenities arranged with elegance: a sink with a long metal counter devoid of any standard toiletries, faucets, or fixtures, a toilet large and white with no visible knobs or seat cover, and a large area toward the back that seemed to be empty space. There was no indication it was a shower until she moved into the space. Water began to pour from the ceiling and spray from the walls, failing and draining through the floor without an obviously visible drain. The entirety of the bathroom, from the metal counter to the tile floor, didn't have a single speck of dust anywhere.

She moved out of the bathroom as she completed that portion of her morning routine, heading back into the bedroom. The bedroom looked eerily similar to the bathroom in its simplistic design. There was only a bed protruding from a wall into the middle of the room and two doors at either side of the foot of the bed. She moved toward one that opened when she approached. Her closet was well organized, although it was easy to keep it well organized with only two types of outfits. One side had a precession of bright white lab outfits, all recently pressed and hung tightly together. The other side was laid out the same way but with black outfits resembling a UNIC officer uniform. She put on the lab outfit and proceeded to the other door, revealing a small living room and kitchen area.

The living room had one white couch with a black framed glass coffee table in front of it. The kitchen consisted of a fridge, a glass surface, a short metal counter, and a metal island set in front of the fridge. She moved to the fridge and opened it. The barren fridge contained only a carafe of orange juice. She leaned down to the shelf located within the kitchen island and grabbed the one glass that was available, in fact, the only glass that she owned. She poured and drank the orange juice, putting the glass and carafe back where she got them. She then proceeded through the main door and into a corridor. She navigated the desolate hallways as she headed for her office.

She paused for a moment before entering the door to her office as she waited for the validation, the light on the door turned green. As it did, the door opened, she moved to her desk and sat in the chair. She wasted no time tapping on the screen embedded in her desk as it began projecting screens that seemed to float in front of her. With the swipe of her hands, she progressed from one file to the next, one communication to the next, as she got herself caught up on the information gathered through the night. She stopped on a particular screen, a list of the operator teams assigned to the Forge. The status of each team displayed next to the names, almost all showed *active: ready* next to the team names. She tapped on Delta team as it read *inactive: KIA*. The screen then showed the personnel files from Delta Team. It listed them in order showing ID and status along with their record. She read: *ID: 3O103, Age: 20, Status: KIA; ID: 3O201, Age: 19, Status KIA; ID: 3O312, Age: 21, Status: KIA; ID: 3O408, Age:19, Status: KIA; ID: 3O505, Age: 20, Status: KIA*. She swiped the files away and immediately pulled up another file. She read: *ID: A101, Age: Unknown; Status: KIA*, she kept the file up, staring at the photo of him. Her eyes began to tear for a moment before she shook herself back to reality.

"Get a grip Barnes," she said to herself in a whisper as she swiped that file away as well.

It had been almost twenty days since the attempt to take the commander. There had been no unusual chatter from the resistance about the raid and no word on the status of the commander. Although she ordered the complete destruction of the resistance base, not knowing the status of the team or the target upset her precise nature. Her thoughts were interrupted by an audible tone.

"Come in," Barnes said.

Barnes' secretary, Mr. Kinston, walked through the door. He was a man built like a brawler, 5'11" and weighing 250 lbs., almost all muscle. He was clean-cut and very precise in both the way he spoke and his actions. Barnes and Kinston were a perfect match, their personalities and mannerisms went hand in hand. They understood each other in a way that few could.

"Director, the counsel has requested an audience. They

would like to see you in the SQC room," he stated as he remained perfectly still.

He knew the level of professionalism and decorum that was required for this position, as he had held this job for most of his time with the UNIC. It had become second nature to him. Although in the beginning, he often ran afoul of Barnes's very particular expectations.

"Very well, let's get this over with," she said as she stood up and proceeded toward the door.

Mr. Kinston allowed her to walk past him as he turned to follow closely behind. They entered the door to the communications room and proceeded to the secure quantum communication room. As Barnes entered the room, Mr. Kinston remained outside, turning his back to the door to ensure no one interrupted. Barnes stepped toward a circular platform a short distance from the door. As she stood on it, the platform began to glow as light emanated toward the ceiling from the perimeter of the platform. There was a moment of silence before the images of five people began to form in front of the platform.

The Ministers that made up the council came to life through a life-like full-body digital projection, with Minister Gantley being the first. He appeared in the middle of the group, a tall man who appeared to be around the same age as Barnes. It wasn't difficult to determine from his appearance that he was originally of Indian descent. He was clean-shaven with a full head of slicked back hair that showed off subtle gray streaks. He wore the typical minister uniform: a black shirt with a collar that came half-way up his neck, black slacks that seemed to be tailor-made, and a long sleeve black coat that reached down to his polished shoes. Minister Halin appeared to his right, a Caucasian woman of similar age with short silver hair, wearing the same uniform. Minister Yamato appeared to his left: he seemed to be of Asian descent with black hair that reached to his shoulders. Minister Sarpong, a man of African descent, and Minister Guerrero, a woman of South American descent stood at the far left and right end, respectively. Barnes bowed slightly once the avatars were fully formed, acknowledging the presence of the council.

"Good morning to you all," Barnes said after only a second of silence.

"I wish we could say it was, Director," Minister Gantley, the man in the middle of the group spoke first. "The council has reviewed the report from the latest mission to take out the resistance leader. Three operator teams KIA, no confirmed status on the target, and the resistance base has been completely destroyed. Quite an effort for such results, wouldn't you agree?"

"If I may sir, the destruction of the resistance base should be a welcomed act. One less base for them to utilize in the future and a nice propaganda piece for the people," Barnes replied.

"I would agree except for the fact that if we would have allowed the base to exist, we could have potentially gathered valuable intelligence on other resistance efforts. Instead, the base was reduced to dust and we are no closer to eliminating the resistance. You had actionable intelligence on the location of the resistance leader and your team failed," Minister Gantley said as he paused, allowing for the others to speak.

"If we were simply looking for a PR stunt, we could've easily staged another attack. There was a clear objective, and it was either ignored or botched. Either way, the outcome is unacceptable," said Minister Halin.

Her vague European accent combined with her shrill tone was something akin to nails on a chalkboard to Barnes. Minister Sarpong interjected before Barnes could respond.

"We don't question your loyalty, we are very aware of the sacrifices you have made for the UNGA, but this type of failure cannot be left without consequence," the minister continued. "The resistance must be brought to justice. We cannot continue to risk the exposure when we are so close to our objective."

"With all due respect to the council, we have all made sacrifices and we have all experienced failures. These sacrifices and failures have brought us to where we are today, on the precipice of completing something that could once again change the course of humanity. These failures and sacrifices are what strengthen our resolve. We will eliminate the resistance and change our destiny once again," Dir. Barnes said as she stood tall.

"The last time we embarked on an effort of this scale, we created the UNGA itself, this will allow us the opportunity to expand humanities' reign throughout the cosmos. I...we will not allow anything to jeopardize that," she continued.

"Good, then we are in agreement. Confirm the fate of the resistance leader and eliminate the remaining resistance. Do what you must, we will not delay our plans," Minister Gantley concluded. "We expect the welcomed news will come soon."

"Yes minister," Barnes replied.

With that, the projections of the ministers faded, and the light went dark. Barnes exited the SQC room as Mr. Kinston followed closely behind once again. She kept a brisk pace as they walked in silence to her office. She sat in her chair and pulled up the files for Operation Alexander.

"Mr. Kinston?" Barnes called and looked up at him.

"Yes ma'am?" he asked with a mild sense of tepidness.

"Humanity is a fragile thing. I assume you understand something of the sacrifices that have been made in order to ensure the human race continued to exist. You've read about the great war, the climate crisis, and the creation of the UNGA. The sacrifices made during those pivotal moments in history are ones that only a few can ever truly understand," her voice cracked ever so slightly as she paused to ensure the next words out of her mouth were unwavering.

"The only thing standing between humanity and eventual annihilation, Mr. Kinston, are these," she said.

She moved her hand to spin the seemingly floating screen in the direction of Mr. Kinston. He looked at the screen, his expression suggested he was beginning to put the pieces together. He was, after all, the doctor's right-hand man.

"The incorporation of these assets will allow humanity to forge ahead. They will allow us to secure our place in the universe," she said as she motioned to move the screen back toward her.

"Forgive me if I'm being too presumptuous, but are these to be the next generation of TITANs?" Kinston asked, unsure if she had even expected an answer or if he had overstepped his bounds.

"Not TITANs, Mr. Kinston, something more...the future. This is the future of humanity," she said in an intensely soft voice. At that moment, a tone cut through the silence indicating an incoming transmission.

"I'll be outside ma'am," Mr. Kinston said as he let himself out. Barnes tapped the screen.

"Director Barnes, we need you on level 13 immediately," the voice said in a bit of a panic. Barnes recognized the voice and immediately jumped to her feet, moving quickly out of her office.

"Director, is everything ok?" Mr. Kinston asked as she moved through the door.

"Yes, everything is fine. Please make sure you have the

personnel files for the lab workers on level 18 on my desk ASAP," she said, looking for an excuse to keep Mr. Kinston busy as she continued to level 13.

"Yes Ma'am," Mr. Kinston responded as he moved in the opposite direction. The Director entered the elevator and placed her hand on a discolored portion of the elevator wall next to the door. When she did, a separate set of buttons lit up where the normal levels would be. They included levels that did not show up on the normal panel, level 13 was one of them. She pressed the button as the elevator moved quickly to its destination. As the doors opened, the Director moved quickly from the elevator to one of the labs. The lab doors opened as she approached. A scientist moved toward her with a look of concern on his face.

"What's the situation?" Barnes asked.

"Well, we've followed the procedures on test subject 50010. The subject has displayed some unusual reactions to the process," Dr. Winslow said as he motioned her to follow. He led the Director through the front of the lab to a door in the back. Once through the door, they walked quickly down a hallway to yet another door. The security on level 13 was strict, each door further restricting unauthorized access.

"We contacted you as soon as we saw what happened, but it was too late. We lost four good technicians..." the doctor said.

The door at the end of the hallway opened to a large room housing thousands of cylindrical containers. Each container was approximately nine feet tall and five feet in diameter. The base of each container was large, at least six inches in thickness, and a foot tall. The top of each container had several hoses connecting the container to larger pipes running across the entire room. The liquid inside was thick, making it difficult to tell what was inside of the containers.

The Director and Dr. Winslow made their way through the container room and entered another.

"It's always hard when we lose team members, doctor. We must remember that it is sacrifice that has propelled humanity forward and it will be a sacrifice that continues our progress," Barnes said as they entered the room.

The room they entered was an observation area, peering down into a surgical room of some kind, that allowed the observer to witness a procedure while remaining protected. As Dr. Winslow hit a button on a control panel in front of them, a door within the procedure room opened. A creature began to slowly appear through the door. At first, long pointed fingers reached out from the darkness to grab the edge of the door's opening. It seemed to pull itself forward.

"About three minutes into the procedure, we began to notice changes taking place and attempted to pause the process. As we tried, 50010 became aware and stopped the technician before she could cut off the supply. He ended up getting a full dose, we tried to evacuate the room but..." Doctor Winslow paused.

A leg extended from the same darkness as if the creature was testing the environment. It had two large thick toes about seven inches long connected to the ball of its foot. The foot itself seemed to angle up as if it walked on the balls of the feet. As the creature found its footing, it seemed to become more comfortable as it moved. It began to come out of the darkness faster, revealing more of itself. The creature ducked through the door, standing almost eight and a half feet tall. The creature seemed hunched and contorted, resembling a human but with distorted features. The lower jaw appeared exaggerated, the ears looked as though they were unformed, the face seemed to have rigid bone structures on the forehead and cheeks, and the eye sockets extended outward toward the ears slightly.

"Wonderful..." Barnes whispered to herself as she studied the creature.

"Excuse me?" Doctor Winslow asked, confused.

"You have recorded all the data I assume. Exterminate it," Barnes said.

"Yes Director," the doctor said as he pressed a button on the panel in front of him.

The door that the creature emerged from closed and the room that now trapped it began to fill with a heavy gas. As the room filled, the monstrous creature began to writhe until it could no longer be seen. The director and the doctor waited for a moment before the doctor moved his hand toward the button labeled *purge*.

"Wait," Barnes said before Dr. Winslow hit the button.

The creature slammed up against the glass that was protecting the Director and the doctor. Winslow jumped out of his skin as Barnes stood there motionless. The creature then fell to the floor with a loud thud.

"Simply wonderful," Barnes said.

They waited another minute until they were certain the creature was no longer moving. This gave Winslow some much-needed time to compose himself. He hoped that Barnes was not paying attention to his reaction, although he knew she had noticed.

"Ok," Barnes said.

The doctor hit the button and cleared the gas out of the room. The retreating gas revealed the motionless creature that laid on the floor. They watched as a team of six scientists entered the room and prodded it with a long electrified rod. The creature didn't react. The scientists loaded the creature onto a rolling table and left the room.

"I want all of the information on subject 50010 sent to my office immediately. I want to see all of the footage, notes, formulas, and analysis from concept stage to this. I expect it will be there before I return," the director said as she turned to exit. "And I want that thing under the microscope immediately. I expect full biological and technical composition reports by morning."

"Yes ma'am," the doctor said in a less than enthusiastic tone.

He knew full well he would have to make the team work through the night to complete all of the reports Barnes was requesting, regardless of how long they've already been working. Barnes acknowledged the doctor with a simple head nod as she made her way back to her office.

Barnes didn't waste a moment upon her return, opening all of the files that Dr. Winslow had sent. She studied them intently, swiping and tapping while chart after chart appeared before her. While this was not the intended result of *Project Olympians*, she was amazed by what she saw. She watched the lab videos intently, absorbing every detail of each second. The first video showed the staff preparing the table in the same room that she witnessed the creature. As they did a human, larger than normal was wheeled in on a gurney. He seemed to be unconscious, with several tubes and wires protruding from his skin, connecting him to various bags of fluids and several monitoring devices. Additional staff entered the room as they brought him next to the clean surgical table. It took six hefty-looking technicians to transfer the man to the table. Just after they placed him down, the six technicians who helped lift him left, and the video ended.

The next video started, showing a technician walking into the room with a small metal case, roughly the size of a laptop but about seven inches thick. The technician opened the case, revealing a container. At that point, another technician entered the room, wheeling a larger device. The device looked like a cylinder turned on its side. There were coils on either end with four nozzles at each end. The tech that brought the device in began connecting the hoses going into the patient. The tech that opened the case brought the contents to the device, two black orbs the size of a bocce ball. The tech placed the two orbs side by side in the device. All but one of the technicians left the room as they prepared to begin the process. The video ended and the doctor began the next.

The device emitted a faint light as dark material was seen flowing through the hoses. The veins in the subject began to turn black as involuntary convulsions tested the limits of the restraints. As the restraints appeared to hold, the subject's skin started to change. Dark spots emerged before morphing into boils that then evolved into a rock-like texture. These textures spread rapidly over the subject's body and the convulsions began again. Three technicians came rushing in, attempting to remove the hoses and shut off the device before it was too late. This time, the restraints did not hold. The subject lunged off of the table, grabbing one technician by the throat, and threw him across the room. His body hit the wall, leaving a splatter pattern as the force of the impact killed him instantly. The technician's body laid on the floor as the others were frozen in a split second of sheer terror. The remaining technicians scrambled to make it through the open door and attempted to close it. They watched in horror as the creature hobbled their way. Just as the door was about to shut, the creature reached its arm in, stopping the door from sealing closed. The creature lifted the door with ease as it proceeded inside the dark room. The video ended abruptly.

"Interesting," the director said to herself as she replayed the videos over and over again.

Comparing charts side by side with the video as if she was looking at a puzzle that had only a few missing pieces left, it took a while before it clicked. She looked at one of the charts and sat back in her chair with a smirk. She reached her hand down toward a drawer at the bottom of her desk and pressed her thumb against a small square pad that seemed to be part of the drawer. It lit up for a millisecond before the drawer popped open. Inside she had a quantum connection encrypter and an old thumb drive. She held up the thumb drive to take a look at it. It seemed like archaic technology at this point, but it wasn't what was on it she was interested in, rather what it represented. As she sat back holding the thumb drive in her hand, she reminisced about the day she came into possession of it.

The sunlight streamed through a small crack in the drapes, the drapes themselves a dark thick fabric blocking out all of the other sunlight that would have otherwise filled the room. Her mother laid on the bed, IVs and monitoring equipment seemed to wrap her in tubes and wires like a monster stretching out its tentacles to devour its prey. The constant humming and beeping of the equipment provided a depressing and deviously hypnotic background soundtrack. The room was a cluttered mess, papers spread haphazardly, computers and monitors sat powered on but collecting dust, the walls covered with news articles and photos. Barnes had been working with her mother for her entire career. At this point in time, her entire career was all of 10 years, but her aptitude and connections had easily earned her a top spot within the scientific community.

She was relentless in her pursuit of knowledge, focusing all of her time and effort on being the best scientist she could be. She had become the lead scientist on some of the most cutting-edge technology projects within DARPA. She owed everything to her mother and her father. Her father, a lead engineer sought after by almost every major technology company in the world, had pushed her to be everything she could. Her mother, a top biologist with the United States Military and highly respected Officer, had helped her through any and every difficult time in her life. It only felt right for her to take care of her mother once she got sick.

"I brought you some soup," she said, trying to muster a cheerful tone.

Every day it pained her to see her mother like this, but in her mind, it was better than the alternative. Barnes couldn't bear the thought of losing her mother, it was what drove her every day. She was determined to find a cure and save her mother, though that had proved to be a very difficult task.

"Thank you Ashley, just lay it down over there, I'm not that hungry right now," her mother replied.

"You have to eat something though," she tried to push back, but they were both stubborn.

"I will eat, just not right now. I want to hear about your day. How was work? Any breakthroughs?" she asked, genuinely interested in how the project was progressing.

"No major breakthroughs today, but I think we're close. We figured out that the device itself isn't generating energy, it's harvesting it and drawing it from somewhere," she replied. She paused for a moment, always a bit paranoid when talking about work outside of her office.

"It's only a matter of time before we figure out where the energy is coming from," she said, still trying to maintain a cheerful attitude.

"Well they have the smartest mind I know working on it," her mother replied with a smile.

"Maybe I'll try some of that soup now," her mother said as she attempted to sit up a bit.

"Here let me," Ashley said and moved over to the bed to help her mother up, bringing the soup over as well.

As her mother started eating the soup, Ashley took out her MP3 player, put one earbud in her left ear, and hit play. Her mother shot her a look as Ashley seemed entranced by the music.

"I know I'm just an old lady but am I that bad at conversation?" she asked.

"No, not at all, I was going through some of your old files and found these old audio recordings. I had the team convert them to MP3s so I can listen. It almost sounds like someone talking, but I've been listening for a while now and can't figure out what it is," Ashley said as she appeared to strain more than usual to listen.

"I think this might have something to do with it, but there's no way to know for sure," she continued.

"Mind if I have a listen?" her mother asked as she finished the remaining bit of soup.

"Sure," Ashley replied then walked over and crouched down next to the bed, being overly cautious that she didn't get tangled in any of the tubes or wire. She gave her mother the other earbud. Her mother put the earbud in, and almost instantly, her face dropped. The beeping from the monitor that had been fairly steady and almost unnoticeable had begun to beep faster.

"This...I know what this is..." her mother was starting to scare Ashley.

"It's Them," she said in a soft voice as she continued to listen.

Ashley was confused. "Them?" she asked.

"You know the story behind the core," her mother said, seemingly waiting for Ashley to confirm the story.

"Yeah, we recovered it after that crash in the desert way back when," she said.

"That wasn't the only thing that was recovered from that crash though," her mother said, sparking Ashley's curiosity.

"We found the core, yes, but there was more," her mother began to talk in a whisper. "The beings that piloted that craft were up to something. The core was a significant discovery, powering the ship, but it was the existence of the beings and the cargo they had on board that was significant. We weren't able to determine much, but If you can figure out the core it might help you discover the purpose behind their visit."

Her mother turned sharply, looking at a vent in the corner of the room. She motioned her head slightly toward the vent, indicating what she did not want to say out loud. Ashley vaguely understood and moved toward the vent. She looked up, noticing the screws that held the vent together, then looked over at her mother for confirmation. Her mother nodded slightly to confirm. Ashley looked around and moved a chair under the vent. She left the room for a moment to find a screwdriver. She came back into the room, hopped up on the chair, and began unscrewing the vent. After removing the dust-covered vent, she reached her hand into the ductwork, feeling around until her hand happened upon a small, rectangular object. Ashley removed the object, a small USB drive.

Ashley smiled like a kid at Christmas who just found one last present after believing all of the presents had already been opened. She looked at her mother who motioned back to the vent. Ashley put the USB drive in her pocket and screwed the vent cover back on. After jumping down off of the chair, she moved it back to its original place. She walked back over to the side of her mother's bed.

"Make sure you hold on to that, it has all of my research. If you...when you figure out this core, you're going to have to see the bigger picture...this could help," her mother said as she removed the earbud. She handed the earbud back to Ashley, holding her hand as she did.

"There are things happening that will change the very nature of humanity. Don't trust anyone's agenda; it's never what it seems. Use your logic, try to understand what someone can gain and find a way to turn it into your advantage," her mother said in a serious whisper.

"Everyone will try to use you for your talents, if you can make them think they are while pursuing your own goals...you can achieve anything," her mother said.

"Now get home to your husband. I'll be fine here," her mother said, knowing that the drive she had just handed Ashley would make her crazy with curiosity

Ashley wasn't exactly sure what to think, but just as her mother suspected, her curiosity began to overtake her. The anticipation that there could be something on this device that would help her unlock the secrets of the core was too much for her to argue with.

"Ok Mom, I'll see you tomorrow," Ashley said as she leaned in and kissed her mother's forehead.

"I'll be here," her mother replied with a smile.

"Love you!" Ashley said, not knowing that would be the last time she would see her mother alive.

The image of her mom laying in that bed stuck with her as she opened her eyes, revealing the reality she had escaped, if only for a moment. She put the thumb drive back in the drawer but kept her QCE on the table. She began to work on the other projects that were under her jurisdiction. The personnel files for the lab workers on level 18 were left on her desk, just as she had instructed Mr. Kinston. While she was responsible for the TITAN program and its various branches, she was also responsible for research into energy-based sciences, the nanites themselves, and quantum communication applications. She poured through the personnel files and other reports sent to her by the various departments. Before she knew it, the day had gotten away from her. When she noticed how late it was, she decided to head back to her room. As she moved down the corridor toward her room, she received a call from Mr. Kinston. Barnes accepted the call by tapping just behind her ear. Cell phones were a thing of the past since Barnes had helped develop a communication device resembling a clear plastic film that stuck to the skin just behind the ear.

"Is everything ok Doctor?" he asked.

Although it wasn't abnormal for her to leave at such a late hour, Mr. Kinston was very protective.

"Yes Mr. Kinston, I'm fine," she said, matter-of-factly.

"Ok doctor, if you need anything, please let me know," he said as he paused for a moment.

Barnes said nothing as she hung up the phone. Although her responses would've seemed terse coming from anyone else, Mr. Kinston knew her well, this was typical behavior. Barnes went back to her room although she did not go to sleep. The results of the subject on level 13 consumed her thoughts. The how and why became an obsession. She moved right to the coffee table in front of the couch upon entering the room. She placed the PC from the inside of her coat pocket on the table. A projection appeared above the PC. The screen was red, with a flashing option that read *Accessing private secure server*. Barnes selected the option while text began to appear and fade. *Procuring secure connection, quantum communication in progress, quantum connection established, and connection secure.* A type of keyboard appeared in the glass of the coffee table, not a typical old-fashioned keyboard but a customized command keyboard. She began pressing the keys without hesitation. Screens popped up above the glass of the coffee table. They would appear and disappear, some would linger off to the side, others would move to the background. She continued working through the night, before she realized the window displays indicated it was dawn. The dim red of the sunrise beamed through the forest, growing brighter as the minutes flew by. She was undeterred by the display, knowing that the reports from the subject would be reviewed by the council soon enough. She continued working to determine what happened, a mistake, or the next evolution of the Olympus program.

Three days had passed as she worked tirelessly on the problem. She had slept for all of a combined eight hours. It was approximately 0700 based on the light coming through the window projection when she cupped her hands over her face in disbelief. Her investigation into the incident with subject 50010 led her down a rabbit hole she never saw coming. She swiped all of the screens away and removed the PC from the table. After tucking the PC under the cushion of the couch, she leaned back in deep thought. While she had figured out what happened, she had another problem to deal with...how to throw the council off her trail. She needed to give them something...she knew that if she focused for this long on the problem, the council would expect some results. She began working on calculations, including the main components while leaving out key information.

This should work, she thought to herself as she sat back once again.

Barnes went through her typical morning routine, although late, grabbing the PC she had tucked under the couch cushion on her way out. She proceeded to her office, going over and over her plan in her head. As she approached her office, she spotted Mr. Kinston, standing outside the door like a soldier at attention.

"Good morning Director," Mr. Kinston welcomed Dir. Barnes.

"Good morning Mr. Kinston," she responded politely.

"I assume you did whatever it was you needed to," he continued as he moved with her through her office door.

"Indeed...what gave it away?" she asked curiously.

"Well, with all due respect, you look terrible. I have only ever seen you look this way twice. Once when you pulled back-to-back all-nighters to solve the QC variant bug and the other when you had to send Echo and Charlie team to the breach. Two very interesting problems and both issues solved," he said. The doctor smiled as she moved to her desk.

"This has been the most interesting few days in quite a while," she said as she laid her PC on the table.

"There are some interesting variations in the genetic makeup of the new subjects," she said, seemingly excited.

"I'm surprised the council hasn't requested my presence yet," she said before Mr. Kinston could speak.

Mr. Kinston remarked, "Well before you jump the gun, the council informed me that they would like to speak with you as soon as you are ready."

"Understood," she said, knowing they must have a pretty good idea of what's going on by now.

"I will go establish comms with the council and will let you know when we're ready," Mr. Kinston said.

"Perfect, thank you," she replied.

As soon as Mr. Kinston left the room, she pushed her thumb to the drawer and opened it, sliding the PC out of her coat pocket and into the drawer. She got right to work, looking through all of the other work that she had neglected for the past few days. Not ten minutes had passed, and Mr. Kinston arrived at her office door once again.

"Doctor, the council is ready," he said in a very serious tone. Dir. Barnes knew Mr. Kinston well, well enough to know when his tone held a deeper meaning.

"Thank you Mr. Kinston," she said in an equally serious tone.

It was an unspoken understanding, letting him know with her tone that she got his message. She got up and proceeded to the door, as she passed Mr. Kinston, he slipped something into her coat pocket. The two then continued to the SQC room. As always, Mr. Kinston waited outside as Barnes entered. Before she stepped onto the platform, she reached in her coat pocket and pulled out a small piece of paper. She knew almost instantly that something was very wrong. Paper was a rare commodity as were pens...everything was done electronically. The only reason someone would use paper was to keep something a complete secret. She unfolded it, staring for a brief moment before putting it back. She then took a deep breath and exhaled before stepping on the platform.

FIVE
VANISHED

TWO DAYS HAD PASSED since Delta team was first brought back to the resistance headquarters. After their talk with the commander, they were given more freedom than they had expected. They took this opportunity to scope out the resistance operations and from what they witnessed, it seemed to focus on helping citizens. They caught word of an operation in progress, only to realize it was to drop supplies to ailing people in several remote outposts.

Try as they might, they found no evidence to back up the theory they were told by the UNIC. The resistance seemed more like an underground supply network than a terrorist organization. Many of the deployed resistance soldiers were assigned to protect transports, rescue prisoners, and smuggle resources.

They did, however, continue to look for a way out. They checked every hallway they could, testing the security of doors and hatches. It didn't take long to reach the conclusion that without the proper clearance, they weren't going anywhere the commander didn't want them to.

The lieutenant caught up with the team in their quarters. "I trust you have been taken care of," she said.

"When are you going to let us go?" Jossen asked

"Yeah, if you're going to kill us just get it over with. All this waiting around doing nothing is driving me crazy," Toa said.

"Let's take a walk, there's something I want to show you. It will definitely be better than just sitting around here," the lieutenant said.

They followed her out into the hallway. As they did, they noticed the commander making his way toward them with an intense look on his face. His serious demeanor instantly instilled the sense that something was very wrong.

"Lieutenant," he said as approached.

"We need to mobilize. We've just received a report that outpost 12 has gone silent," he said with an insistent tone. "I will accompany our soldiers. Please ensure that our guests are all set and then meet me in the briefing room," he commanded as he continued walking past the group.

Jossen looked at the rest of the team, giving them a look they had all seen before. He cocked his head slightly to the side while each member gave him a quick nod of approval before he spoke.

"We would like to go with you," Jossen said firmly as he stepped forward next to the lieutenant.

The commander stopped in his tracks and turned around to see Jossen. He stepped closer and looked him square in the eye before turning his gaze to the lieutenant.

"It might be worthwhile to bring them, at least they would see firsthand that we aren't the terrorists they think we are," she said confidently.

"Agreed...but we would need to make a few adjustments

first," the commander said as he motioned for the team to follow him.

They made their way to a lab, one that looked far different than the lab they had seen at the compound. This lab was large, far more technologically advanced than they thought possible for the resistance. It was staffed with nine technicians who seemed to be working on exoskeletons. Next to each of the exoskeletons, there were multiple screens displaying the accompanying armor designs.

"These men will need to make a few adjustments to your nanites and their housing," the commander said.

"Woah, wait a minute, no one is touching my nanites," Toa barked angrily.

"Take it easy. They need to adjust your nanites or you won't last five minutes out there. Your exoskeleton and nanites are linked to AIDA. The minute you step foot out there, AIDA will either send a fleet to take everyone out or just dust the entire area," the commander said.

"What do you mean out there, why wouldn't they know we're here now?" Taylor asked, slightly confused.

"Your nanites have been suppressed since we captured you on outpost 8. This place keeps them suppressed. We developed a way to disable the nanites, these systems are embedded in almost every outpost and fortified resistance compound. It's our best defense against UNIC forces, specifically reapers," the commander said.

"If the nanites are suppressed in every outpost, how were we able to enter outpost 8 and get all the way down to where you were?" Taylor asked.

"We deactivated the nanite suppressors all the way to where I was. We couldn't risk giving away our secret if you came into the base and decided to turn back once you realized your nanites didn't work," the commander replied.

"When you leave here, they will no longer be suppressed, meaning they will once again transmit back to AIDA...and I can promise you, they won't wait to find out the details of your capture. They'll take no chances, you're probably already listed as KIA, and they won't risk a return from the dead," he continued.

"No way, they'd definitely come for us. Send another team of operators to bring us back or at least try," Jossen said, dismissing the fact that they would be killed.

"Actually, thinking back, I don't think I've ever heard of an operator listed as MIA...they come back successful or die trying...no operator listed as KIA has ever *come back to life,*" Coughlin interjected.

"That's right," the commander said. "And if you think you're the first operator team to be captured, you'd just be wrong again."

"Ok, I'll go first, what needs to be done," Harden stepped forward, volunteering to be the first from the team to get their nanites adjusted.

"They'll disable the quantum communicator embedded in the nanite core, reconfigure comms, and if you're up for it...customize your armor," the commander said with a smile.

"Customize our armor?" Toa asked.

"You have standard-issue operator configurations. They have been designed to be the most effective universal configuration because AIDA doesn't believe in an individual, they believe in uniformity. We are quite the opposite," the commander replied and stepped back.

He took off his suit jacket, removed his dress shirt, and dropped his trousers. Under all of that revealed a thick skin-tight black fabric, almost identical to what the team was wearing, and his exoskeleton. He activated his nanites as the armor formed around him. He stood there for a moment, allowing them to see his modifications.

His armor was a deep ocean blue in color. His helmet had a different design than they were used to with a slight lip above the visor. The helmet bulged slightly at the sides as if it was creating a bit more room around his ears. The base of the helmet at the back of the skull also seemed to protrude as the armor seemed thicker there. The torso seemed beefier with thicker plating on the chest, two ridges that began to rise from the top of the chest between the shoulder and the neck and extended down to the shoulder blades. The shoulder plates appeared thinner than the typical shoulder plate. The back had three large bulges along the horizontal frame of the exoskeleton, the ZPE core, and two micro thrusters. The ZPE core in the center being the smaller of the bulges and the two micro thrusters on either side being slightly larger. The thigh plates seemed to have additional plating and what appeared to be either holsters or protrusions that something could clip to. The shin armor seemed fairly basic, with armor for the knee cap extending up from the top.

"Hey, how can you activate your nanites? I thought you said the nanites were inactive here," Toa said with a hint of jealousy and anger.

"Your nanites have been disabled. Once we modify your core, you will be able to activate your armor here as well. Of course, I'm not going to give too much away...you are still technically UNIC," the commander said.

"Each of you is an individual. You each have strengths and weaknesses. I assume AIDA is still assigning classes based on their analysis?" the commander asked.

Jossen responded, "Yes, each TITAN is assigned a class based on where we stand on the AIDA Assessment Test.

After that, your nanites are modified based on your class... team leader, engineer, scout, tech, and heavy."

"Well, we don't believe in classes. That was established after the first phase of the TITAN program. We believe in individuals and their unique skills, insights, and abilities, combining them with a team of other individuals to complement and enhance each other," the commander said.

"So you're telling me we can hack the nanites so I can design my own armor. I'm in." Toa said excitedly.

Jossen then stepped forward as well. "I want Taylor to review everything they are doing to the nanites. We may be willing to listen and even tag along to see what's happening for ourselves, but I won't put the team in danger by allowing you to just tinker with our suits," Jossen said and motioned for Taylor to step forward.

"Understood," she said as she moved toward the commander.

"I would expect nothing less," Hanlon remarked as he looked at the other members.

"Give them the quick version, we have to get moving but we can tweak and detail when we return," Hanlon said to the engineer.

"Assuming we are coming back...that's some confidence you have," Jossen said.

"Well...you and your team seem like a smart bunch. I think that once you see who we are and what we stand for, you will be surprised...surprised enough to want to learn more I think," Hanlon replied.

"Let's get them customized, equipped, and ready to go. We leave within the hour," the lieutenant said in a stern voice as she turned away from the group continuing to command as she walked out of the room. "I want the ships armed and ready in 30 minutes, Sierra and Kilo teams are to be assembled and ready to deploy."

"Well, I'll leave you to it," Hanlon said, turning to leave the room.

The team began their nanite customization while Taylor watched everything the engineers were doing. Hanlon and the lieutenant met down in the hangar. The hangar was a large, cavernous space, a mix of rock and concrete. It was hard to distinguish where the concrete ended and the rock began, running together as if battling for dominance.

"This mission could get rough," Hanlon said to the lieutenant.

They stood next to a large ship called a Javelin, a combat dropship capable of transporting large payloads of personnel and equipment. It was perfect for deploying a sizable force in a short amount of time, a critical vehicle in any large-scale combat mission. Although it looked impressive when dropping its payload, it looked somewhat diminished while parked in the hangar.

"Can't they all?" she asked rhetorically.

"You're right though, I don't like it, losing all communication...it would be unlike the UNGA to try to take outpost 12...they would just dust it if they knew what it was," the lieutenant continued.

"Well, we know it wasn't dusted, power systems are still online according to the satellite data. Could be a trap, take down comms and wait for us to come check it out, try to get us and their wayward team in one shot? Still, I don't feel like that's the case either...there's been no reports of UNIC movement in the area. Either way, we need to find out what's going on," Hanlon said.

"Agreed," the lieutenant said with a cautious tone.

She looked at the Javelin, watching as it was loaded with

weapons and ammo. The missile bay was being stocked and the mechanical systems being inspected. The ship's claim to fame was its size and speed; large enough to transport a strike squad consisting of four teams, four badgers, a rhino tank, and two stinger PAVs. Hanlon paid particular attention as the vehicles were being loaded.

"Seems like a bit much maybe?" he remarked.

"Like you said, this could get rough," she replied with a smile.

"Well, if it does come down to a fight, at least we'll see what he's capable of," Hanlon said in a tone that was just slightly above a whisper.

"I hope you're right about him sir," the lieutenant replied in the same tone.

Sierra and Kilo teams arrived in the hanger and approached the commander. Each team was composed of five soldiers. The soldiers were outfitted in resistance gear, from the black combat boots to the olive green tactical pants, everything about their gear seemed standard. The black helmets provided the most basic protection. Their olive green shirts were covered by a protective vest. The vest was bulky, bulging in several vital areas, protecting these areas with a resistance-developed ballistic material. Unlike the UNIC's uniformity, the soldiers seemed to have modified their uniforms to fit their personalities. Some had short sleeves while others had extra pouches. No two soldiers who stood there looked exactly the same. Two of the soldiers stepped forward, one from each team. They seemed very disciplined, remaining in formation as they approached and saluted both the Lieutenant and Commander.

"Sierra team reporting for duty sir," team leader Jennings said while team leader Santos followed.

"Kilo team reporting for duty sir."

"Get your teams situated on the Javelin. We will be launching as soon as the new team arrives," the lieutenant said.

"Understood," Jennings said as he motioned his team to follow him onto the ship.

Santos gave a similar order and both teams boarded the ship. When they saw the vehicles that were loaded on the ship, they knew that this was not a typical reconnaissance mission. The commander and the lieutenant remained outside of the Javelin, waiting for Jossen and his team.

"Let's hope they are ready for this," the lieutenant remarked as she looked to gain more insight from Hanlon.

"We'll know soon enough," he responded as he looked back at the javelin.

At that moment, the doors leading from the hangar to the rest of the facility opened. The team walked through the door with Jossen in front, Harden and Taylor just behind off to the right and left respectively, followed by Coughlin and Toa behind them again slightly offset to the right and left, respectively. They approached the commander and lieutenant.

The commander and lieutenant noticed right away that they had done some considerable work in such a short amount of time with regards to the modifications. The team had already activated their armor before they entered the hander. Their new armor looked impressive as most of the resistance personnel paused what they were doing to get a look.

"Looking good, I wasn't sure how far you would get with the armor given the short notice," the commander said.

Jossen said as he approached, "Commander, I want to make one thing clear although we're going along on this mission, we are not a part of the resistance. I just want you to know I will do whatever I need to do in order to protect my team."

"I can respect that," commander Hanlon continued. "Just know that if you have any ideas of double-crossing us...going back on your word, I will take you and your team down myself. Just as you would do anything to protect your team, I will do anything to protect my people."

"As long as we are all busy protecting our people, we shouldn't have to worry about fighting each other," the lieutenant said in an attempt to lighten the mood.

The commander and lieutenant stepped aside, clearing the way for the team to board the ship.

"And your call sign?" Commander Hanlon asked.

"Delta team," Jossen responded.

"Ok...Delta team, let's load up," Hanlon replied.

He watched as Jossen walked onto the ship, taking a look at his armor. He kept his black base color, while keeping much of the original design the same. The commander did notice some small changes though. Jossen modified his communication module located at the base of his helmet. He also modified his forearm armor to provide a better balance when using the standard AAR-10 that was secured to his back.

When Taylor approached, he noticed her modification immediately. A metallic purple made her stand out. She had modified her armor for flexibility, opting for streamlined armor plating, keeping any protrusions to a minimum. She had an upgraded terminal interface on her forearm and chose to go with enhanced armor on her backside, adding a force-deflection unit. The two small MMGs would provide her with quick rapid-fire offensive capabilities.

Harden, chose a forest green color with recon enhancements. The helmet was modified to include a scanning module above the visor and motion detection units just behind where his ears would be. The chest plate was enhanced to provide the most protection up front. *Interesting,* Hanlon said to himself as he noticed the TSR on Harden's back.

Toa went with a gunmetal gray color for his armor while Coughlin opted for an off-white. They both chose a variant of the assault armor. Heavy fortified with extra plating, of course this style sacrificed mobility for durability. Toa was equipped with an ARS (Arrow Rocket System) and an AAR-10. His leg armor had stabilizing protrusions that would allow for a more secure footing when using the ARS.

Coughlin's white armor had heavily fortified modifications similar to Toa, but she opted for the additional back panels instead of the stabilizers. She was equipped with a TRS (Tactical Repeating Shotgun) and AAR-10. She walked quickly past the commander and lieutenant, not amused by the perceived runway that was taking place.

Delta Team boarded the ship and sat in their seats. As they looked around, they noticed that both Sierra and Kilo Teams were staring at them. Jennings and Santos were very suspicious of the new team, not sure why they were there, but no one was about to question the commander...or lieutenant for that matter. The commander, followed by the lieutenant, came aboard as the cargo door closed on the ship.

"We are not sure what we're about to get into. We've lost communication with the outpost and need to determine why. Satellite relays have confirmed that the power systems for the outpost are still active. There have been no reports of UNIC activity in the region and no indication that the location has been compromised...but we need to be ready for anything," the commander said as he turned to the lieutenant.

"When we deploy, Sierra Team will take point. The

objective is to access the command center of the outpost and re-establish communication. Kilo Team will locate personnel and secure defensive positions," the commander continued.

"Delta team will be joining us strictly to assist with the civilian population. We want the world to know who we are and what we stand for, so let's show Delta team that the resistance is for the freedom and prosperity of humanity," he said as he motioned to the lieutenant.

"Ok, prep for takeoff," she said as she sat down and strapped in.

The engines started up, creating an intensifying low pitch noise that soon filled the cargo bay. There was tension in the air, more so between the two resistance teams and Delta team than the mission they were about to go on. The lieutenant noticed and tried to distract everyone, she began to go over the plan.

"When we touch down; I want Sierra team with two of the badgers heading straight for the command structure, we need to get the comms up ASAP. I want Kilo team split between operating the rhino to take up a defensive position and on foot looking for our resistance personnel. Delta team will take two badgers and assist civilians. The commander and I will take the stingers and head for the control facility," the lieutenant said as the ship became airborne.

Moments later, a voice was heard. "Destination set, engaging SDD."

The ship disappeared into the distortion. After a short time, the space above the planet where outpost 12 was located became distorted and blurry, the ship emerged, and the distortion dissipated in their wake.

"SDD disengaged, we've reached the destination," the voice was heard as the ship began to descend to the planet below.

All three teams began to stand, preparing for the drop. The commander and the lieutenant moved to the stingers while the other teams moved to their respective vehicles. The ship positioned itself just outside the outpost about twenty feet from the ground. As the cargo bay doors opened, Sierra team drove the badgers off the back, cutting it close as the door wasn't fully opened yet. They were airborne for a moment before they landed with a heavy bounce onto the surface below. The ship dropped a metal ring to the ground via an opening below the rhino. As the platform below the rhino began to drop at a quick pace, it didn't slam into the ground, instead, it slowed to a snail's pace just before touching down gently. The use of the GR, Gravity Ring, was instrumental in supply logistics. The rings, powered by the ZPE cores, allowed the loading and unloading of supplies without direct contact with a surface other than the ring. This same technology was fundamental for space exploration as it allowed supplies to be sent to space cheaply and efficiently.

Delta team departed as Sierra had, only after the commander and lieutenant took off in the stingers. They watched as the commander and lieutenant darted across the sky toward the outpost.

"Looks like they were able to activate the outpost's defensive measures. The whole place looks like it was under lockdown protocol. There's some extensive damage, Jennings, can you confirm?" the lieutenant asked as they approached the outer perimeter of the outpost.

"I've got eyes on the gate," Jennings said as he continued his observations. "Looks like it's been destroyed, blast marks look strange though."

There was a pause in the communication for a moment as Sierra team rolled over the damaged doors that used to secure the gate. The doors were thick, reinforced blast doors capable of withstanding multiple shots from the rhino's mounted weapons.

"Looks like parts of the door were melted," he said with concern.

"Moving into the outpost now," he said as they continued.

"I've got scorch marks on the ground in various locations. Doesn't look like a grenade or rocket blast though...something else," the lieutenant remarked as the commander and her made their way to the control facility.

"We've got a lot of debris," Jennings remarked as they approached the Command structure.

"Approaching command structure now. It appears defenses have been activated here as well but the doors are open. Moving in now," Jennings said as Sierra team moved into the building.

"There's an awful lot of rounds here," he remarked as they moved through the main corridor.

"Looks like we missed all the action, there are bullet holes everywhere," he continued as they came to the end of the corridor, "the walls are like swiss cheese, I'm surprised they're still holding this building up,"

"They must have gone with the spray and pray method cause we're seeing the same thing here," Santos said as they got in position. "Rhino is set and ready, rest of Kilo will begin personnel round up."

"Something's wrong," Commander Hanlon said.

He and the lieutenant landed on the roof of the control facility. They stepped out of the stingers and moved to the edge of the roof. The commander and lieutenant surveyed the situation on the ground; the front gate had been destroyed, scorch marks peppered the ground, and not one trace of human existence.

"This many bullets and not one body, not one injured soldier, not one drop of blood..." he said as his demeanor grew somber.

"Everyone, keep your eyes open, it's too quiet...could be a trap," the lieutenant said.

"I want those soldiers and civilians found, they have to be held up somewhere," the commander instructed.

"I want each of you to search these structures and let's do it fast...something's not right here and I don't want us getting caught up in the middle. Let's find these civilians and move out," Jossen instructed as the team split up and began searching structures. *Clear* was heard from each of the team members as they moved through each of the buildings. Jossen grew worried. No soldiers, no civilians, he began to ask himself if this was indeed a trap.

"Sir, communications have been established but there's no sign of anyone. It looks like a serious fight but no bodies... not ours or theirs," Jennings said.

"We've checked the control facility, no one home but we were able to check the logs," the commander said. "We need everyone to meet here."

After regrouping with the rest of Delta team, Jossen made a gesture with his hand. Taylor tapped a couple of times on her screen. She had made a few modifications of her own, programming a separate communications channel, allowing the team to speak to each other without anyone listening in. She signaled to the team that they were all set with a nod.

"We're not doing that right?" Coughlin asked.

"It's sounding more and more like a trap. Modify our

armor, lure us out here, and take us out. I don't like it," Jossen responded.

"Well, it seems to me that it would've been easier to take us out when we had no armor while we were unconscious on those cots," Harden replied.

"Good point, but what if they needed some information from us?" Taylor asked.

"Well I say we go...what's the worst that happens?" Toa asked as he immediately answered his own question. "Two teams of resistance soldiers surround us, and we have to take them out?"

"Don't forget the TITAN and his lieutenant," Coughlin added with a hint of sarcasm.

"Let's see what's going on...I don't want a repeat of the last mission. Coughlin and Harden stay here, Toa and Taylor are with me...let's go see what's what," Jossen said as he started toward the control facility.

As Jossen, Toa, and Taylor approached the rest of the group in the control facility, they all appeared to be huddled around an array of screens. The control facility was the hub for all infrastructure to the outpost. It housed the controls for all essential facilities including water, HVAC, electricity, and security. The group didn't seem to notice as the three approached, their eyes glued to the screens at the security station.

"So what'd you find?" Jossen asked the commander.

"Come take a look, it's bizarre," the lieutenant responded.

As they continued to watch the screens, it appeared to be a surveillance camera, showing a group of unarmed soldiers and civilians all walking out of the facility. The people moved in an orderly fashion, seemingly of their own free will, like it was a fire drill.

"That looks like all of them," Jossen said as he had

already formulated an opinion. "Looks like they're going on strike...the resistance not taking care of their people?" he continued, irritating both the commander and the lieutenant.

"Just watch," the commander snapped.

As the last of the soldiers and civilians walked past the camera, there was a blurring motion as some type of interference was preventing the camera from providing a clear image.

"There!" the commander said as the blurring motion appeared to be a form of the active optics.

"The UNIC must've rounded everyone up," the lieutenant said.

"That's a pretty ballsy move," Jennings remarked. "Sending a squad of operators to take an entire outpost into custody."

"I'm not entirely sure that's what we're seeing here. Something else is going on," the commander said as he began thinking out loud.

"If it were the UNIC, there would be some casualties, injuries, something left behind. I have a feeling this is something else," the commander said. He paused as he thought. "Even if they sent enough operators to round everyone up, why would they take the injured or dead? Why would there be an effort to leave no trace? How would their nanites still work?" the commander seemed as confused as he was angry.

"We need to get this footage cleaned up. There has to be more than this, something else that can give us a better idea about what happened here," the commander said as he looked around.

"I might be able to help," Taylor spoke up as she moved to a nearby console that was badly damaged.

"I'll search the system to see what I can find...it's going to take some time though, it's in rough shape," she continued as she noticed Jossen shooting her a glaring look. She rolled her eyes and connected to the console.

"What are you doing? Helping the resistance gather evidence against the UNIC? That's not what we came along for," Jossen said in a hushed voice.

"No, we came along to help the civilians...and if we're going to do that, I for one would like to know what we're up against. I'm not gathering evidence for the resistance, but something happened here, and I'd like to know what," she replied.

"Who else could it be? Only the UNIC would be able to pull something like this off," Toa asked.

"But why?" asked Harden over the comms.

"Why would the UNIC storm the outpost, take everyone into custody including civilians, and then take the wounded and dead?" Harden asked again puzzled.

"We would probably already know the answer if we were back on the Forge," Jossen said, growing more and more frustrated with the team's attitude.

"Well I say Taylor finds out what she can, and we discuss it before letting anyone know what she finds," Coughlin finally chimed in.

"Fine," Jossen said, relenting to the group. "Let us know when you find something."

"I think we're past the point of an ambush by the commander, Jossen," Harden said as he indicated that Coughlin and himself would join the team.

"Yeah," Jossen said reluctantly.

Back on the Forge, Barnes stood in front of the holopad, preparing herself for the coming discussion. She slowly stepped onto the pad and it began to glow as the images of the ministers began to materialize.

"Good Afternoon," Barnes greeted the ministers.

"Again I find myself with the same response...I wish it were," Minister Gantley said with disappointment. "Your tone-deaf approach to this meeting leads me to believe that you are slightly behind on current affairs."

"I hope your sequestration has proven fruitful," Minister Yamato interjected.

"Well yes, I have been focused on my work, and made a very interesting discovery," Barnes was set to continue but was interrupted.

"I'm sure you have but there are more pressing matters that require your undivided attention," Minister Gantley continued in a solemn tone. "You are not aware, but yesterday at 2200 hours, the resistance launched an offensive against colony C2032. The entire population has been lost."

"The entire population?!" Barnes asked as if the minister had misspoken.

"You heard correctly Director Barnes, the entire population," Minister Gantley reiterated.

"Been lost? What does that even mean? How is that possible?" Barnes fired off the questions in rapid succession.

Minister Halin interrupted, "The entire population of the colony is no longer there. We have received reports that they have been captured by combatants that utilized a form of active optics to shield their identity. They transported everyone from the colony to an unknown location."

"The use of active optics by the resistance is indeed troubling. Time and again they have shown us their ingenuity and adaptability. It seems as though the threat we face from the resistance is as dire as it has ever been," Minister Yamato said.

"This resistance attack cannot stand, we will not allow them to openly assault the UNGA. They have been playing the long game...only attacking when an opportunity presented itself...but now, with this blatant attack on the UNGA, on humanity itself..." Minister Sarpong paused, seeming distraught, "we must show strength in the face of this tragedy."

"And indeed we will. We will utilize all of our resources to eradicate the resistance and bring its leaders to justice," Minister Gantley interjected.

"I understand this council's grief and anger but what evidence is there that this was a resistance operation? It seems rather sophisticated for them to pull off wouldn't you say? I wouldn't think twice if the population had been killed or injured...but abducted? I don't believe the resistance has the resources to abduct and hold hostage that many people," Barnes said to the dismay of the council.

"This has always been your greatest weakness, you underestimate your opponents. While you underestimate them, they use that to their advantage. Your trivializing of their abilities makes you vulnerable and gives them the advantage," Minister Sarpong said.

"Well, I think that it would be prudent to evaluate all possibilities to ensure we take the proper course of action," Barnes tried to appeal to the council.

"Spoken like a true scientist, however, the council exists to protect humanity and that's what we intend to do. We have already given the orders to the Admirals and the UNSS Forge will lead the effort, they will be departing stationary orbit shortly. Admiral Vincere has been given full authority to utilize any means at his disposal to bring the resistance to an end," Minister Yamato said, standing tall as he did.

"You propose a more steadfast course of action Dir. Barnes? And what information do you possess that would indicate it is anything other than a resistance operation?"

Minister Guerrero asked, attempting to draw something out of Barnes. "What was the discovery you spoke of earlier?"

"It is unrelated to this but there was an issue with one of the subjects. It seems that the process for fusing the nanites had a less than desirable effect on one of the subjects," Barnes replied.

"Less than desirable effect?" Minister Halin seemed very intrigued.

"Yes, although the incubation of the subjects worked as intended, the nanite infusion failed. It ultimately took over the cells and the resulting subject had to be terminated," Barnes responded.

"We weren't concerned in the slightest about the incubation of the subjects. I would like to know what you believe constitutes a failure," Minister Yamato said with a hint of skepticism.

"The subject exhibited severe nanite syndrome resulting in extreme deformation and elevated aggression. We lost several scientists during the procedure," Barnes stated.

"It seems that we do in fact have different definitions of failure. The nanites did fuse to the subject and the subject's strength and lethality were subsequently enhanced?" Minister Guerrero asked.

"Yes, but not in the way we had hoped," Barnes replied.

"If the subject met the critical parameters then we cannot call this a failure. You will send us what you have on the subject in question, we would very much like to see this *failure,*" Minister Gantley said stoically.

"Yes, I will send the videos. I have reviewed them extensively and believe that I have found the issue with the fusion. I have already begun work on the solution," she responded.

"It took me a while to figure out that the cellular makeup of the subjects resulted in the absorption of the nanites, creating a hybrid nanite. I was able to reprogram the code for the nanites and will be testing them on the next subject shortly," she continued.

"Well, keep working on it. Project Olympus is instrumental to the future of the human race, Director. While Admiral Vincere ensures the resistance is destroyed, Olympus should be your main focus. We will need this to be operational to re-enforce the Admiral's plan," Minister Yamato said.

"Back to the issue at hand, if the resistance has the ability to launch an assault of this kind, we need to find out how and from where they are getting their resources immediately," Minister Halin stated.

"I will find out," Barnes offered before being soundly rejected.

"You will do no such thing Director. That task will fall to the Vincere. You will continue your work on Olympus and provide the Admiral support as is requested by him. I know it can be hard for you to handle sometimes but this is not an order to be taken lightly," Minister Gantley said sternly.

"Understood," Barnes said curtly.

She didn't want to seem overly concerned about the Admiral's appointment. She knew that with Vincere in charge, her entire life's work could be jeopardized. The appointment of Vincere solidified the meaning behind the note that Kinston had handed her. It had become apparent to her that time was no longer on her side.

"We need results, Director, and we need them now," Minister Yamato said before ending the transmission.

Barnes stepped down off the holopad and moved to the door. As the door opened, Mr. Kinston turned to face the doctor. Barnes was barely able to get through the door before two UNIC soldiers approached from behind Kinston.

"Sir, you're to come with us," the soldier said.

Kinston asked, "On whose orders?"

"Admiral Vincere's," the soldier replied.

Barnes knew as well as Kinston what was about to happen. She gave him an apologetic look as his face tightened. Mr. Kinston was a rare type of man, dedicated to principle and strong-willed. He would be difficult to break, but Admiral Vincere was known as a ruthless man, a dedicated man without the same moral compass Mr. Kinston possessed to guide his character. The soldiers began to lead Mr. Kinston away. Barnes knew she didn't have much time before they came for her. She went back to her office to go over the events of the last few days. She played through several scenarios in her head before deciding on a course of action. She always knew this day would come, but knowing it and living it were two different things entirely.

Meanwhile, on outpost 12, Sierra and Kilo teams took their time searching the outpost looking for any clues that could shed some light on the current situation. Taylor continued to pour through the surveillance system, her demeanor changing slightly when reviewing one of the feeds. She looked over at the team as inconspicuously as she could, not wanting to alert the commander and lieutenant. Harden saw her as she slightly motioned to the screen with her head. As Harden began to move toward Taylor, he grazed the arm of Jossen. Jossen immediately recognized that he was moving toward Taylor and held back for a moment. Just then, the commander received a communication from Resistance Operation Command. It played over all of their communications.

"Commander, we just received intelligence that colony C2032 has been attacked. The entire population of the colony is gone. It sounds like whatever happened on outpost

12 happened there as well. We are also receiving reports that the entire UNIC fleet is mobilizing...you and your teams need to get back here ASAP," the transmission ended.

"Ok, you heard them. Let's get back to the dropship now," the commander said as he moved toward the door.

The lieutenant and the rest of the group made their way to the door. They noticed that Delta group was still in the room, huddled around one of the consoles.

"It's time to go. We don't want to be here if they decide to dust this place," the commander directed his comment to Delta team.

"You may want to see this," Jossen said.

"Unfortunately, it seems as though we're out of time," the lieutenant remarked.

"I think you'll make time for this," Taylor insisted.

"Sierra and Kilo, get back to the javelin. We'll meet you there," the commander instructed.

The commander and lieutenant then made their way over to the screen. Taylor rewound the footage and played it from the beginning. As the footage played; screams, gunfire, and yelling provided a soundtrack to a room full of men shooting toward an open door. As a moment passed, a blur of what appeared to be bent light entered the room. As bullets approached the bent light, they seemed to ricochet off of it. During a particularly large volley of gunfire, a grenade is thrown and exploded. This explosion seemed to be enough energy to temporarily disable the active optics, revealing a distorted being. It was humanoid but had exaggerated and distorted features. The elongated arms, slouched head, and deformed legs sent a chill through their spines. The active optics quickly re-engaged, and the operative took out the room full of men with ruthless efficiency. The operative was not very fast but deliberate in its movements. It didn't seem to have a firearm as it incapacitated the soldiers with physical force.

"If that's a new breed of operator, then I think we're out of business," Toa remarked as everyone was still fixated on the video.

"We need to move. Taylor, can you extract that video?" the commander asked.

He pulled himself away from the screen, knowing that the UNIC was undoubtedly on their way there right now.

"Working on it now," she said as she tapped the screen a few times.

After a moment that seemed to last an eternity, she said, "Got it!"

"Everyone get back to the javelin now!" the commander shouted.

The commander and the lieutenant moved quickly to the roof. Delta team darted to the badgers that were parked out front. Everyone made their way to the javelin as fast as they could. Sierra and Kilo teams were already loaded on the ship when Delta team rolled up to the ring. Once they were on the ring, it lifted into the ship with an echoing thud.

"Let's move," the commander said.

The ship took off into orbit as a field of distorted space formed in front of them. The javelin disappeared into the distortion.

SIX
BETRAYAL

DR. BARNES PACED in her office as she thought about her conversation with the council. The knowledge of what Mr. Kinston must be going through under the direction of Admiral Vincere infuriated her. She knew this was a necessary step in her plan but that didn't make it any less painful. It kept interrupting her thought process as the more pressing matter of the council stood before her.

She knew the council was aware of all of the work she was doing. It was all part of her plan, but one slight misstep could jeopardize everything. If the council really knew what she was up to, they would never have let her walk out of that room.

"If they did know what I was up to, why let me leave?" she asked herself out loud.

"If Vincere and the council knew about Kinston, then the only reason they would let me go would be Olympus." She paused for a moment as Vincere and Kinston took over her thoughts once again.

That man will ruin everything. He may be a great military

mind, but he lacks subtlety and finesse, and they know that. Why would they give him this kind of authority? She asked herself while attempting to answer immediately, *because they must want to make a show of it.* All at once it clicked in her head, that they must want to use Olympus as a way to publicly end the war.

"So if the council has the subjects here, why would they take a colony of humans? And where would they take them?" she asked herself out loud once again.

Ok, they create a war with the resistance, knowing that it would be a human tragedy, it allows them to continue developing new weapons of war while using the resistance as a scapegoat. The goal hasn't changed though, create a new breed of soldiers to ensure humanity's survival...they wouldn't need colonists or an escalation now, she thought to herself as she began to grow frustrated.

I must be missing something. They've always played the long game...they wouldn't be doing this now unless it was to their advantage, and now with the abduction of the colonists. Was it the council who had the colonists abducted? To fan the flames of war? To create a diversion large enough to keep all eyes off of what they're doing? Her frustration got the better of her as she fell into her chair. She knew she needed to get this right, to understand what their goal would be taking this new information into account.

Director Barnes knew better than most the lengths the council would go to in order to achieve their goals, not unlike herself. As she sat in her chair, she remembered the first time she met Gantley, long before he was Minister Gantley.

She had just left her mother's house. Thumb drive in hand. She felt an excitement as she anticipated what may be on the drive. She walked down the stairs of the house, the warm June sun shone in her eyes. Ashley continued down the walkway toward the driveway, a gentle breeze lofting through the oak tree in the front yard. I need to get the landscaper to stop by, she thought to herself as she looked at the grass that had become overgrown. As she approached her car she noticed another vehicle coming down the road. The surrounding fields that had once been green with corn had become a lifeless brown, drought had set in and turned the once vibrant fields into a wasteland. As the vehicle approached, she noticed that it began to turn down her mother's driveway. She paused while opening the driver's side door of the car, wanting to see why there was someone there to see her mother. It became clear that the driver was either lost or not there to see her mother. A limousine pulled up behind her car while the driver got out and moved around it to open the back door. A man stepped out while the driver closed the door and waited there. The man walked up to Ashley as she took a moment to scope him out. He was in his thirties, slicked-back dark hair with a tailored blue suit. His shoes looked like they had never been worn before, a shade of brown that seemed to match the dirt at his feet. Ashley would always look for any details that could give her additional insight and the shoes told her all she needed to know.

"Hello Miss," the man said as he approached.

"It's Mrs.," Ashley replied.

"My mistake, hello Mrs.," he corrected himself.

"Can I help you?" Ashley asked.

"I hope so. I'm looking for Doctor Barnes," the man replied.

"I might be more apt to help if I knew who was asking," she replied.

"Yes, my manners—you must think I have none - my name is Adam Gantley," he said.

"Ok Mr. Gantley, I'm not sure that I'll be able to guess

what you would want with Doctor Barnes," she replied as she pretended not to know who he was.

In fact, everyone at least knew of Adam Gantley. He was the CEO of three global companies, the richest man in the world. He ran the largest technology, energy, and supply companies on Earth. His value at the time was around two trillion dollars. He supplied every household with almost everything they needed, from food to electricity to cell phones.

"Well," he responded, knowing that a doctor of her reputation would absolutely know who he is, "you must not get out much."

"I didn't say I had no idea who you were, but I'm a little confused as to why you're here," she responded.

"Fair enough," he said as he approached a bit closer. "I would like to discuss your future."

"My future is pretty well on track, thank you," she responded, not wanting to hint at the curiosity that was welling up inside of her.

"Indeed it is, but I wanted to discuss the expansion of that future," he said as he leaned on the hood of the limo.

"Look around...I see the coming climate crisis, it's already begun. The leaders of the world isolating themselves with their short sighted policies. The global population continues to climb while resources become scarcer and scarcer. It's only a matter of time before that track you think you're on is no longer there," he said as he looked at the landscape around them.

"I know you're trying to pitch me something, but I can't say exactly what it is," Ashley responded, preferring a more direct approach.

"I would like you to come work for me. I would be able to provide more resources than you can imagine, far more than the government is allowing you. I want you to be on the

ground floor of something that can change the course of humanity forever," he said, trying to cut to the chase.

"Just being honest, kind of sounds like a cult thing," Ashley said, again playing coy.

"Take a ride with me, let me lay out the vision I have for the future. If you decide it's not for you, I will bring you right back. If you decide you are interested, I would like you to start immediately," he said.

"Well I'm on my way home, my husband is waiting," she replied.

"I understand. I can have him picked up to join us if that will help. Unfortunately, I can't waste a moment because I don't think we can afford to. There are things happening right now that could change everything, and I would love to explain more, but I need you to come with me," he said as he motioned to the limo. Ashley's curiosity began to overcome her common sense.

"What about my car?" she asked.

"I will have it picked up and brought to us," Adam said.

"I just need to call my husband and talk to him first," she replied.

"Understood," he said as he moved to give her some privacy while she called her husband. They spoke for a few moments then Ashley hung up the phone and moved towards Mr. Gantley.

"Let's hear what you have to say," she said as the driver opened the door to the limo.

"My husband is awaiting his ride," she said. Mr. Gantley motioned to the driver and he immediately got on the phone.

"Don't you need the address?" Ashley asked.

"We actually have a driver in front of your home right now. As I said, we don't have a moment to waste," he replied.

Ashley and Adam entered the limo as the driver closed the

door. A notification alerted Ashley to the text message she had just received from her husband Jonathan. It said that he was on his way, at least that put Ashley's mind at some level of ease.

"You have quite a talent, doctor," Adam said as he situated himself in his seat.

"How's that," Ashley asked.

"I've been following your research. To have accomplished so much while still looking after your mother, that's some feat," he said.

"I do what I need to do," she said instinctively. She had been used to people saying that to her ever since her mother got sick.

"But how have you been following my research?" she asked, puzzled by the fact that her research was considered top secret by the US Government.

"I understand that you have been working on some sensitive projects. In fact, my teams have been working on those very same projects. We enjoy a certain level of cooperation with many governments of the world," he said.

"We?" she asked.

"Yes, me and my associates have recognized the coming perils. The human race will soon be, some may say is at, a crossroads," he said as he reached for a briefcase.

"The impending climate crisis, already creating worldwide disasters, combined with the current political climate will create a global catastrophe, the likes of which we've never witnessed," he said, trying not to sound too dramatic but failing, nonetheless.

"Me and my associates have been working on ways to mitigate these disasters. We have been working with the governments of the world to advance a new way of thinking. A mindset that will be needed to adapt humanity for survival,"

he paused, seeing that Ashley had begun to look uncomfortable.

"What is it that you're suggesting Mr. Gantley?" she asked, slightly confused as to what would constitute a new way of thinking.

"Take a look at these," Adam said as he opened a brief-case and removed a small stack of papers, handing them to Ashley.

"The world will soon be at war Mrs. Barnes. A war that will without a doubt draw every country to arms. A war that will devastate the planet. There is no way to stop it," Adam said in a very matter-of-fact way.

"How did you get these?" Ashley asked as she read the papers.

"I told you that me and my associates enjoy a certain level of..." he said before he was interrupted by Ashley.

"Yeah, cooperation. This is not just cooperation, this is something else. How were you able to get these readings from the core? Are these results from the nanites on human test subjects?" she asked.

"Yes, they are. As far as the readings, those are theoretical. Which brings me back to you. I believe that you would be instrumental in helping us advance this technology. If we weren't burdened by the red tape that hinders your progress, you probably would've been far beyond where we are now," he said.

"We might even be able to save your mother," he added, waiting for the opportune time to drop that on her.

"What are you talking about?" she asked, intrigued but skeptical.

"Look at the data on the nanites. We are so close to unlocking what they could do. Imagine the possibilities once we figure out how to adapt them to the human body. We

would be able to eradicate disease, cure genetic defects, and eventually stop the aging process," he said.

Ashley looked over the data. Flipping through page by page, looking for something that could dissuade her from pursuing this course of action. There it was, she thought to herself.

"Even with this information and if I worked non-stop with an equally dedicated team, it would take more time than my mother has to work out the details," Ashley said.

"I figured you would say that, you truly are the one we need on this team," he said as he opened the briefcase again. He removed one piece of paper and handed it to Ashley.

"How is this possible?" she asked as she looked at the paper.

"We have been working on this for some time. We have already tried it with moderate success. It wouldn't take you long to crack this one I'm sure. It would buy you as much time as you needed to figure these nanites out," he said.

Ashley sat there stunned. What this man was offering, what he was talking about, was nothing short of a miracle for her mother. A way to cure her of her disease. Ashley, now faced with a difficult decision, found it hard to grasp.

"Ok...you understand that you're putting a lot on me right now. You're asking me to what, help you overthrow the governments of the world?" she asked, recognizing the absurdity in the phrase.

"Not overthrow. We are talking about a shift in the way the human race exists on this Earth. We can no longer afford to exist as anything other than a species, united. For our entirety, we have existed as a divided people, focused more on our differences than our similarities. If we can't unite the human race, if we can't change the way people view this planet and each other, there will be no future left for humanity," he said.

"How do you shift the way people think? This isn't something you can buy, not something you can force people to do, and it certainly won't come on its own," she said.

"You are correct. The only way that people will change is if they truly want to change. I have found that the best catalyst for change is...trauma," he said

"Trauma? What kind of trauma?" she asked.

"The kind that can change the world forever," he said in a solemn voice. "I told you earlier that the world is headed for war. That is not something that can be stopped. We can, however, prepare for humanity's existence after the war. Prepare the people for a world where all humans are free to travel anywhere, where energy comes from a clean and renewable source, and where sickness and disease are a thing of the past. We can prepare the human race for a brighter future. All of this is dependent on a key factor, Doctor Barnes," he said, pausing to allow for her to ask the inevitable question.

"Dependent on what?" she asked.

"Quite frankly – you," he answered with a smile.

As he answered her, the limo pulled up to the tarmac of the airport. A private plane was parked, awaiting their arrival. The driver got out of the limo and came around to the door. He opened the door as Adam stepped out, holding his hand for Ashley to use when exiting the limo. She ignored the symbol of help and stepped out on her own.

"Obviously, you will need to convince my husband," she said as she looked around.

"Obviously," he responded as another vehicle pulled up with Jonathan.

Director Barnes felt a pit in her stomach. Knowing now what impact that first meeting had on her life, the lives of everyone she loved. It pained her to remember how naive she was then, someone who just wanted to help.

"I have to be certain if I have any chance of surviving this," she whispered as she removed the piece of paper from her pocket. She read the piece of paper, it said, *Be careful, they know everything*. She got up out of her chair and moved to one of the bookcases in her office, sticking the piece of paper into one of the books. She made her way back to her unit. She grabbed the QC that she left under the couch cushion and held it for a moment. She looked out at the digital landscape through her so-called window for a moment before putting the QC on the table. After the device made a secure connection, she began searching through files before finding the one she was looking for. "That could work, but it's a long shot," she whispered to herself.

Barnes headed down to Lab 10A at a brisk pace, knowing that she could be called by Admiral Vincere at any moment. She walked up to the door for the lab and softly held her breath. The door opened, she breathed a sigh of relief while maintaining her composure, not sure if her clearance was still active. She proceeded to one of the stations where an engineer was buried in her work. The engineer was so focused on what she was doing that she didn't notice the director standing behind her. She was working on a type of probe that was used to map the coordinates in space needed for interstellar travel. The probe had its own micro SD drive and would travel to a set of spatial coordinates and begin mapping the area to ensure that we had a detailed map of space. This was critical when using the space distortion drive as if you were to use it on unknown coordinates, you could very well re-emerge in a sun, an asteroid belt, or a black hole. The doctor made her presence known to the engineer by bumping her chair slightly. The engineer turned around.

"Director Barnes," the engineer said, surprised to see her in this area of the lab.

"Can I help you with something?" the engineer asked.

"Actually you can, I need to verify classified information, and I need a probe to do it," Barnes said as she picked up one of the new microprobes.

"Classified?" the engineer asked. "You know there's a whole stock of these in A&E."

"Yeah, but I think that guy down in A&E is a little off," Barnes said as she had to think on her feet.

Going down to Asset and Equipment meant signing out a commissioned piece of equipment, and that meant it would be tracked by AIDA and the UNIC. As soon as she signed it out, it would be flagged, putting her entire plan at risk.

"Oh...that old guy with the bad breath?" the engineer asked, unknowingly helping Barnes make her story more believable.

"Yeah, I think he has a thing for me. He's always asking if we can grab something to eat, or if he can take me to the deck, or if he can call me some time," Barnes said as she tried her best to fake her way through a social situation.

These types of conversations were not what the director was used to and would never carry on this way under any normal circumstances, but desperate times called for desperate measures.

"I just really don't want to deal with him right now," the doctor said, trying to sound genuinely creeped out.

"I get it, come to think of it he always looks at me weird when I drop stuff off," the engineer said as her eyes looked up in an exaggerated attempt to think back.

"Do you have any commissioned probes up here?" the doctor asked, knowing full well she didn't.

"I don't," the engineer said, "but does it need to be commissioned?"

"It doesn't need to be I guess, I just need to send it out to take a map of some coordinates we found in an old file from Admiral Yinsman," Barnes responded.

"The UNGA wants to confirm that is where...." she stopped herself.

"I'm not supposed to say anything but," Barnes paused, she sat down beside the engineer.

"I'm sure you can keep a secret right?" Barnes leaned in and whispered to the engineer.

"It could very well be where Admiral Yinsman lost a ship full of hexatriton. We think we may have found the coordinates while going over some old research," the doctor said, trying hard to believe her own lie and sound excited about it.

"Wow, that's gotta be worth a fortune. I won't say anything, but I'd be interested to know if you found it," the engineer replied, thrilled with the fact the doctor had trusted her with what seemed like classified information.

"I'll definitely let you know. That's the least I can do for your help," Barnes said as she got up.

The engineer grabbed a non-commissioned probe off of one of the many shelves and handed it to the doctor. These probes were small, about the size of a basketball, and weighed little more than 10lbs.

"Remember not to say anything. I don't want us both getting in trouble," Barnes said as she turned to leave.

"I won't," the engineer replied with the biggest smile on her face.

Barnes knew that any excitement would provide a much-needed escape for so many scientists and engineers working for AIDA. While it provides stability, for the average person, it also provides a level of tedious boredom and isolation unmatched in humanity. Barnes smiled as she exited the lab. She went back to her unit and got right to work. She opened a part of the probe and pressed the QC against it. She then set the probe down on the table and began typing away. It took some time, but she finally reached for the probe, touched the QC to it again, closed it up, and sat back on the couch. She was done with this phase but needed to get the probe out into space. The AIDA engineer might have been easily fooled due to the relationship with the director, knowing that ultimately all AIDA personnel work for the director, but the others wouldn't be as easy.

There was no easy way to open an airlock on this ship. There were strict protocols for accessing airlocks. She technically did have the authorization, but if she were to authorize an airlock opening and a subsequent space distortion was detected, she would raise suspicions, and at this point, suspicions were probably high enough. So she thought to herself, *how can I get someone else to authorize this probe's departure?* She sat on the couch running scenarios in her head and finally found one that could work.

She grabbed the probe and headed down to hangar bay 9. A UNIC soldier standing guard near the elevator greeted the doctor as she stepped off the elevator.

"Director Barnes, we weren't expecting you down here," the soldier said as he approached. "But that doesn't mean we don't appreciate the visit."

"Sergeant..." she said, making it obvious she didn't know his name.

"Sergeant Dimitri, Director," he responded.

"Of course, Sergeant Dimitri," she said as she held out the probe.

"Is there something I can help you with?" he asked, not understanding why she was holding out the probe.

"Ah, I take it they didn't inform you about the launch," the doctor said.

"Launch?" the Sergeant asked.

"I'm telling you, if it doesn't involve the deployment of ships and soldiers, then it must be of little to no importance," Barnes responded, seemingly annoyed.

"Ok, it may not be a full-scale mission, but we need this probe launched immediately. We have found a transmission source coming from a classified location. We need to get this probe out there immediately to ascertain if we can mobilize," she continued.

"Uhhh," the sergeant said as he looked around, "I'm not sure if I can do that without the proper authorizations."

"Sergeant, I may be a doctor but I'm also the director of AIDA. I'm telling you that in order to act on the intelligence we have, I need to map those coordinates. When I have to speak with the council, I don't want to have to tell them that there was nothing we could do because we couldn't get this probe out...that we had to wait for an authorization as the sergeant wouldn't make a call. It's going to be me in that room, and I don't want to throw anyone under the bus, but I will name names...Sergeant Dimitri..." she looked him straight in his eyes, unwavering in her confidence and boldly believing her own words.

He looked back in her eyes, perhaps waiting for a moment of weakness, a sign that would give him reason to pause but he found no such thing. Her well-developed gaze exuded only confidence, well-honed during her many years of service.

"Right away director," he said as he grabbed the probe and began to move.

"I trust that you can handle launching that so I can begin sending coordinates and working on the analysis?" she asked in a louder tone as he was walking away.

"Yes Doctor, I'll take care of it myself," he said as he turned the corridor and disappeared.

Barnes turned back toward the elevator and went back to her office. There was nothing she could do now but hope that the probe would be launched without anyone realizing the modifications that she made.

Back on the javelin, the commander worried about what they found at the outpost. Everyone was on edge, not knowing what to make of everything they had just seen. They made their way back to the resistance base. Once they were back in the hangar, the commander addressed the group.

"I have some things I need to take care of. I don't want this escalating out of control before we know what the whole story is. There are bound to be some people who don't take this news sitting down and will want action," the commander said to the team.

"Taylor, I need you to work with our scientists to find out everything you can about these things. We need to know what we're up against. If you find anything else that might be relevant in that surveillance data, please let me know. I want to save lives, and the older I get, it seems the best way to do that is to be informed," he continued.

Taylor nodded at the commander as he turned to the lieutenant. The commander and lieutenant both walked away, moving with a purpose as they navigated the loading bay and back into the complex.

Taylor approached Jossen as the team was left in the loading bay. "There's something funny going on here," she said.

"I don't think these are operators or UNIC at all. There's a part in the video that I'm trying to clean up, but the data is telling me that whatever these things are, they're causing the interference. They must be emitting something that interferes with the signal as they approach. It seems to get worse the closer they are to the camera," she told Jossen.

"Well keep trying to clean it up. I want to know before they do," he replied.

"And the rest of you, let's continue our recon while everyone is distracted. Commander Hanlon knows quite a bit about us, I'd like to find out more about him and what they had planned for the future. We need to be cautious, tensions will be high if the resistance thinks the UNIC staged this attack. Talk to whoever you can, look through whatever you can, but be careful. We can meet back at the mess hall," he told the rest of the team.

Everyone nodded as they moved into the complex. Taylor went to find a tech station where she would be able to work quietly. She eventually found one as she wandered down corridor after corridor. As she walked in and sat down, she felt a strange feeling, like someone was watching her. She looked around but saw nothing, so she went back to working on the video interference. As she continued to work she felt that strange feeling again...she turned quickly to see a girl, not quite eight years old. The girl stood there, unsure whether she should speak to this person.

"You're new here aren't you?" the little girl asked.

"You can say that," Taylor responded.

"What's your name?" the girl asked.

"Taylor," said Taylor, realizing that the questions probably wouldn't end there.

"My name is Emma," the girl said, offering her name even though she wasn't asked. "Whatcha doin?" she asked as she moved closer to Taylor and peered up at the table.

"Working," Taylor replied.

She hoped that if she gave short answers, the child would get the hint, but Taylor didn't have much experience with children or childhood for that matter. As she looked at the girl, she couldn't help but feel a strange swirling of thoughts and emotions. These new feelings took her by surprise, but she quickly dismissed them by focusing once again on her work.

"Whatcha working on?" the questions from the girl continued.

Taylor turned and looked at the girl, realizing that focusing on her work was not going to get her out of this. Emma's auburn hair was stringy and stood out against her complexion. Her eyes bright and full of curiosity, not at all scared or nervous about talking to a complete stranger. Maybe it was the fact that her own childhood was lost that made her soften just a bit.

"I'm trying to figure something out, but it's a little harder than I thought," Taylor said as she turned her gaze from Emma back to the station.

"Some things are really hard," Emma said as she nodded in confirmation. "I had to make a book in class today. It was about my favorite day," she said. She paused for a moment.

"Writing can be tough, but my teacher told me to start with a beginning and an end. Then I just filled in the middle," she said with a smile.

The words resonated with Taylor. *Start with a beginning and end, fill in the middle* Taylor thought to herself.

"Emma, you're one smart little girl," Taylor said with a smile.

"Little girl?!" Emma said. "I'm almost eight!" she said in a matter-of-fact manner.

"True," Taylor said. "Thanks for the help."

"Anytime," Emma said with a smile, then turned and left the room.

Taylor got right to work, pinpointing the signal before the interference then after. She then began to piece together the signal working from both directions. *It may not be the cleanest, but it should work,* she said to herself.

While Taylor continued to work on the signal, the rest of the team wandered around the complex. As they did, they noticed that most of the people here were normal citizens. The corridors were alive with activity. You couldn't walk down a single hall without walking past a construction worker, a technician, or a group of kids. It seemed like a close-knit community, everyone stopping for a moment to catch a glimpse of the newcomers. The team could sense the tension, hear the whispers as they passed. There were soldiers stationed at various points around the base but having their nanites active again, they knew that the soldiers couldn't stop them if they tried.

"I have to be honest, the resistance is nothing like I thought it would be," Toa said as they continued walking.

"Yeah, I was expecting to see a bunch of soldiers gathered around a table plotting their next attack," Coughlin said.

"Don't let your guard down. I wouldn't expect them to be doing anything like that out in the open. In fact, I suspect we may not find anything at all while we're here. They may let us walk around, but there's no way they'll allow us into areas they don't want us," Jossen cautioned.

"Well, they haven't given us reason to believe that they're responsible for anything but defending themselves," Harden pushed back.

"Whoa, these are the same people responsible for the attack on IRIS, the same people that tried to kill us when we were sent to outpost 4, and the same people that have killed so many during the course of their campaign. Don't think for a second that if presented the opportunity that they wouldn't take us out or the entire UNIC....the UNGA for that matter," Jossen said as he stopped and confronted Harden.

"You need to get the fairytale stuff out of your head. You're a UNIC operator. We were sent on our mission to bring Commander Hanlon to justice. Right now may not be the best time but if an opportunity presents itself, we are completing our mission," Jossen said.

He turned to face the other team members as his look grew more stern. He knew what was happening, that the team was beginning to sympathize with the resistance. Jossen had to get the team to focus on the mission.

"And I need to know that we are all on the same page," Jossen said.

"Listen, I'm all for finishing a mission. You know us, we always find a way to get it done...but I feel like there's more happening here than what we've been told," Harden said as both Toa and Coughlin nodded their heads in agreement.

"There's stuff that both the resistance and AIDA is not telling us. I don't like being used by anyone, but the more I see, the more it seems like AIDA views us as tools to complete a job," Coughlin said.

"Of course they do!" Jossen yelled in frustration.

He immediately realized it and brought his tone back to normal before continuing.

"We are tools, the most effective tools to get the job done. The entire UNIC is a tool, even the UNGA is a tool...a tool for humanity to ensure its survival. I have no delusions about my role in this. That's why they chose us and that's why we're here now. We know what we are and who we are," Jossen said.

"We know what we are and who we are?" Harden said curiously.

"Honestly, I don't think any of us know who we really are. This is probably the longest we have been away from AIDA and it makes me realize that AIDA is all we know...

and as for what we are..." Harden said, looking down at himself, holding his hands out to see the nanite housings. "I would like to believe we are more than what they made us".

"They made us more than what we were, they gave us a chance when no one else would, it's what we do with that chance that will define us. We wouldn't be who we are now without AIDA...we could've ended up like any other orphans," Jossen continued.

"They took us in when we had no one," he continued. Jossen's tone had shifted from passionate anger to despair.

"That's assuming the orphan story is true," Harden replied.

"Do you have any reason not to believe it? Other than what the commander said?" Jossen asked.

Harden remained silent. The images from his dreams nagging at his waking self, giving him pause and not allowing him to answer the question. Harden looked away, not wanting to divulge the reason for his pause, allowing Jossen to believe whatever he wanted.

"I think it's hard to answer that question because I don't even remember a time before AIDA," Coughlin chimed in.

"Neither do I," Toa recalled.

"Look, I get it. I have a lot of questions too. None of us have the answer and I don't trust the *answers* from Hanlon. The bottom line is we need to finish this mission, I think we owe it to Zhou. He gave his life for the mission and we can't let that sacrifice be in vain. We can talk to Barnes when we get back and see if we can learn more about our backgrounds and how this all happened but for now, we need to stay focused. I promise we will do whatever is necessary to get those answers when we get back, we'll make that our next mission," Jossen said.

"Fair enough," Harden said.

Jossen was great at redirecting people. He knew how to prioritize and focus a group. The team was satisfied with his response because they knew that a statement like that was not to be taken lightly coming from Jossen. The rest of the team nodded in agreement, the thoughts of who they were and who they should be still weighed heavily on their minds.

"Let's get back to Taylor and see if she found anything, then we can figure out how to get back," Harden said.

"Let's do it," Toa said as he grabbed Coughlin and Jossen on his left and right.

Coughlin and Jossen in turn grabbed Harden. They put their foreheads together for a moment, each understanding that they were their own family, that they would always be there for each other. As the team made their way to Taylor, she was finishing up her analysis. As she got up to go meet the team, they came around the corner, almost running into each other.

"Guys, you aren't going to believe this," Taylor said in a nervously excited tone.

"What did you find?" Harden asked.

"Well, I had to piece together the data from the start and end of the video. Those two reference points had the least amount of distortion. Then, I created an algorithm to re-create the signal and propagate it over the interference."

Toa interrupted her, "Ok, you lost me at *well,*" Toa said. Toa didn't have any interest in faking an understanding of what Taylor was going to say.

"I was able to re-create the video," Taylor dumbed it down for Toa. "You have to see it," she said as she showed them the screen.

The video began, showing people fleeing through a corridor. Shortly after a group of people run by the camera, the gunfire starts. A hail of bullets flew down the hallway, flashes from the gunfire reflected off the walls creating a strobing effect as smoke and dust lightly floated in the air. As the blurred objects began to move into the frame, the team witnesses the bullets deflecting around the blurred objects.

"It's like they're bulletproof," Toa said, pointing out the obvious to the rest of the team.

The objects moved slowly, deliberately, toward the gunfire. A small metal object was seen sliding along the floor to the base of the blur. A bright flash temporarily blinded the camera, obscuring everything from view. As the flash dimmed, the blurring effect that had obscured the objects seemed to fail, as the light-bending effect appeared to twist in on itself. The exposed portion of the object showed what appeared to be an arm, elongated and distorted, black in color similar to the operator's nanite suit...but different, not a suit, it appeared to be their skin. The distorted light then appeared to fill back in as if the explosion had only temporarily disable parts of the effect. The objects then continued down the hallway. Just before the objects would have left the frame, a soldier was seen running up to the objects. As the soldier attempted to engage, the objects swiped at him with what the team believed was an arm, the soldier was lifted off of his feet and sent hurtling toward the wall. The impact of the soldier against the wall suggested that this object had incredible strength.

"Did you see that?" Coughlin asked rhetorically. "They just swatted him away like a bug."

The other team members barely noticed that she spoke, each one glued to the screen. As the objects continued out of frame, the video switched to a view within a room. The room appeared to be a mechanical and electrical room. There were soldiers still moving people out through the back of the room. The camera was facing the entrance to the room which had a hardened blast door. As the soldiers braced for what was coming, a soft red glow began to illuminate the left and right sides of the door. As they began to glow brighter, the door came exploding inwards landing feet from where it once stood. The soldiers opened fire as once again the objects approached, seemingly unconcerned about the gunfire that ricocheted around them. Another soldier decided to engage but with a different tactic. He was seen doing something with his vest just before running at the objects. It looked like it was going to be the same outcome as the last soldier's attempt but just as the object attempted to swipe at him, the grenades that the soldier armed just before running at the objects went off. It appeared as though the soldier pulled all of the pins as the explosion was dramatically larger than the last. The flash that once again blinded the camera fades. The two objects stood there stopped in their tracks as whatever cloaking field around them was disabled. They were tall, at least eight feet, slim figured, and hunched slightly as their shoulders leaned forward. Their arms were long, long enough that it looked obviously disproportionate. Their legs looked different, as if they walked on the balls of their feet. It looked as though their legs would be able to bend in a way that didn't seem human. This was disturbing to watch but what threw the team off the most was the armor they were wearing, or rather the armor that was part of them. Taylor had paused the video on this scene.

"Those can't be TITANs right?" Harden asked, shocked.

"Some kind of new nanite suit maybe?" Coughlin suggested.

"Well, whatever they are, it appears they have some kind of magnetic field that's strong enough to bend light. It's not just active optics, the bullets change trajectory as if they're being guided...deflected," Taylor said.

"It makes our armor look like regular skin," Toa remarked.

"Ok, all the more reason to get back to AIDA and figure out what's going on. If this is a new generation of TITAN, we could have a problem. I still don't understand why the UNIC would take the entire outpost, but it doesn't seem that the resistance has the answer either," Jossen said as he turned his focus away from the screen.

"We need to find the commander and see about getting back," Jossen commanded.

The team set out to find the commander. They arrived at the door to the command center, a large room the size of a football field. It consisted of one main room with a dozen smaller rooms around it. The soldiers standing guard outside stepped to the side, allowing the team to enter. The thick transparent doors opened but as they closed behind them, they turned opaque. The room had multiple teams of people working at ten large stations. The back wall was an array of screens showing important information relating to resistance activities throughout the outposts and colonies.

"I'm glad you're here," the commander said without looking up from his chair.

"We need to talk to you about what we found," Jossen motioned Taylor to come forward.

"Hold on," the commander instructed as he swiped something from the desk he was at to the large array of screens on the wall.

It was a message, the message read:

Commander, I know you have no reason to trust me. The past has been more than slightly complicated between us. I am contacting you now because I will soon be labeled a traitor to humanity. You can no longer rely on your source, as he has been compromised. This fight has exacted a heavy toll on us all. I have discovered something that could potentially end this conflict and may indeed be a turning point for humanity. I need you to meet me at the coordinates stored in this probe at the exact time specified, although I cannot explain, this is the only opportunity I will get to try to set things right. This message and the potential that it represents is far greater than you or me. I truly hope that you are able to understand the significance of this message and will anticipate one last rendezvous. Director Barnes.

The team looked shocked.

"Why would Barnes be contacting you?" Harden asked, being the first to fire off the question that was on everyone's mind.

"Obviously, something's wrong. She must have nowhere else to turn and if that's the case then things are more dire than I thought," the commander said.

"We recovered this from a probe that entered through a space distortion near the compound where you dropped in on us. All systems on the probe were disabled except for the SDD and the distress signal. She somehow sent this probe, which tells me she couldn't trust anyone. The abduction at outpost 12 must play a role in this. We received intel that there was a similar incident at colony C2032," the commander said as he turned his chair toward the team.

"There's more," he got up from the chair and moved toward the team. Coming face to face with Jossen, he said, "Your team's mission was to fail."

"No, our mission was to bring you back to AIDA, alive if possible but either way," Jossen responded as he took one step closer to the commander.

"That's what you had to believe if you were to succeed in your mission," the commander responded without instigating any further.

"You had to fail in order to give us something you didn't know you had," the commander said as he saw the confusion and frustration begin to build in Jossen's face.

"You were in possession of something more valuable than reaper armor or nanites or a ship. You are in possession of a second-generation TITAN," the commander said as he continued staring at Jossen.

"You really think that, don't you?" Jossen asked.

"How would we have a second-generation TITAN? There's no such thing," he continued.

"That's what we've all been led to believe it seems," the commander said as he turned his gaze toward Harden. "You... are a second-generation TITAN."

It didn't seem real, the entire room froze. A silence that seemed to thicken within every empty space, becoming a presence in itself. Harden felt his stomach turn, the weight of the recent revelations manifesting physically.

"What?!? You're a second-generation TITAN?!?" Toa exclaimed in excitement.

"How is that even possible?" Taylor asked as she looked him up and down.

"Well there's only one way to make a second generation TITAN," the commander said, squaring up with Harden. "We verified it though, his DNA is different than anyone in this room, fundamentally changed by the unification of two TITAN genetic codes. He has nanites as well, although they don't seem to affect him the same way as the rest of us."

"You son of a TITAN," Coughlin said as she moved to get a look at him with a smile. "I can't believe it!"

"I'm not sure I believe it either," Jossen said with a jealous tone. "We're supposed to just trust what you say as fact? Even if it were true, why would the doctor want to send him to you?" Jossen asked the commander. "Unless..."

"I'm going to cut you off right there. While it's true that some TITANs did attempt to reproduce, the countermeasures employed by AIDA were supposed to prevent that. Apparently, someone found a way around this or AIDA merged the DNA of two TITANs," the commander cut Jossen off.

"I'm still not sure why Barnes would send you here though. I need to meet with her," he continued.

"You really think that's a smart idea commander?" the lieutenant asked, "it sounds like a setup to me."

"It may be, but either way, we need some answers," the commander replied.

"We're coming with you, we need some answers of our own," Jossen insisted.

"Fine with me...I wouldn't mind some backup based on the way things are going," the commander said.

"Let's get something clear commander, we're not your backup. We are UNIC operators, and if this is a trap, it wouldn't be wise to rely on us to help you out of a jam," Jossen stated firmly.

"That's fine, once we meet up with Barnes, you can decide what you want to do. I'm sure things aren't as normal as you think they are back on the Forge," the commander said.

"You keep acting as though there's a chance we're going to end up joining the resistance, we will be going back with the director," Jossen said defiantly.

"Then it's settled, we'll go meet with the director," the commander sounded as if he had just won the argument.

"We don't have much time. The coordinates also have a time stamp. We'll need to be ready to deploy in four hours, we'll meet in the hangar and move out," the lieutenant said. "And you guys might want to make sure you're on the same page...if she orchestrated this whole thing, I'm certain she has a good reason...and a plan."

The team moved into one of the secure rooms on the perimeter of the main room of the command center. As the door closed behind them, they engaged the security, the glass turned opaque, and the door indicators turned red. The room was small, enough space for the five of them. There was a small round table in the corner with two very basic chairs.

"So we aren't showing him the footage?" Taylor asked, not addressing anyone in particular.

"I'm not sure we should," Jossen replied. "If they are part of a new AIDA program, I don't want to be the one who helped the resistance with intel that could compromise them."

"And if they aren't a new AIDA program? If they're something else?" Taylor asked in a concerned tone.

"Whether they are or not, we need to be prepared. I want to know what, if any, weaknesses we can identify based on this footage. We also have the issue of Barnes, why is she meeting with the commander? Maybe she's trying to get the resistance to surrender because of these new TITANs...or whatever they are. Maybe she truly has been a traitor this whole time. We don't know but we need to be prepared for whatever happens," Jossen said.

"And then there's the issue of this guy right here," Coughlin said as she walked up from behind Harden and patted him on the back with a heavy hand.

"Yeah, a TITAN mix...or some kind of TITAN hybrid?" Toa said. "That's gotta mean something."

"Well right now it means nothing," Jossen said, a bit of jealousy seeping out through his tone once again.

"He's still just Harden, a member of this team...and a hell of a shot," he continued, trying to conceal his jealousy.

"That's right," Harden affirmed. "I'm still me, the same guy I've always been."

Taylor smiled at Harden as he caught her look. Coughlin rolled her eyes, *just get it over with already,* she thought to herself. As soon as she thought that, she looked at Toa, although his mind seemed to be elsewhere.

"Ok, so what's the plan boss?" Toa asked Jossen.

"Right, I want Taylor and Harden to pour over the video...I want every frame of footage that shows these things scrutinized. Any information we can gather about them will help. I want Toa and Coughlin to find out what ship we'll be departing on and prepare some means of escape. There's got to be a way to sneak something on the ship in case things go south. I'll see if there's anything else I can find out from the commander and lieutenant. I want to stay close to them and make sure what preparations they're working on don't negatively impact us," Jossen instructed.

The team got to work. Toa, Coughlin, and Jossen left the secured room while Taylor and Harden stayed behind to review the footage.

SEVEN
REUNION

THEY POURED over the footage for hours, staring at the screen, hoping to find some useful information from the footage. With each passing minute, Harden found himself thinking solely of Taylor watching her every movement while she seemed obvious to him. He moved his chair closer to her and felt his pulse quicken. He thought it could be the fact that they'd been away from home for so long, or that there was something different about him, some reason that could explain the sensation that was overtaking him. He couldn't focus on the video, he could only see her. He didn't understand, the attraction was always there but never this strong, it had begun to consume his every thought until she snapped him out of it.

"Harden, look at this," Taylor said as she stared at the screen.

"There's something on this thing's back. It looks like two devices of some kind," she said as she tried to zoom in. "It almost looks like it's part of the..."

"Like it's growing out of its back," Harden unintentionally interrupted her.

"I think that's generating this field. Almost as if it was designed to be a part of them," she finished her thought.

"It doesn't seem to have any weapons though. How could they get through the blast doors?" Harden asked as he stepped back.

"Well, we'll keep looking to see if we can find any other details, there's still quite a bit of footage to pour over," Taylor suggested.

"Yeah, you're right," he said as he leaned back over her.

"You ok?" Taylor asked as she looked up at Harden.

"Yeah...why?" he tried to play it cool.

"Well you seem, I don't know, like you're holding something back," she said as she looked back down at the screen.

"Well we have had some heavy stuff dropped on us in the last couple of days," he said, trying to brush it off.

She recognized what he was doing and turned in her chair to face him. His pulse quickened again, staring into her eyes. She stared right back, keeping a serious look on her face. She turned her head slightly as if she found a tell in his facial expression.

"Something's up," she said with a smile.

"What..." he went from coy to nervous, "nothing that we all aren't going through."

"Nope. Not buying it," she said.

Harden paused, hoping she would let it go. He was in no way mentally prepared for this. He tried to think of something to say, anything to end the awkward silence. His mind raced, doing laps at lightspeed trying to say something that would convey his feelings without sounding hapless.

"You know, well at least I hope you do by this point, we've known each other for a long time and have been through a lot together," she began.

"Yeah..." he replied, again hoping that they weren't doing this right here.

"We have no idea what we're going to run into when we leave here, it could very well be a trap...and I feel like something needs to be said," she paused.

She tried to give Harden a chance to speak up. His brain began doing flips in his head. He knew where she was going, or at least he hoped he did. He pulled up the chair next to her, sat down, and took a deep breath.

"I'm really no good at this..." he said as he leaned in toward her.

"I feel like there's always been something between us, something unspoken. Even though we were assigned to different teams, we always *happened* to run into each other," he said and waited to see if she would interject.

She didn't but the slight smile on her face was enough to motivate him to continue.

"I'm here now with you, we're faced with questions about who we really are, facing an enemy we know nothing about, the world seems to have gone crazy, and yet the thought that keeps coming up in my mind is that we should've just stayed on that white sand beach together," he couldn't just come out and say how he really felt as his self-preservation instinct took over.

"Finally, it's like pulling teeth to get anything out of you sometimes," she said as she looked in his eyes.

"Then it's a date," her smile beamed. "Just as soon as we make it out of this."

As they both smiled at each other, they leaned closer. Harden's senses heightened, the sound of his heartbeat became as loud as a drum, his breathing like a gust of wind. He felt almost intoxicated as he grabbed her hands to pull her closer, no longer able to resist.

"Taylor, Harden," Jossen said as he and the others interrupted their moment.

"What are you two doing?" Jossen asked, confused by what he witnessed.

"Just waiting on you guys," Harden replied coyly.

Harden and Taylor both smiled, comforted by the fact that they at least got this far. Coughlin and Toa understood immediately what was happening. They too felt the same attraction as Harden and Taylor, although they did not have the same inhibitions as them. While they were searching the base, they wasted no time exploring their attraction but wouldn't dare lead anyone to believe they had. The team left the room and made their way to the hangar where the commander and the lieutenant were already waiting next to a falcon.

"It's time to go," the commander said as they loaded into the falcon.

The falcon quickly made its way to a safe distance and activated the SDD. As the falcon emerged from the distortion, the SDD disengaged. The falcon continued to the planet, making the descent to the surface below. A crater was now visible where the UNIC had dusted the compound previously occupied by the resistance. The falcon approached a clearing flying just above the treetops, as it did, the trees began swaying from the force of the falcon above. The falcon touched down and the cargo door opened. The commander was the first off the ship followed by the lieutenant and then the team.

"Everyone stay alert, we don't know what to expect," the commander instructed.

The lieutenant surveyed the landscape, making mental notes of cover, high ground, and any other natural advantages they may be able to gain if things took a turn for the worse.

They were there for only a few minutes before their comms became active.

"Commander, we have confirmed SD," a male voice said.

"One ship has exited the distortion, a sandpiper," the voice continued to relay information as it was received.

"The SD has closed. Confirmed, one ship on descent," the voice paused only seconds between updates.

"Sandpiper on approach," the voice gave one last update.

"We have visual confirmation," the commander said.

The sandpiper; a small, low-profile transport ship used to ferry high-ranking UNGA officials, looked more like a personal leisure plane than a military ship. The ship landed about fifty feet from the falcon. As the door to the ship opened, the door panels formed a type of staircase reaching just above the ground. The lieutenant turned slightly, trying to hide the slow movement of her right hand to her sidearm, a modified magnum pistol that she had holstered just to the right of the small of her back. The team tensed up, assuming the director would emerge from the doorway, but the level of anxiousness swelled with each passing second of uncertainty. Finally, a few moments after landing, Barnes appeared in the doorway. She made her way down the stairs slowly with a metal case slightly larger than a briefcase in each hand, assessing the situation she has just put herself in. She maintained eye contact with the commander as she stepped onto the grass. As she walked toward them, the commander stepped forward and began walking toward her. The lieutenant and rest of the team did the same, staying just a few steps behind Hanlon. Barnes and the commander came face to face as she placed the two cases on the ground. There was a long uncomfortable silence before the commander finally spoke.

"Director Barnes," he said, simply acknowledging her presence.

"A101," she replied in the same tone.

"Sorry...Commander," she corrected herself.

She knew that she had to take the high ground which was not an easy thing for her to do. She would have to be the one to relent as she was the one who requested the meeting. She knew calling the commander by his ID alone was not the way to start the conversation.

"A lot has happened in such a short time and every moment counts," she acknowledged before getting down to business.

"The UNGA is preparing to wage open war against the resistance. The council has given Admiral Vincere discretion and authority to conduct operations as he sees fit," she said.

"Admiral Vincere huh, that won't end well for anyone," the commander said.

"Agreed," Barnes acknowledged.

"You work fast, I didn't know how receptive they would be to joining you," she said as she looked past the commander at the lieutenant and then the team.

"We haven't joined the resistance if that's what you're implying. Our armor may appear different, but we are still with you," Jossen said as stepped forward and stood at attention.

"Well, if you *were* with me, you wouldn't want to be now," Barnes said.

"103...you are a great leader, your loyalty is an admirable quality...but you need to turn that loyalty to where it truly matters...your team. Things have changed. AIDA, the UNIC, and in fact the UNGA are not what you think they are," she continued.

"They are still what they have always been...a mechanism to suppress the people, disguising it as necessary while keeping the powerful in their positions. Don't let her fool you, they will take everything you can give and when the time comes that you no longer have anything left to give they will break you and toss you aside," the commander remarked.

"Barnes?" Harden stepped forward.

"Ah yes, 201. I'm sure by now they've told you and I bet you have many questions," she said with a feeling of both relief and guilt.

"So it's true then?" Harden asked.

"I can tell you that there are no answers that will ease your mind. The only answers I have lead down a path of hurt and heartbreak," Barnes said.

"This goes for each of you: the past is the past. None of us can change that now, you all need to focus on the future. I believe that whatever happens, you will need each other to get through it. Not knowing the past may have been difficult but learning the truth would be far worse," Barnes continued.

"Whatever happens?" the commander asked puzzled.

"With Admiral Vincere in charge, there will be a push like nothing you've seen before. He will take over every outpost, use every UNIC asset, he will execute anyone if it will bring him his victory. There was an abduction of an entire colony," Barnes said as she was cut off by the commander.

"C2032, we know, we heard the reports. The same thing happened to outpost 12," Hanlon said.

"What you don't know, Commander, is that the UNGA has put all blame, for both attacks, squarely on the resistance. During a meeting with the council, I hinted that this may not have been the resistance, as they too fell victim to the same type of attack, the council would hear nothing of it. It led me to believe that they are in fact behind this, although something still eludes me," Barnes said as she took a minute to form her next thought.

"If they are behind this, where did they take everyone?" she asked in general, assuming that there wouldn't be a response.

"I still have a few questions for you like what were those things that took the colonists?" the commander asked.

"What do you mean the *things that took the colonists*?" Barnes asked.

"Director Barnes. Harden...eh...201 and I have gone over footage we salvaged from the attack on the outpost. I was able to filter out the interference and we found some interesting details," Taylor interjected nervously, not knowing whether she was still to operate under UNIC protocols.

"Interesting, go on," Barnes said as she motioned for Taylor to step forward.

The lieutenant shot the commander a look that seemed to scream I told you so while the commander acknowledged she was right with a quick nod. The commander knew the lieutenant was referring to the fact that the team was able to analyze the video but didn't share their findings.

"Well, based on the video, we were able to determine that they are humanoid, they have some type of force field, and it's generated by something on their back...best guess is a modified EM-Field Generator. They possess the strength of a TITAN and their skin seems to be similar to our nanites, but from what we can gather, it doesn't appear to be a suit. They were unarmed and only attacked when engaged directly. I don't think they were there to kill anyone, just gather them," Taylor described their findings.

"Do you have the video with you?" Barnes asked.

"Of course," Taylor replied as she brought up the video.

Taylor played it for her as the commander and lieutenant

crowded in to get a look as well. Barnes didn't seem at all surprised by the video. Meanwhile, the commander and lieutenant watched the video with intense focus.

"It's far worse than I thought. We need to move and move quickly," Barnes said.

"How bad did you think it was before seeing that video?" the lieutenant finally spoke up, not sure if she wanted to know the answer.

"That...that thing in the video is...that's very much in line with what we saw from the results of Project Olympus," Barnes said.

"Project Olympus?" the commander asked.

"Before the titan program existed, before the UNGA, UNIC, and even before AIDA, I worked for DARPA...a group that was the foundation for what would become AIDA. DARPA worked for years trying to figure out what the nanites were. No one knew at the time what the nanites could do. We had no idea that they could be controlled, programmed, replicated. We tried various experiments; we introduced them to animals, plants, and inanimate objects which all ended with the same result: the nanites would take over the molecular structure and repurpose it. It wasn't until after the war and the formation of the UNGA and UNIC that we were able to make significant advances with this technology. With the creation of the UNGA came access to resources that were previously unavailable. We had access to the most brilliant minds of humanity and almost infinite financial resources...those two things combined with enough time and anything was possible. Once we figured out what the nanites could do, we became confident...overconfident in our own knowledge and abilities. We began experimenting on humans," she paused for a moment as if the memories were too harsh but continued.

"The first experiments were rough. We were brought subjects, we didn't ask, and they didn't tell. The subjects were not able to find an equilibrium with the nanites, we didn't know at the time, their biological systems couldn't support the nanites. As time went on, we realized that the subjects would need to be stronger. We found a way to alter human DNA, reprogram the cells, to give them the ability to withstand the absorption of the nanites. This altering of DNA proved to be fatal in adult humans. We found the only way to successfully alter a human's DNA is when they are still growing, able to adapt to the changes in the body," she said as she turned her focus to the commander.

"That was when the TITAN program we know today was conceived so to speak. It was also that time when each and every member of AIDA sold their souls," she stopped talking, knowing that if she continued she would undoubtedly choke up.

"That's when you started experimenting on children," the commander intervened.

"You took children from wherever you could...the streets, orphanages, loving families," the lieutenant said.

"The TITAN program was built on lies...each of us believing our parents abandoned us, making yourselves out to be the heroes, coming to our rescue, providing us with everything we could need," the commander said, his tone growing angrier as he spoke.

"Providing for us while at the same time taking everything. You took our futures, condemning us to a life of war with no purpose in peace. And when you finally couldn't take it anymore, when watching parents pleading for the return of their children was too much to take, you chose another path...one with less direct impact but the same level of abhorrence. You began growing children, genetically altered children, infusing them with nanites," the commander finished, so disgusted he didn't want to continue.

"That's right!" Barnes shouted, almost in tears.

"We did what we had to do. We did things that haunt me every moment of every day, but you weren't there during the climate crisis or the war. I've seen suffering that no human should ever have to endure, both before and after the UNGA. You don't understand that no matter who is in charge, suffering is a part of being human. Are there things I regret? I could spend a lifetime listing them all. The work we did, we did for a reason. The things we've done will haunt us for the rest of our lives and beyond...but even still, it won't be you who judges me. We set out with a purpose, a goal, regardless of what the government or any other authority that came after dictated..." Barnes said defiantly.

"We set out to save lives. That was always our goal. We knew there would be sacrifices that would have to be made. I did what I had to do to save the people I loved. I'm doing what I need to do now to save the people I love once again," the doctor said as she composed herself.

The team was standing silent. The shock of everything they had just heard left them without a voice. They, like the TITANs before them, had always been told that AIDA, the UNIC, the UNGA had saved them, rescued them from the life they would've been doomed to inherit. A future so bleak that being a TITAN was the single greatest thing that could've ever happened to them. They were selected for the operator program because of their potential, the genetic qualifications...well it turned out that one of those was true.

"We trusted you, even when we may not have completely trusted AIDA or the UNIC, we completely trusted you. I completely trusted you. How could you?" Jossen asked angrily.

"You trusted me and look at where you are, alive. I didn't send you on that mission by mistake. If you would have brought the commander back and completed your mission then I would've been the one who failed you. What do you know about the retirement of an operator?" Barnes asked.

"It depends on which story is true. If I were to believe AIDA, the operators receive a retirement ceremony and are sent to TN9932. If I were to believe the resistance, we are sent for a ride that takes us to oblivion," Jossen responded.

"If I were you, I would put your stock in the resistance story," Barnes said then paused.

"You haven't been retired though, have you? I didn't send you on this mission unprepared. I sent you with him," Barnes said as she looked at Harden.

"I have lied to you all. I have lied about your past, the how's and whys and when's...but I have not lied about who you are. I have not lied about who you were meant to become, what you were meant to do. I can't expect that you will understand now, but I promise the day will come when you do," Barnes replied with regret and passion.

"And what good did sending him with us do?" Jossen asked, keeping his eyes focused on Barnes.

"Well, you're still alive for starters. If he wasn't with you, the entire team would've been killed. That was the plan, they would capture you, extract every bit of information they could...and when they did, they would realize who was with you. Although I still don't think they know everything," Barnes hinted there was still more to the story.

"If you have anything else to share, now's the time," the commander said.

"Indeed. 201, Harden has TITAN lineage. Harden is the result of a TITAN born into the world," Barnes agreed.

"Born? You mean created," the commander corrected

Barnes.

"No, I don't mean created. Harden is the result of the natural birth of a TITAN," she insisted.

"Birth of a TITAN? TITANs aren't able to reproduce, you and your lab rats saw to that," the lieutenant asked, seeing that the commander may have been a little too shocked to speak.

"True, we did take precautions to ensure the TITANs would not be able to reproduce, but it seems that we weren't entirely successful in that endeavor. There was a TITAN who came to me, scared of what might happen to her unborn child. After discussing this with the council, it was decided that the original TITAN program would be terminated along with every last TITAN. They had set everything up, a ship would carry the TITANs on one last mission, a mission none of them would be able to come back from. We were ready to execute the plan, but I couldn't let it end that way. At the last minute, I made some adjustments to the plan. I ensured that there were supplies on that ship so some of the TITANs would be able to escape. They were sharp soldiers, I knew they would find the clues that I left to lead them to the truth. I also had to get the TITAN who came to me to safety," Barnes explained.

"Who was the TITAN?" the commander demanded angrily.

"I will get to that," Barnes replied.

"I arranged for the child to be brought into the operator program discreetly, to not arouse suspicion, I falsified records so that he appeared in the system as subject 50201. We then had to inject that child with the nanites. I honestly wasn't sure what to expect...it had never been done before. To my surprise, the nanites had no immediate effect. They existed within the child but remained mostly dormant. The best I can figure is the nanites spent their energy fighting him for control. In fact, I believe that if the nanites are removed, this TITAN would become more powerful than an average TITAN. The nanites in his system are at odds with the DNA's nature to correct deficiencies, spending its energy on trying to get rid of the nanites instead of reaching their full potential," Barnes explained.

"Who was the TITAN?!" the commander demanded once again.

Hanlon was on the verge of shaking, his fists clenched tight. Barnes was on the verge of collapse. She had dreaded this moment since she first found out about the child. She always knew that this moment would come, but now that it was upon her, she was speechless.

"Who was it?!" the commander yelled, insisting as he stepped closer to Barnes.

"It was..." Barnes paused.

She had to work up the courage to utter the name, knowing that the commander's reaction may mean her death. She took a breath, knowing it might be her last, and spoke.

"A109," Barnes said.

The commander instantly dropped to his knees as if they had turned to jelly, unable to physically support himself. The lieutenant's face turned white as a ghost as the rest of the team stood there, unaware of the significance behind the name.

"Who is A109?" Harden asked.

"I'm truly sorry that I couldn't save her," Barnes began to sob, ignoring Harden's question.

"I tried...I did everything I could to save her, but it was her or the child. She insisted the child be saved. She believed that he would somehow change the world, that he could bring hope to the remaining TITANs, that he represented what the TITANs could become," Barnes continued between sobs.

"How could you?" the lieutenant said in a low heated voice.

"Vaile, meant everything to me, she was my entire world, and you took her from me," the commander said in a voice so soft, even those standing right next to him could barely make out what he said.

The commander suddenly jumped to his feet and in the same motion wrapped his hands around Barnes' neck. He squeezed his hands, tightening his grip with each memory that came to mind. He came dangerously close to crushing her windpipe.

"You took her from me!" he exclaimed in pure rage as he lifted her off the ground.

She didn't fight back, she seemed to almost welcome it, believing that it was only fitting for him to be the one that took her life. As the team and the lieutenant moved to remove his grasp, he released her. Barnes collapsed to the ground, coughing and gasping for air. The commander took a few steps back, knowing how close he had come to killing her, he looked around at the team and the lieutenant. Without saying a word, he turned his back to everyone and walked away, needing a few minutes to compose himself. As Barnes brought herself back to her feet, the team approached her.

"Are you ok?" Jossen asked as he helped her to her feet, unable to ignore her situation.

"I'll be ok. I knew this day would come, I've been living in fear of this inevitable moment. I knew that I would have to destroy him twice," Barnes said.

"Director Barnes, I have to ask. I have had these vivid nightmares for as long as I can remember, and I have never told another soul. Do you know anything about that?"

Harden interjected, not knowing if he would get the opportunity again.

"I see, what kind of nightmares?" Barnes asked.

"Well, I'm under a bed...I feel an incredible sense of panic...dread. I can only see what I can see from under the bed. I can hear crying in the other room, a woman's cry. Then several people enter the room, there seeming to be a scream before a hand reaches down and pulls me out," Harden said as he described the nightmare.

Tears welled up in Barnes' eyes once again. Although this had happened before, she was unable to hold them back as they streamed down her face. The team found it difficult to process any more of these emotional moments. They were always taught to stuff their emotions down, unleashing them during combat.

"How....how can you remember that?" she asked as she continued to sob.

"Remember?" Harden asked.

"When each TITAN is injected with nanites, they undergo a process that utilizes the nanites to erase their memories," she said.

At that moment, the look on her face said it all, she realized why and how he had the nightmares. She knew that because the nanites didn't have the same effect on him, he still retained some memories.

The commander moved toward Barnes, coming within inches of her face. Barnes didn't flinch but stared the commander in his eyes. As they both stood there for a moment, their eyes laid out their emotions for each to see, and while it was tough for both of them, they at least could still see humanity in each other. The team along with the lieutenant positioned themselves behind the commander in case they needed to intervene.

"Director, you came here for a reason, and while I'm sure trying to clean your conscience is one reason, I don't believe it's the only reason," the commander said.

"Indeed," she replied.

"We had been working on a new variant of the TITAN program: Project Olympus. This was supposed to be the last phase of the TITAN program. One that would see TITANs spread throughout the galaxy and the universe. We had created tens of thousands of subjects, all to be injected directly with nanites, no need for discs or housing. These TITANs would be living operators, their armor would be a living armor. We recently had a test subject, after the nanites were injected, the subject transformed...not that dissimilar from what I saw in that video...apart from the shield generator. It wasn't supposed to work like that, all of the calculations I performed were verified. After reviewing all of the data, it seemed to me that this change in the nanite program was ordered by the council," she paused for a moment before continuing.

"Project Olympus was created to ensure that we could provide protection for all, stationing these new TITANs at every outpost and colony. They were to be the instrument of peace, finally providing the security that was needed to ensure the resistance was no longer able to continue their *attacks*. I believe the council has hijacked the project and are attempting to use it for a different purpose. While I still don't know exactly what their endgame is, they must have a reason to change the nanite programming. Now they are using the colonist's abduction to give them cause to deploy this type of weapon," she said.

"If they have an army of these things coming for our people, we're going to have a problem," the lieutenant chimed in.

"Not to mention the question of why they would actually abduct these people and not just kill them. I mean why wouldn't they just kill the colonists?" Toa asked.

"I've been asking myself the same thing...the only reason I can come up with is that they may have found a way to inject the nanites into mature human subjects, increasing the numbers of this new nanite army. Whatever their plan may be, I have one of my own," Barnes replied.

"I know I don't have long...that as soon as I get back, no matter how it goes, I don't survive this. Commander, your AIDA contact is certainly dead by now. I knew what I was doing, all that I have done in the name of science, would eventually come back to me in the end. I knew all of this, but I had to try to help change the course of humanity one last time. Hopefully, this time will be different than the others. If we do nothing and leave the UNGA to their own devices, the human race will march to its own destruction," Barnes said.

"He was working with you? I actually thought for a while it might've been you," the commander asked.

"No, it was Mr. Kinston...a man I trusted, a man who wanted to do the right thing, and a man who ultimately gave his life for it," Barnes said.

"So what do you propose?" the commander asked.

"We need to expose the UNGA to all of humanity for what they are, and there's only one way to do it," Barnes said.

Barnes leaned down to one of the cases and unclipped the latches. She opened the lid, a screen slid up revealing a keyboard. As the screen was displayed, coordinates appeared along with a schedule. It showed meeting times, locations, agendas, all of the information they needed related to the council's activities.

"This is a complete list of minister schedules along with locations for various meetings. It took me quite some time to gather all of this information, but it has proven reliable," Barnes said.

She tapped on the screen and typed on the keyboard for a moment. Videos began to appear on the screen; one video showed the council members present during a TITAN subject harvest, the other showing the UNIC launching an attack against colony 2110, and yet another showed the council entering an unknown facility.

"This could be the one that helps turn the people against the council," Barnes said as the video continued.

As the ministers walked into the facility, a UNIC soldier was seen reaching out for help as he was badly injured. The ministers looked at him for a moment while talking amongst themselves. Minister Gantely then turned to the man and shot him dead with a pistol.

"Oh my God!" Coughlin said in horror.

"Yes, this was a UNIC false flag attack on its own people. This footage was from the assault on C2026, a so-called resistance attack," Barnes confirmed.

"We were ordered to destroy all of the footage from these attacks and any footage showing the ministers in sensitive situations," Barnes continued.

"Ok, so we have this footage. We can disseminate it from anywhere, what are we waiting for?" Jossen asked.

"Because my guess would be if you tried sending this to anyone, the UNGA would have it scrubbed in less than an hour. You would need to disseminate it within their network so their people would be able to see it immediately. The question remains though, how do we get this into their system without them knowing?" the commander asked.

The doctor smiled coyly. She had a plan but knew it would require everything the team had, in fact, everything the resistance had. She began to lay out her plan.

"You will need to get to Earth, to UNGA headquarters, in order for this plan to work," Barnes began.

"Earth? The most heavily fortified planet in the system? There has to be another way," the Lieutenant said.

"True, it is the most heavily fortified planet in the system, but I will be disabling all security systems," Barnes replied.

"How do you plan on doing that? As soon as you get back, you will be branded a traitor," the commander asked.

"Yes, I'm actually counting on it," Barnes replied.

"You and your people need to be ready. Once I return to the Forge, Admiral Vincere will no doubt look to interrogate me then transport me back to Earth. Once there, I doubt there will be a trial, just a guilty verdict. After that, I'm sure they will stream my judgment for all to see. Make sure you are watching, there will be a signal. That's when you will need to strike," Barnes said confidently.

"So...I just want to make sure I have this correct...you get caught, somehow disable planet defenses while also disabling security in the UNGA headquarters, we fight our way through a literal army, upload the files, kill the ministers, and then what? Wait for the people to turn on the UNGA?" the commander asked.

"And if the people don't rise up? If they are so apathetic that they decide the risk isn't worth it and do nothing, what then?" the commander continued.

"Then you would have to do the only thing you could at that point, destroy the UNGA," Barnes said in a solemn voice.

This suggestion would give anyone who heard it pause. Killing the ministers, while always a top objective for the resistance, carried with it dire implications. Removing the ministers and the UNGA from the equation could incite more violence, alienate the resistance, and lead to a coup by the military...namely Admiral Vincere. If Vincere were to gain control, the consequences for humanity could be catastrophic.

"If Vincere were to gain control of the UNGA..." the commander suggested.

"I will handle Admiral Vincere," Barnes said pointedly.

"If we don't do something now, Vincere will tear the resistance apart and he will destroy anyone who gets in his way. If we do nothing, I have to watch another loved one die," Barnes said.

"I think we're past the cryptic references at this point. Just come out and say it," Coughlin said.

"I won't stand by and do nothing, watching my family be hunted down by Vincere," Barnes said passionately.

The commander looked at Harden who seemed to be having some trouble processing everything he heard.

"Wait what?!?" Toa asked.

Toa was confused, he thought they were past the dramatic reveals. It seemed as though there were still a few secrets that needed to come out.

"Commander, you know that you were the reason that Jonathan had to leave?" Barnes asked.

"Yes," the commander replied stoically.

"How do you think I was able to stay under the radar for so long? When we all went our separate ways after we got off that ship, I wanted nothing more than to take my revenge right then and there, but Jonathan found me...taught me all about what I was up against. He told me everything. Well, almost everything it seems," the commander said.

"Then you know why I had to stay," she asked

"I understand why, but that doesn't change how I feel about it," he replied.

Harden stepped forward. "This is all a bit ridiculous

don't you think? Like something out of a bad movie?" he asked.

"This changes nothing for me. Director Barnes, you are just another liar in my book...you've lied to me for my entire life, and not just me but all of us. The one thing that I do care about right now is getting my life back. I'm done with the UNGA, the UNIC, AIDA, and the resistance. If it were up to me, I would destroy them all," Harden said angrily, turning his back to everyone.

"So are we really talking about taking down the council? Not a matter of days ago we were on a mission to take out the leader of the resistance. Now we're supposed to go back to Earth and kill the people that we were trained our whole life to protect. I don't know if I can do that. With everything going on, it's hard to tell what the truth is...and if we're wrong and we kill the council, then what? The world...humanity is left in chaos and anarchy?" Jossen asked.

Jossen was beside himself, for the first time in his life completely unsure of what to do. No clear direction, no clear objective, he stood there looking at the rest of his team. He did not know where to begin, the events of the past couple of days wore on him mentally.

"We need to make sure that there are good people ready to take command when the council falls," the commander said.

"And who gets to decide which people? From what I can tell, there's no telling good from bad and vice versa," Coughlin asked.

She also had become frustrated by the fact that everyone else seemed to be deciding the next course of action. Harden turned back around and paused for a moment, taking the time to look each person in their eye before speaking.

"We'll get this done, take out the council, but after that,

I'm gone. I don't care who takes over after they die. In my mind, they did this to us, along with every complicit official, and they have to deal with those consequences. I don't know why everyone is so set on saving humanity, from what I've seen and heard, all we do is create misery," Harden said as he walked off toward the falcon.

Taylor followed, concerned that Harden had lost a little bit of himself today. She kept quiet and followed just a few steps behind him. The rest of the team watched, knowing where their allegiance would end up.

"Harden's right, I'm tired of being used like a pawn. It ends after this," Jossen agreed.

Coughlin and Toa turned to face each other, feeling like Harden and Jossen already said what needed to be said. The three of them hurried to catch up with Harden and Taylor. As they caught up to them, the team huddled up, overlapping arms while putting their heads together.

"I better go with them, don't want them doing anything stupid," the lieutenant said, looking for an excuse to leave the awkward situation.

"Well, seems like as good a time as any to put an end to this story," the commander said.

Barnes handed the commander both cases. "You'll need these," she said.

"What's in the other case?" the commander asked.

"That's why you are who you are Hanlon...everyone is so consumed with what's happening that no one else noticed. Just some gifts...it won't mean much now but might come in handy in the future," she responded.

"I want you to know that Jonathan meant everything to me. Without him, there's no way that we would be here now. And just so you know, I always loved him, just like I always loved you," she said.

"I know, Dad told me the same," the commander replied.

"Look after him, he is a special one, always has been," Barnes said while looking in the direction of Harden.

"I will," the commander said as he started to walk away.

"He may be done with humanity, but it's only because he has seen the worst of us...he hasn't had the chance to live, to love, to see the good in life. I hope he gets that chance...until he does, he will just carry the worst of humanity with him," Barnes said.

She tried to draw out her time with Hanlon, taking her time handing him the cases. She walked slowly backwards as the commander turned away. She finally turned toward her ship, knowing it was the last time she would see the commander like this. The commander kept walking toward the falcon as Barnes boarded the sandpiper. As the sandpiper took off, everyone boarded the falcon.

"Well, I wasn't sure what to expect, but it was definitely not that," the commander said.

Everyone situated themselves on the falcon. The lieutenant strapped in while the team took their seats. The feeling of betrayal clouding the reunion that had just taken place. The lieutenant being the only one there that wasn't emotionally invested in the situation had to redirect everyone's focus.

"We need to begin preparations immediately. If we are going to do this, it's going to take everything we have. I can't imagine what everyone is going through right now, but we can't do this alone, this is going to take everything we have," the lieutenant said.

"Engaging SDD," a voice said as the falcon disappeared into the distortion.

EIGHT
REBELLION

ON THE FORGE, Admiral Vincere emerged from a door, dressed in his formal admiral attire. He carefully removed a handkerchief from his front breast pocket and wiped his brow. He grabbed his hat that was tucked under his left arm and fit it over his salt and pepper military crew cut. His face was serious, no emotion, only dedication in his eyes. He meticulously folded the handkerchief and put it back in his front breast pocket.

"We're done here, make sure this traitor is disposed of," he told the chief petty officer standing guard at the door.

"Yes sir," the chief petty officer responded.

He turned to look in the room, a broken and bloodied Mr. Kinston lay in a heap on the ground. The Admiral made his way to the SQC, moving with determination. He stepped onto the holopad while the holograms of the ministers appeared.

"Council," the Admiral spoke sternly, dismissing any need for pleasantries.

"It appears as though Director Barnes has been assisting

the resistance, with the help of others, for quite some time. She has recently stolen a sandpiper and we believe she has made contact with the resistance leader. It appears as though they are working together, although we still don't know to what end. It is my belief that they are plotting a coup to overthrow the UNGA," Vincere said.

"We've had our suspicions, but we appreciate your diligence in getting to the bottom of this," Minister Gantley responded.

"In my opinion, we need to prepare for an assault by the resistance. The fact that she has made direct contact would lead me to believe whatever her plan is, the wheels are now in motion. I believe their intent is to come directly after the council," the Admiral advised.

"With all due respect Admiral, do you truly believe the resistance would be foolish enough to come to Earth and stage an assault on UNGA headquarters?" Minister Takamoto asked.

"Not foolish sir, strategic. Their forces wouldn't be able to overwhelm the UNIC in a front-facing battle, they would need to deploy forces to specifically target the council. The guerilla tactics they have utilized so far would not be enough to bring about meaningful change. If the former director is indeed aligned with them, I would assume they believe it is possible," Vincere replied.

"And if they believe they have the element of surprise, I wouldn't discount their courage in carrying out such a plan. While I don't believe they have a chance at succeeding, it would appear to be the best option they have," Vincere continued.

"Understood Admiral, I would ask that you have the UNSS Spirit head to Earth and make any other preparations you deem necessary for an assault on headquarters," Minister Halin said.

"Minister, I believe that the Forge would be better suited for this type of assignment. While I have the utmost confidence in Admiral Capetolli, I believe that my experience would be valuable to this assignment," Vincere replied.

"We also believe that to be true, however, your experience and dedication is far too valuable to be put at risk in this manner. Admiral Capetolli and the Spirit are quite capable of supplying necessary defenses. You will remain on mission with the Forge and contact us when you have an update regarding the status of your mission," Minister Gantley instructed.

"Understood sir," the Admiral acknowledged grudgingly.

The Admiral saluted the ministers before stepping off of the holopad. While he understood the need for the council in its day, he believed that they were now both outdated and ineffective. He knew the only way forward for humanity was military, something the council and the UNGA stood in the way of.

"Perfect," Vincere whispered through a grin as he exited the SQC.

Admiral Vincere went back to the bridge. The bridge was massive, a sprawling three-tiered room staffed with at least one hundred people. Vincere sat in the Admiral's chair on the top tier of the room. Staff scurried around screens, projections, and stations. Digital windows surround the bridge in an elongated horseshoe projecting the expanse of space in front of them.

"Bring up Admiral Capetolli," Vincere ordered.

A moment later, Admiral Capetolli appeared on the large front panel at the middle of the digital window array. He was considered a more lenient admiral, preferring to command with compassion as opposed to an iron fist. He had a less rugged look about him, reflecting his nature. What was left of his white hair was well kept, the sides and back trimmed and combed. His white mustache was well groomed as well.

"Admiral Vincere, what can I do for you?" Capetolli asked.

"We have intelligence that suggests there may be an attack directed at the UNGA headquarters by the resistance. The UNSS Spirit and its fleet are being redirected and deployed to Earth orbit. You will be the first line of defense for the UNGA," Vincere said.

"Understood Admiral. I can't imagine you're happy about this though," Capetolli said, knowing Vincere's inclination to be present for such operations.

"Indeed, but we all have a part to play. The UNSS Forge will continue to play its part. We wish you luck and Godspeed," Vincere said as he signed off.

A captain approached Vincere's chair from the side and whispered something in his ear. Vincere's expression was one of suppressed surprise. He slowly stood up from his chair.

"Captain Rahni has the con," he announced.

He then proceeded back to his office. His office was not unlike the director's, meticulously organized but with many more photos and awards. Among his photos were ones of the Forge christening, a photo with all of the Admirals, and one with him and Barnes. When the Admiral arrived in his office, he sat in his chair and began typing on his desk. When he did, a projection of the sandpiper appeared with a docking request.

"So you've come back Barnes, this should be interesting," he said to himself in a low tone.

He accepted the request and continued to tap and swipe

the displays until he found what he was looking for. He tapped again, contacting the docking officer.

"When Director Barnes arrives, she is to be placed under arrest. She is not to send out any communications, you are not to engage her in conversation, she will be brought directly to isolated holding," the Admiral commanded.

"Yes sir, understood sir," a voice responded.

He ended the communication and closed the projection above his desk. He leaned back in his chair ever so slightly, looking at the photo that sat on the shelf. The photo was of a ceremony in which the director and him were presented with the award for humanities advancement. It was a small metal, in the shape of an infinity symbol, made from hexatriton. This metal was only awarded to individuals who made an undeniable contribution to humanity's advancement. Although the director had been awarded three during her lifetime, the Admiral had only one. He had always secretly resented her for it, believing his achievements were not fully recognized.

This could work out perfectly. If the resistance succeeds in taking out the council, the UNIC could easily assume control of the UNGA. The council may not like it, but the mission won't matter if the council is gone, I need to be in Earth orbit when this happens, Vincere thought to himself as he pictured leading the UNGA.

He quickly formulated a plan to put the Forge in Earth orbit, he sat upright and started typing on the desk. The screen projected above the table displayed the message he was typing to Admiral Farcau. It read, *We have reason to believe there will be an imminent attack on the UNGA headquarters. Admiral Capetolli will be bringing the Spirit to assist with defense. I am asking for your assistance while I track down a resistance lead. This lead will bring me close to*

Earth, but I will not have Admiral Capetolli distracted by such endeavors. Please bring the UNSS Triton to our coordinates in 24 hours. Admiral Vincere. Vincere hit transmit and closed the screen as he got up and prepared to go greet his new guest.

The Admiral made his way to the isolation holding cell 1211. The isolation holding cell looked similar to an interrogation room. It was brightly lit and there was only a small metal table with two metal chairs, one on either side. He opened the door to find Barnes handcuffed, waiting with an emotionless look.

"Hello Barnes," the Admiral said.

Barnes didn't reply.

"So I assume you are aware? We know everything you have been up to," the Admiral continued, assuming she wouldn't respond to anything he asked.

"You have been very busy," he said as he got comfortable in the chair opposite her.

"Not only have you found time to run AIDA's most advanced programs...you also somehow found time to aid the resistance," he said as he tapped on the table.

As he did, several photos displayed above the table. One of them was a security shot of her receiving a probe from an engineer. The other was of her boarding a sandpiper in one of the hangars.

"Here's some of you stealing and reprogramming a probe to contact the resistance, here's some of you stealing a sandpiper to actually meet the resistance, but these are my favorite...you actually meeting with the resistance leader," he said.

A photo of her, the commander, the lieutenant, and the team was displayed. Barnes, although slightly surprised that he had a photo of the meeting, showed absolutely no emotion as the photo was displayed. She was relieved to see that the photo did not show the cases she had brought with her.

"After everything we have been through, all of the sacrifice, this is how you choose to atone for our sins? You assume that you can, what, save your soul? There's nothing you can do that will change the horrific acts we've committed. Nothing that will atone for the death and misery we are responsible for, we have no other choice than to see this through to the end," he said.

"Nothing to say? We have been through a lot together, what could possibly be worth throwing it all away for now?" he asked as Barnes remained silent.

"I want you to know that the attack on the UNGA will not accomplish what you hope it will; the resistance will fall, your friends will fail, and you will die. I will see to it personally that all of these things happen" Vincere said in disappointment as he swiped away the photo.

Barnes sat silently as a smirk became a smile.

"I'm glad you can smile at a time like this, you must have made peace with your situation," the Admiral said before he stood up.

"Enjoy your last hours," he said as he left the room.

The Admiral made his way back to the bridge. He was genuinely irritated with Barnes, the way she handled herself with extreme composure even when faced with death. When he arrived, he motioned for the captain.

"Former Director Barnes is to be transported to Earth as soon as possible to be executed for treason. I want her secured on a falcon with a team of your best men. Nothing happens to that prisoner...she must arrive on Earth to face her sentence. Understood?" Vincere commanded.

"Yes Sir," the captain replied.

The captain set out to fulfill his orders. The Admiral's

irritation was quickly eclipsed by excitement, as everything he worked for was finally coming to fruition. He smiled as he sat confidently in his chair, watching his subordinates continue their tasks as though it was just another day. He knew better, this wasn't just another day, for in a matter of hours his life will be changed.

"Set the following coordinates," the Admiral said.

He typed on a small projected screen that appeared above the right arm of his chair. Once he typed in the coordinates, he sent them to the navigation officer.

"Yes Admiral," a voice from the crowded bridge called out.

"Coordinates set Admiral," the voice called out again only moments later.

"Notify me when the falcon engages its SSD," the Admiral commanded.

"Will do sir," another voice called out.

"Notify all close-range fighters that they are to be on station and ready in six hours, I want all swarms armed and synchronized, and I want the crucible to be charged and ready to fire by the time we arrive," the Admiral continued to shout out commands.

He was preparing for what he hoped would be waiting when they arrived.

Meanwhile, Barnes was led down a corridor surrounded by UNIC soldiers with Captain Rahni leading the way.

"You know that following the Admiral will have consequences for everyone on board this ship," Barnes said as they made their way to the falcon.

"Yeah, the resistance is a formidable force," the captain said with overly apparent sarcasm.

"It's not their size, it's what they fight for—their heart," she said.

"Hearts don't win wars, firepower does, and we have that covered," the captain replied again, wanting to get in the last word.

There was silence as they approached the hangar where the falcon was prepped and ready to take off. As they entered, the size of the hangar revealed a glimpse into what the resistance would be up against. Condor drop ships were lined up, there were easily fifty of them staged in groups of ten. Each Condor had the capacity to carry up to one hundred soldiers. There were Osprey attack ships arranged in squadrons, grouped in ten for each Condor. They had squads of soldiers with stingers stationed with the Ospreys. The Admiral seemed to be preparing for war. Barnes was a bit shocked to see the extent of the preparations, but she knew the Admiral very well. She knew he would send each one of these soldiers to their death, sacrificing every last resource to ensure his victory.

"Impressive, is it not?" the captain asked as he motioned for Barnes to take it all in.

"All of these soldiers with one goal...stopping the resistance. Your people won't have a chance. I almost feel bad for them, then I remember all of the lives they took, all of the devastation they've caused, and I can't wait to watch them die," the captain said.

"You think this will stop them? You have no idea what you're up against. My guess is, you won't even be able to deploy these ships before the Forge is destroyed," Barnes said, hoping she would be able to rattle the captain just a little.

The captain chuckled. "Well I am surprised. I thought for sure the conversation with you would be dull. Maybe a little weeping, some begging for us to let you go, or even just silence."

"I'm glad you have been able to entertain us with your

terribly misguided views on reality but it's time to bring you back to reality. Load her on the falcon," the captain continued.

The two UNIC soldiers that had accompanied the captain and prisoner escorted Barnes onto the falcon. Four additional UNIC soldiers joined them on the falcon while the captain remained on the Forge. The captain motioned toward the pilots of the Ospreys that were to accompany the falcon.

"Secure the prisoner and prepare to depart," the captain ordered.

After a moment, the doors to the falcon closed and the engines began to hum. As the falcon began to lift off, two Ospreys also began to take off, providing support in case the resistance attempted a rescue. The captain watched as the squadron took off.

"Admiral, the falcon has departed," the captain reported.

"Excellent, return to the bridge immediately," the Admiral directed.

"Yes sir," the captain replied.

The falcon and two Ospreys made their way to the safe operating range to engage their SDDs. As the space in front of them distorted, they entered, disappearing into it. A space distortion began to form over the Earth as the Spirit was positioned in Earth orbit.

"Admiral, space distortion detected," a voice was heard over the bustling activity on the bridge.

"Confirm contacts," Admiral Capetolli said.

"Confirmed, falcon S1," the voice said.

"Understood, grant clearance to proceed to Earth," Capetolli commanded.

The falcon flew past the UNSS Spirit heading toward the Earth, with the osprey flanking their position, they appeared as three bees flying past an elephant. The Earth, bearing little resemblance to its appearance in the past, left ravaged by war and the climate crisis. The Earth was now composed of islands of civilization. Large cities built up in the only areas left inhabitable. Large storms loomed around where the north and south poles would be. The once vibrant planet Earth just now coming back to life after humanity brought it to the brink of extinction.

The falcon continued its descent to Earth, bringing more of the desolation into view. Large expanses of charred and scorched earth provide a glimpse into the war that had changed humanity forever. There were several large cities built after the UNGA took over, the largest among them, Renata. It was a sprawling city, housing a population of approximately four billion. There were five of these types of cities constructed on Earth, but Renata was the largest and home to the UNGA headquarters. The size of these cities played a large part in the migration of humans to colonies. They sought the space and freedom they once had on the Earth before it was rendered mostly uninhabitable.

The falcon continued its approach and landed near a large, towering building. There were landing pads at different levels of the building, most housing sandpipers, but the falcon landed at the ground level. As the occupants of the falcon disembarked from the ship, Barnes' memories came flooding back, the Earth triggering a resurgence of feelings long forgotten during her time in space. The smell of the air was the most intense trigger. She looked up at the tower. One hundred floors, 15 landing pads, 500,000 square feet per floor, a massive building with large letters affixed at the top... UNGA. While this building was the largest by far, the compound itself was massive. Serving as central operations for the UNGA, this compound housed many of the other divisions under the UNGA. The UNIC had approximately one hundred buildings, structures, and airfields located here. The UNAF had approximately 70 buildings consisting of barracks, training ground, and equipment supply.

The buildings that surrounded the compound were all cookie-cutter, with the same basic look from the outside. They appeared like a sea of concrete square blocks, each having fifty floors arranged in grid patterns around the compound, stretching as far as the eye could see. The soldiers escorted their prisoner to the main entrance, a series of large glass doors. As they made their way into the building, people stopped, stared, whispered, and jeered at the Barnes...the former Director of AIDA being paraded through the building in handcuffs.

"Murderer!" one voice shouted.

"Traitor!" another exclaimed.

The UNGA had already begun their campaign of propaganda against the former Director. For the last 24 hours, the UNGA had been issuing scathing information about Barnes. The former Director had been helping the resistance, providing them information so they could carry out their attacks. They told the people that Barnes was behind the abduction of the colonists at C2032. The people seemed to feel safe when the UNGA paraded a scapegoat around...the people knew nothing of the truth, only what the UNGA wanted them to know.

Barnes and her escorts proceeded to the elevator, where one of the soldiers hit the button for the 99th floor. The doors opened as they reached the 99th floor, revealing a very narrow hallway. It seemed out of place when you thought about the size of the building. Every hundred feet or so, there was a door on either side of the hallway. As the group reached the end of the hallway, there was a door larger than the rest.

They stood in front of it for a moment before it opened. When it did, the group was standing face to face with a team of guardians.

"You're relieved, soldier," the guardian said to the soldier standing closest to the door.

"Director, come with us," another guardian said.

Barnes stepped forward as the soldiers turned and went back down the hallway. The guardians led Barnes through the mostly empty room to a staircase that led to the 100th floor.

"I'm glad I get to see you again one last time 142, 234, 321, 412, and 519," Barnes said as they began walking up the stairs.

"Wish we could say the same doctor. We still don't understand how you could do it," 142 replied.

"One day soon you will. I'm sure it will take some time to figure out, but you'll realize things aren't always what they seem. Life is complicated," Barnes replied.

They arrived at the top of the stairs to see the five ministers standing in formal ceremonial gowns. A guardian motioned for Barnes to move toward the ministers.

"Former Director Barnes," Minister Gantley began to speak.

"While we can understand your disapproval with the methods of the Council, we are having a hard time reconciling your actions. To go against everything we have built, everything we are trying to achieve not just for us but for humanity seems wasteful. You have personally sacrificed more than almost anyone here, why would you decide to help the resistance now? Why would you render all of your sacrifices, and the sacrifices of others, useless? And to accomplish nothing – a pointless endeavor that can only end in death," Gantley continued.

"While it's true that I have sacrificed a great deal, more than you could know actually, this is not a pointless endeavor. You of all people should know that seemingly pointless endeavors can lead to great things. I remember the first time we met and that ride in the limo like it was yesterday," Barnes responded.

Barnes recalled when they were in the jet on their way to Gantley's compound. It was a long time ago at this point but something that lived with excruciating detail in her mind.

"There are rumors of war, with everyone fighting over access to resources during these challenging times, we have reason to believe that these rumors will prove to be true," Adam began.

"War? War between who?" Jonathan asked.

"Everyone, A truly world encompassing war," Adam responded grimly.

"You're talking about world war three. There's no way," Jonathan refused to believe that what Adam was saying could be possible.

"Why? Is it so hard to believe given the current state of the world and the political climate?" Adam asked.

"It's hard to believe that the same people you say want to hold on to their power would risk it by causing a global catastrophe," Jonathan responded.

"I don't believe they want to risk their hold on power but at the same time, they each need the support of their people. Without that, the very power they covet is at risk. It would be hard for the countries that are struggling to sustain their people to not go to war over resources, resources that are necessary for their survival," Adam countered.

"The people wouldn't allow it, they would rise up before they watched the world laid to waste. You don't have much faith in humanity do you Mr. Gantley?" Jonathan asked.

"Please, call me Adam, and it's quite the opposite, I absolutely have faith in humanity. I know that humanity can and will prevail in the end. What I don't have faith in is people's resolve. If there's anything I've learned from my success, it's that people are more often than not apathetic. They would rather worry about the kind of car they're driving, or where they're eating out, or what their plans are for the weekend than what's happening a half a world away. What they don't realize is that what happens a half a world away could be at their doorstep in no time. By the time it's at their doorstep now, it's already too late," Adam said.

"So how would you prevent this world war?" Ashley asked.

There was a long pause from Adam. He shifted a bit in his seat. This was going to be the most difficult part of the conversation. He took a moment before he spoke.

"I wouldn't," he responded bluntly.

Jonathan was taken aback by his comment. He looked at Ashley who just turned and looked out of the window. She didn't want to indicate to Jonathan that deep down, part of her agreed with Adam.

"You wouldn't? So what exactly would you do?" Jonathan asked.

"If we were to try to prevent it now, the same situation would continue to play out. I truly believe we are past the point of trying to stop the inevitable. What we and several others are focused on is the aftermath and how we rebuild after this war so we can ensure that humanity is able to carry on. Once people are shaken out of their apathy, then and only then can we begin the process of forging ahead," Adam said in a somber tone.

"So let millions, billions of people die, that's the plan? You don't need us for that!" Jonathan barked.

Jonathan became frustrated for thinking that Adam might be someone who could actually help change the world. He didn't give a second thought to where Ashley stood on this, assuming that she was as against it as he was.

"What we need you for is something far more important. We need you both to help reshape humanity's future, to help change the course of existence forever," he said.

He pulled a briefcase toward him. After he unclasped the latches, he removed several papers, handing them to Jonathan.

"What are these?" Jonathan asked.

Jonathan grabbed the papers skeptically and began reading. The look of shock on his face said it all. Adam had not been telling him everything.

"How is this possible?" Jonathan asked as he continued reading.

"I looked them over on the way here Jonathan, they are close. If we are able to help guide this research, we might discover the breakthrough that we've all been looking for. It's not just that, if I'm correct, we would even be able to save her," Ashley said.

Ashley tried to appeal to Jonathan's emotional side. As Jonathan continued to read, Adam sat back and held in the confident smile that was on the cusp of breaking out. He knew that he was close to convincing them.

"Well we have had some setbacks, but we have also made some incredible progress," he said as Jonathan stared at the paper.

"It seems that way," Jonathan said as he became enthralled by what he was reading.

"There are some errors in these equations, but this really is almost there. How did you get this far without the materials? I mean there's no way DARPA would've handed any of this over," Jonathan said as he looked at another page.

"Actually, they did hand it over, me and my associates have very close relationships with your superiors. The goal of all parties was to solve this riddle and now we are far closer than they were able to get. Governments have to deal with bureaucracy and endless red tape while we have a bit more freedom. The government has given us the materials, but we lack one final component to finish the equation and that's Ashley and yourself. I believe that with your talent and our resources, we can solve this. If we can, we would be able to put humanity on a path that would otherwise be unattainable," Adam said as he sat up in his seat.

"So while we work on this, we let the world burn? We keep our heads down while millions die and hope there are enough people left to benefit from what we can hopefully create? Then the survivors get to live in a world under new leadership?" Jonathan asked.

"I, we, want to create a new world. One where every human being has an opportunity to be part of something bigger, where every human being is a productive member of humanity, where the color of one's skin or their beliefs are of no consequence, where we no longer have to fight over energy or land: a better world. We want to bring humanity into a new age, and we can do just that if we are able to complete this work. My associates and I have complete faith in your collective ability to solve these remaining issues and finish this project," Adam elaborated.

Jonathan handed the papers back to Adam. He then turned to look at Ashley, surveying her face for a sense of where she was on this. Adam placed the papers back in his briefcase.

"I need to discuss this with Ashley in private," he said.

"I would expect nothing less. But please understand, while we may lose millions of lives, possibly hundreds of

millions, we have the opportunity to save billions and prevent humanity's eventual and inevitable extinction," Adam said.

Adam leaned a little closer to both Jonathan and Ashley, trying to emphasize his point and connect on a more personal level. He looked then both in the eyes and appealed to Ashley's more primal instincts in a hushed tone.

"And this will give you the opportunity to save her," he said.

Adam leaned back, allowing room for Jonathan and Ashley to move to the back of the plane. They spoke in whispers, going back and forth for most of the flight. They finally approached Mr. Gantley.

"Ok, we're interested, but we need to see everything and know if we do this, we have some requirements that will need to be considered," Jonathan said.

As the memory faded, Barnes found herself back in the presence of the council. She had to compose herself before she continued to speak.

"In the beginning, I truly believed in what we were doing, that what we were doing was for the good of all humanity. Over the years, it became apparent that everything we have done, everything we worked for, everything we sacrificed, was only for the good of a few. While the richest among us enjoy everything life has to offer, the rest of humanity struggles to survive. You stand before me now, in this palace, and talk to me about the greater good? It was never about humanity, it was always about personal enrichment. Power has a way of corrupting even the best of man and those who stand before me, and myself included, have fallen victim," Barnes said.

"We have always worked to ensure that humanity can continue to exist. We now exist without racism, religious bias, disease, drought, or famine. Every human being has the ability to receive housing, food, water, and medical care. The fact that humanity still exists is a testament to what we have accomplished. While you may not be privileged to the same information we are, I can assure you that the only reason humanity still exists is because of the sacrifices we have made and the work that the UNGA, the council continues to pursue," Minister Halin said.

"Your newfound sense of right and wrong seems to have gotten the better of you, Former Director. While it's true that many of humanity's advancements were because of the work you've done and the sacrifices you've made, there was far more happening behind the scenes that allowed for your work to succeed. Each member on this council, like you, has sacrificed everything," Minister Sarpong added.

"I sacrificed my own humanity, my soul, for those advances. I can't allow my legacy of death and misery to continue. I knew it, deep down I always knew, it was a matter of time before we would get to this point. The things that I've done, that I've seen, that I've allowed to happen...all of those experiences laid out a path, a path that undoubtedly leads to damnation. I could choose to continue down this path, doing nothing to change the outcome, or I could take a stand and do what I know in my heart I should've done from the beginning," Barnes declared.

"While I believe that your attempt at redemption is admirable, the fact remains that the course of action you pursue is not one that leads to the redemption you seek, it will only lead to more suffering for the entire human race," Minister Yamato said.

"Although we do respect you, we wish that you would reconsider this course of action, you must know that you are leaving us with no choice. You will be labeled a traitor to us, the UNGA, and to humanity," Minister Sarpong said.

"You can tell yourselves you have no choice but to label me a traitor, you can tell yourselves that everything you do is for the good of humanity, and you can tell yourselves any other bedtime story that helps you sleep at night, but I am tired of trying to convince myself that we're saving humanity while at the same time destroying it. Let's hurry up and get this over with, I'm tired of hearing these lies too," Barnes said in a defiant voice, standing as straight and proud as she could.

"Fair enough, it seems as though you've made up your mind. 142, bring Former Director Barnes to the square, we will commence the sentencing as soon as possible," Minister Gantley commanded.

Guardian 142 stepped forward as his team moved to escort Barnes back down the stairs and out of the door. Once they had left, the ministers moved into another room and the door closed.

"We have lost a valuable asset," Minister Guerrero said.

"True, but we couldn't allow her to interfere with our plan. We have to stay focused on the bigger picture. While it pains me to do this, it could be catastrophic if they were to interfere with the tenuous situation we find ourselves in. We must not lose focus; we are so close," Minister Halin said.

"Agreed," Minister Gantley confirmed.

Barnes found herself in the elevator with the guardian team descending to the ground floor. She felt the weight of the moment, surrounded by TITANs as she went to meet her death. The very things that she helped create had now turned against her.

"I am truly sorry for all that I've done to you. When you all find out the truth, and you will soon enough, I hope that you can forgive me," Barnes said.

"You tell us you're sorry for betraying us? Why wouldn't you tell the council you were sorry?" 142 asked.

"I'm not sorry for betraying the council or the UNGA. I'm talking about you and all of the TITANs, everything I have done to you," Barnes attempted to clarify.

The guardian team didn't completely understand what she was saying as the doors of the elevator opened. They proceeded outside of the main doors at the front of the building. Crowds of people had gathered as word must have been relayed that Former Director Barnes had been found guilty of treason. The people knew that the only sentence to be carried out for this type of crime was death. As Barnes and the guardian team moved toward the square, more and more people began to gather. The square was the nickname for the large tiered circular public gathering area just outside of the UNGA building. In the center was a large UNGA logo and large planters containing flowering plants lined the perimeter as walking paths led in several directions. Many of the people in the crowd were high-ranking officials who had brought their families. For these types of events, officials were expected to attend with their families to ensure that when a message like this was sent, it applied to everyone, no matter their rank. They stood in the square, waiting for the arrival of the council to administer the sentence.

As the crowd still continued to swell, displays began appearing around the perimeter of the square. They were projected in the air and broadcast on all UNGA frequencies to allow anyone not directly in the square to witness the event. The crowd erupted in cheers as the council arrived at the main path leading to the square. They were flanked by two teams of guardians as they slowly made their way to the center of the square. Once they arrived in the center, Minister Gantley held his hands up to silence the crowd.

"Ladies and Gentlemen, we come to you on this day with

a truly heavy heart. We have exposed a traitor among us," he proclaimed.

Minister Gantley had to pause as the crowd moaned and booed the former director.

"Former Director Barnes has made tremendous achievements during her time with the UNGA. She has helped with advancements that have truly changed how we live but we have uncovered secrets she has kept from us all. She apparently was living a double life, one for the people and the other full of treachery, deceit, and lies. Former Director Barnes has been charged and found guilty of aiding and abetting the resistance, treason against the UNGA, and indeed crimes against humanity," Minister Gantley said.

Again, the minister needed to pause as the crowd erupted.

"Former Director Barnes, you have been found guilty of these crimes for which the penalty is death. The sentence is to be carried out immediately. Due to your previous service and contributions to humanity, we have decided on the manner of your death," Minister Gantley continued.

The crowd was silent, waiting for the announcement with such anticipation. The council knew that these moments were extremely important, they were adept at manipulating, bringing the crowd to the edge of their figurative seats.

"Your execution will be carried out by means of the chamber," Minister Gantley announced loudly.

The crowd erupted in cheers as Barnes began reflecting on what was about to occur. A sense of fear gripped her. She swallowed a hard gulp, summoning the courage that had eluded her for her entire life, and stood tall. Not a moment later, a cylindrical device was wheeled out and down the same path the ministers had just traveled. As they brought the device closer to the square, it seemed to be designed for one person. The cylinder had clear windows on the front, a large device on the back that looked like a sphere with various protrusions, and a modified ZPE core in the center. The device was set in the middle of the square as a soldier opened the front of the chamber. Barnes walked to the chamber and proceeded to climb in. As Barnes settled herself into the chamber, a guardian moved toward the council and leaned in to whisper something to Minister Gantley.

Minister Gantley tried to hide a full-blown smile as a smirk snuck out and was visible for a brief moment. He had just been informed that the resistance was preparing for an assault and that the likely target was the UNGA, a possible attempt to save Barnes. He knew that Barnes would already be dead by the time they got there, their attempt to save the former director would fail before it began. The minister nodded at the officer next to the chamber and he closed it. As the officer walked around to the back of the device, Minister Gantley began to speak again.

"We have all made sacrifices. We have all given of ourselves for the greater good of humanity, and today we ensure that our dedication to peace continues. While the former director's death represents our vigilance and determination, we must remember that the fight for peace is not easily won. Former Director Barnes, the Council of the United Nations Governing Authority hereby sentences you to death. Do you have any last words?" Minister Gantley said proudly.

"I have found that no matter what path we take, they all lead to one destination in the end. Our desires for peace and stability often take a back seat to our more basic human tendencies. While there are some who truly want to do good, there will always be those who try to manipulate them,"

Barnes said as her communication from inside the chamber was cut off.

The ministers each nodded one by one, and on the final nod, the officer activated the device. It took about ten seconds for the device to charge, a whining sound grew as it came to a full charge and activated. The chamber emitted a blinding light through each of the clear plates, forcing the crowd and anyone watching to shield their eyes. As the light dissipated, the inside of the chamber became visible again, Barnes' body was no longer in the chamber. It had been vaporized by the reaction that occurred within.

Not a moment after Barnes had been dispatched from this existence, the lights and screens, all electronic devices in the area began to flicker. This was something of a spectacle as communication interference had been all but eliminated with the invention of quantum communications. The people that had gathered began to whisper among themselves. While the people whispered amongst themselves, the council knew immediately that something was wrong.

"The fusion reaction must have been a little more powerful than we anticipated," Minister Guerrero tried to make light of the interference.

"We understand that events such as this can be disheartening, but they serve to strengthen our resolve. We will not allow those who try to undermine our way of life to succeed. The human race has endured through many difficult challenges and we will continue to do so," Minister Gantley said proudly to the cheers of the crowd.

The ministers then turned and began to walk back toward the building but paused as they heard alerts and alarms ring throughout the crowd. The high-ranking officials who had filled the square began receiving messages. Regular people who had gathered to watch grew concerned as the officials began moving with urgency toward their respective positions.

"We need to move quickly," a guardian escorting the council said.

"What's going on?" Minister Halin asked.

"There's been a security breach. All planetary defenses have been disabled. We need to get you inside and secured as soon as possible," the guardian replied.

As the council moved quickly into the building, the crowd dispersed just as quickly, running for their posts to find out what was going on while their families scrambled back to their homes. As the council made it up to the 100th floor, they gathered in their meeting room.

"How were all of the planetary defenses disabled? How is that possible?" Minister Yamato demanded an answer.

"Get me Admiral Vincere," Minister Gantley commanded.

A screen projected in front of the ministers; however, Admiral Vincere did not appear on the screen.

A familiar voice responded to the minister's command, "I'm sorry Minister Gantley, Admiral Vincere is not available."

The face of each member of the council dropped at once, now understanding the seriousness of the statement and who had said it.

NINE
UNITED

MEANWHILE, the team along with the commander and lieutenant made their way back from their meeting with Barnes.

"SSD disengaged," a voice was heard within the falcon.

The falcon, carrying the commander and his team, approached the resistance command center. The commander sat in his seat looking straight ahead at the wall, still processing everything Barnes had just told him. The team just sat in their seats with their heads down, unsure of what all of this meant for them and their future. The lieutenant attempted to avoid eye contact with anyone, feeling like anything that might be said would trigger an unwelcome response. The falcon landed in the hangar and the crew disembarked.

"Well, we've been going nonstop," the commander said. "I think we all need to get some rest."

"Like any of us will be able to sleep," Toa said.

"Well we aren't all TITANs," the lieutenant interjected.

"True, let's get some food and rest. We're going to need it

before we figure out our next step," the commander said as he led the way to the mess hall.

Everyone grabbed some food, remaining silent as they ate. Once they were finished, the commander attempted to address the TITANs.

"Ok, we know that what we are attempting won't be easy and we need everyone at one hundred percent if we have any chance at succeeding. Do what you need to do and then we'll all meet back in the comms room in a couple of hours," the commander said.

The commander and lieutenant left the team to begin preparations for an assault. The team made their way to their room to discuss what had just happened.

"I'm not sure how we're supposed to feel, that was a lot to take in," Coughlin said.

"I know how I feel. I wasn't under any illusions that we were a tool, a means to an end, but it seems we have been used for all of the wrong reasons. All of our hard work and training has led us to this point. It may not be the mission we thought it was, but we still have work to do," Jossen said.

"I agree. We have all been put in this situation. We lost friends in the pursuit of a false ideal, to the greed of others, and still, our family is in danger. We still have fellow TITANs who don't know the truth, the truth about who they are and what they're fighting for. Like I told Barnes, we will take down the UNGA and humanity can do as they wish, but all TITANs need to know the truth and decide for themselves how they want to live," Harden said.

"Listen, the commander is right, if we're going to do this, we need to be prepared," Jossen said before being interrupted.

"Did you just say the commander is right?" Toa asked with a smile.

"Ha ha, funny guy. Let's try to get some rest, just a couple minutes of shut-eye to refresh ourselves," Jossen remarked.

The team laid down and began to fall asleep. It was easier than they thought, the events of the last couple of days wearing them down mentally and emotionally. As Harden fell asleep, his dreams resurged with a new intensity. The same dread washing over him as he lay under the bed. While he still couldn't understand what was being said, a sensation overtook him. The conversation, the voices that seemed to be arguing before, were discussing what to do with him. As the people enter the room, the feeling of familiarity that seemed vague before became clear, they were there to save him. The hand reached in to pull him out, this time he wasn't blinded but was able to see them. Four UNIC soldiers stood next to Director Barnes. He believed his mother was the sixth person but was unable to see her face. The feeling of dread that overwhelmed him was replaced with a feeling of despair and longing as Barnes held out her hand. His mother put his hand in hers as the crying continued. As they began to walk out of the bedroom door, the light from the other room blinded him. At that moment, he jolted himself awake.

"You ok?" Taylor asked.

She had woken up just a moment before him, watching him as he slept. It was apparent from his twitching that he was having some kind of nightmare. More than likely the same one he had previously.

"Yeah, I'll be alright," he replied.

"The nightmares?" she asked.

"Yeah, but they're different, more sad than terrifying. At least I know what happened now," he explained as the rest of the team woke up.

"Everyone get some rest?" Jossen asked as he sat up.

"Yeah, a bit, should be good to go though," Toa responded while Coughlin nodded her head to agree.

"Ok, let's head to the comms room and see what our next move is," Jossen said.

The team left the room and headed to the comms room. As they all made their way to one of the secure rooms, the commander and lieutenant arrived.

The commander, Harden, Taylor, and the lieutenant took a seat while Jossen, Toa, and Coughlin remained standing. The atmosphere was tense, everyone understood that the mission they would be embarking on was extremely difficult.

"I'm going to cut right to the chase. All of us need to make our own decisions about what to do next. Obviously, there are some things we need to discuss, like the fact that there is the only living second-generation TITAN among us," the commander said.

"Look, I wasn't expecting to hear any of that, but it changes nothing about who I am," Harden cut in.

"Bullshit, it absolutely changes who you are," Toa responded.

There was an awkward pause before Toa continued.

"You're the son of a freaking TITAN! All that stuff we learned about the TITANs, what they did and who they were, well it may not all be true but man I for one am excited. Ok, was it the greatest news, everything we just found out? No, but in my mind, it wasn't the worst either. We had a mission. We succeeded by failing but still a win. Now we know the real story or at least most of the real story and we found out some pretty amazing things about ourselves. Now it's time for a new mission, probably one of the greatest in TITAN history," he said.

Toa felt as though his two cents might motivate everyone.

Harden couldn't help but smile when hearing what Toa had to say. The rest of the team appeared to be on the same page.

"I was thinking on the way back that we have been a team since we were able to walk. There's nothing that could diminish what we've been through together. All of the lies, the deceit, has brought about one outcome that no one counted on: our team. They thought their lies would somehow control us, that we could be manipulated, but I know our strength. I know that when the council sees us again, they won't be able to hide behind their lies. I just can't help but feel I'm responsible for dragging you all into this, that it's my fault we are about to storm the UNGA headquarters," Harden said.

"Dragged into it? I don't know if I speak for everyone else but like you said, we're a team. I don't consider being a part of this as dragged into anything. We follow each other, we support each other, that's what a team does, that's what a family does. So maybe your family looks a little different now, but we'll make sure we all come out of this together," Taylor replied.

"So we know where Taylor stands, but I think we already knew that. Me though? I'm actually pretty pissed. The UNGA has been lying to us for our entire lives. God knows how many lives we've destroyed over the countless missions we've been on in the name of the UNGA. I hope you don't take any offense, but your mother had this coming," Coughlin said as she looked at the commander.

"And I'm happy to say that she isn't anything to us anymore," Coughlin finished as she leaned back against the wall allowing others to speak.

Jossen stood there silent, remained stoic as he didn't react to any of the words being said. An uncomfortable silence began to fill the room. Just as Toa was about to say something, Jossen spoke.

"Every mission we've taken, we've completed. So far, there's been nothing we couldn't accomplish as a team. The UNGA, UNIC, AIDA, and anyone else that would stand in our way will learn that we're not that easy to get rid of. They thought they could make us into their weapons, that we would only serve them, and when we were no longer useful, they would toss us aside. I made a promise to protect this team, each and every member, with everything I have, I intend to keep that promise, whatever it takes," Jossen declared then walked behind Harden and put his hand on his shoulder.

"Then it's settled. We'll go to Earth, break into UNGA headquarters, and get this footage uploaded. We don't have much time though according to Barnes' timeline, we're going to need a plan," the lieutenant said.

The commander put the two cases from the doctor down on the table.

"Let's see what we've got to work with," the commander opened the first case.

The video screen popped up again, revealing the keyboard beneath. The commander removed a thin plastic-looking card from the case.

"This must have the videos on them. We'll need to bring this to upload the videos," the commander said as he handed the card to Taylor.

The commander then opened the second case. That case had another card, an old USB drive, and a couple of hundred transponders. The commander pushed the case over to Taylor.

"Can you run an analysis on these? We need to know

what's on that old drive, what these transponders are programmed for, and what's on the data card?" he asked.

"Let me take a look," Taylor replied as she began investigating on the spot.

"I'm not sure how the people will react when they see these videos. Barnes seemed to have faith that they would stand up to the UNGA, but I don't share her optimism. There's a chance that the people believe it's a hoax or worse, they're just too scared to do anything. In my opinion, we need to be prepared to finish this," the commander said.

"We'll go after the council, they're the ones responsible for all of this and they'll no doubt have guardians on security detail," Jossen added.

"Well these are UNIC transponders," Taylor interjected.

She handed one of the transponders to the commander. He took a quick look at it, already putting the pieces of Barnes' plan together.

"It's probably going to take a little time to crack this data card, it's heavily encrypted. As for the USB drive, that's some old tech, finding a transfer method might take some time," she continued.

"Ok, so we somehow get down to Earth's surface, get into UNGA headquarters, upload the videos, and take down the council. The biggest question I have is, how do we get past Earth's planetary defenses and down to the surface?" the lieutenant asked.

"Don't worry about that, I think I have an idea, but we'll need every resistance ship available to pull it off. We'll also need some more firepower," the commander said with a sly smile.

"Now you're speaking my language," Toa quipped.

"Jossen, Toa, and Couglin, you come with me. Lieutenant, rally the troops. Taylor and Harden, you two seem to make a good team, try to figure out what's on that data card," the commander instructed.

The lieutenant moved with purpose, knowing they didn't have much time to get everything ready. She was shouting orders at soldiers in passing, it seemed random, but each officer took her orders and went right to work.

"You," she said. "Get the falcons armed and ready."

"Which one?" the soldier asked.

"All of them. Put the call out, all resistance ships are to report here asap," she responded as she continued walking.

"Yes Lieutenant," the soldier responded.

As she passed a room, she peeked her head in. "Make sure each ship knows to grab a transponder," she insisted.

"Yes ma'am," a voice responded.

As a soldier walked toward her, she instructed, "We're going to need to open the reserve armory."

"Yes Lieutenant," the soldier replied as he changed direction and moved down a hall.

The lieutenant arrived in a briefing room where it appeared that almost every soldier in the resistance base was gathered. She took a quick breath before beginning the briefing.

"Ok," she began to address the room.

"We have an opportunity to turn the tide on our war against the UNGA. I'm not going to sugarcoat this for any of you. This is not a slam dunk, this is not a shoe-in, this is a dangerous mission that not everyone will survive, including myself. There is a chance that we can expose the UNGA and everything they have done while taking down the council. This is not about any of us though. This is about our family, our friends, the future generations that will have to live with the outcome. Their future is what's at stake, a life of perpetual war or a chance at peace. While I can't promise we will be successful, what I can promise is that this is the best chance we have at changing the future," the lieutenant paused, gauging the reactions of the soldiers in the room.

"I ask you all to fight – fight for yourselves, fight for your family and friends, and fight for the future of humanity," the lieutenant said. She stopped then.

The group of soldiers remained silent for a moment before cheering the lieutenant. After the cheering subsided a bit, the lieutenant continued.

"We will all need to be ready within the hour. I know that's a tall order, but our window of opportunity is a narrow one and it will take everything we've got to make it happen," the lieutenant paused again.

"Now let's go change the future!" she shouted as she dismissed the room.

The room roared with soldiers ready to do whatever it takes. Meanwhile, Taylor continued decrypting the data card. After a short while, she was able to break the encryption.

"What is all this?" she asked herself out loud as if no one else was in the room.

"What is it?" Harden asked as he was sitting off to the side.

It startled Taylor for a moment as she was so absorbed in what she was doing, she thought she was alone. When she dove into something difficult, she gave it her all and the encryption required that level of attention. She blocked out everything around her in order to figure it out, but Harden's words pulled her back to reality.

"It looks like this is information regarding Project Olympus. There's quite a bit in here on the research and development but the data doesn't seem to make any sense. It looks like there are hundreds of thousands of subjects. I'll have to transfer all of this over to my unit and see what I can find out," she answered.

She activated the nanites from her wrist, forming the screen from her armor. She started the transfer of the data card to her own system. She then reached for the USB drive, looking at it suspiciously.

"I'll need to find some way to transfer the information off of this and onto my system. I'm not sure we'll have what we need here to make that happen," Taylor said.

"I don't think Barnes would've given it to us if she didn't think we could figure out what's on it," Harden said.

"You're right, let's see what we can find," Taylor said as they made their way out of the room.

Not a moment later, a resistance engineer came running up to the pair of TITANs. He seemed out of breath as though he had just run from one end of the base to the other.

"Excuse me, the lieutenant asked me to give you this," the technician huffed as he approached.

He handed Harden a six-inch thick disc, an old data transfer pod. These pods allowed the transfer of information from almost any type of electronic storage to a data card. He also handed Harden a blank data card.

"That should work," Taylor said.

"Perfect, thanks," Harden responded.

They walked back into the room and she put the USB drive on the pod, inserting the data card into the slot on the pod. It began transferring almost immediately.

"Ok, this shouldn't take too long," Taylor said.

They waited a few minutes in silence and the transfer was complete. A soft green glow from around the edge of the pod indicated that the transfer was successful.

"Alright, let's see what we've got," Taylor said.

She removed the data card and initiated the transfer to

her system. The transfer was quick, and she began swiping through information on her keypad. Harden didn't recognize any of the faces she was making as she poured over the information. They appeared to be looks of concern, or maybe fear, he wasn't sure.

"This is incredible!" she exclaimed, stunned at what she had found.

"This is the research from before the UNGA was created. This is the original research on the ZPE cores, but it also talks about how they found the first one," she said as she continued to swipe her screen.

"What do you mean found? They were created, invented, not found," Harden asked and immediately answered.

"This is telling me otherwise. This research says that a ship crashed on Earth in the year 1947. That's when they found the original core. They had tried for years to figure out what was powering the core, how it functioned," she said as she continued to feverishly read through the screens.

"The ship that crashed was not from Earth and apparently occupied. The being in the ship offered the nanites and the ZPE cores as a way for Earth to defend itself," she said.

"Defend itself from what?" Harden asked, growing more concerned about what Taylor was saying.

"It doesn't say anything about that, it does say that a treaty was signed that would guarantee peaceful existence while certain limitations are maintained," she said.

"Limitations? What limitations?" Harden asked.

"It doesn't say. There's not much else regarding that, just a lot more research on the core itself and the nanites," she said as she appeared frustrated.

"There's nothing else here about the treaty, the limitations, or the occupant. The rest is just them trying to figure out the cores and the nanites," she said, growing more frustrated.

"We know about the damn cores and the nanites. Where's the rest about the treaty?" she asked, desperately wanting to find out more about the occupant.

As she continued browsing the files, she came across several files that contained additional encryption. She appeared to be growing more frustrated as she attempted to break the encryption.

"Ok, let's see what's on the data card, is it finished transferring? Maybe there's something on there that can tell us more," Harden suggested.

"Only 35%," she said, annoyed at the pace.

"Listen, she gave us this USB for a reason. If she had to sneak this out, then the UNGA doesn't know we have these. We need to keep this thing somewhere safe," Harden said as they put the USB back in the case.

"It can't be a coincidence that Barnes put this in the same cases we would need for this mission. We need to let the others know," Harden said as they set off to tell the others.

While Harden and Taylor were busy searching Barnes' files, the commander, Jossen, Toa, and Coughlin were busy in the armory.

"Ok, so we know we will be up against a whole lot of UNIC troops and at least one guardian team. These will be TITANs that you know that you grew up with, that know you. We need to make sure we're prepared. After our last encounter, I had our guys start working on a magnet similar to the one that trapped you guys but modified to be launched from a weapon. They're small and won't last indefinitely, but it should hold them long enough for us to get away or disable them," the commander explained. The commander grabbed one of the new weapons and showed it off.

"Disable them? Look, if you didn't inject us with those anti nanites and if that field wore off, we wouldn't have stopped...TITANs keep going until they can't, or the mission is complete. You say disable them, but I don't want to have any delusions here. If we are going to stop them, we will need to kill them," Toa said.

"He's right, I wanted to kill you when you walked into that room as soon as we woke up. If I had my strength then I would have done it right there," Coughlin agreed.

"We also made these," the commander said as he held up a pistol.

"I'm not sure you could kill a rabbit with that," Coughlin said.

"Not a rabbit, something much smaller—the nanites. This pistol will shoot a projectile capable of introducing a small number of nanite inhibitors. This will, in effect, disable their abilities temporarily. It's not as much or as strong as the doses we gave you, but it should do the trick," the commander replied.

"OK, so we have to look at our loadouts and make sure we have what we need to get this job done," Jossen said as he grabbed the pistol from the commander.

Toa moved to the magnet launcher and picked it up. It was a large, bulky rifle but it suited him just fine.

"How do I look?" he asked Coughlin as he struck a pose.

"Like a tool," she responded with a chuckle.

They took some time gathering the weapons they needed for the coming assault. They also decided which resistance groups would create diversions and which would land for the assault on the UNGA headquarters.

"Guys, we found, well Taylor found something," Harden interrupted.

"So did I," Toa said as he struck another pose with the magnet launcher.

"There was more to what Barnes gave us in those cases. The USB contained information about how the ZPE cores and nanites were found," Taylor said.

"Found? The nanites and cores weren't found. Director Barnes and AIDA developed them," Jossen said almost immediately.

"I said the same thing," Harden followed.

"Not according to the data on the USB. I finished encrypting the data card she gave us. It seems that a ship crashed on Earth in the year 1947. This ship and its crash led to the discovery of the ZPE cores, nanites, and apparently the discovery that we are not the only intelligent species in the universe," she said with a bit of excitement in her tone.

"The lies don't seem to end," Harden said.

"I'm sorry, what? You're going to drop a bomb on us like that? So pretty much everything that our society is built on now comes from aliens?!" Toa asked excitedly.

"Well when you put it that way, it does seem kind of far-fetched but yes," Harden said.

"This alien apparently brought the nanites and the core to help the human race defend itself," Taylor explained.

"Defend itself from what?" the commander asked.

"We're not sure. The information in the USB talks about a treaty that was signed, and that the treaty has some kind of stipulations. From what I can gather from the data card, it says that the treaty has something to do with the nanites and their use. It seemed that the director was about to uncover something, but I haven't been able to break the encryption around one of the folders though," Taylor said.

"That sounds heavy, but I think we need to table that for now. The time is fast approaching and there's a lot of prep going into this. The resistance has a lot on the line, pretty much everything. If this fails, there will be a lot of casualties and their families will be left with nothing. Let's focus on this mission, then we can figure out what's going on with this treaty later," the commander said.

"Understood, let's grab our gear and head down to the hangar," Jossen instructed.

"And if we run into those things in the video, those nanite-infested things?" Coughlin asked.

"I think we'll have to get up close and personal and maybe a little low tech. One of these in the EM field generator should do the trick," the commander said as he removed a ten-inch long thick blade from a rack.

"Right, and hope we can get that close," Toa said.

"Well, I don't have an anti-magnetic field gun, so it'll have to do," the commander replied.

The group grabbed their gear and made their way to the hangar. As they walked into the hangar, it seemed like pandemonium. It looked like a full-scale invasion. Soldiers were everywhere, loading weapons, vehicles, and personnel. Ships were preparing for takeoff while vehicles were still being loaded.

"We'll take off, remain in orbit, and load the coordinates. We'll tune to the UNGA channels and wait for the signal. Once we see or hear the signal, we move," the commander said.

"Commander! Over here!" the lieutenant's voice carried over the incredible amount of noise.

The team approached the lieutenant, giving a much-needed boost of confidence to her as the TITANs looked like they could take on the entire UNIC. She was standing in front of a fully equipped falcon.

"This is our bird, Sierra and Kilo teams are already on board," she said.

"Perfect, let's not keep everyone waiting," the commander said.

The team boarded the falcon, and before the doors were fully closed, they began to take off. The ships moved to a safe distance to engage the SDD and held there as they awaited the signal.

"Pilot, I need you to tune to UNGA channels. I'm looking for anything out of the ordinary," the commander requested.

"Yes sir, let me see what we've got," the pilot responded.

"So, you missed some information lieutenant. Apparently, aliens exist," Toa made small talk with the lieutenant.

"What?" the lieutenant responded.

"Yeah, it seems that humans and these aliens signed some kind of agreement," Toa continued nonchalantly.

"Ok, sounds like one hell of a story," the lieutenant said as she dismissed his comments.

"He's not kidding, it seems that the UNGA put a lot of faith in alien technology to propel humanity's future forward," the commander confirmed.

"Wow, just going to drop a bombshell like that right before we start the most important mission of our lives, like we don't have enough to deal with already," the lieutenant snapped as she struggled to process that.

Sierra and Kilo teams began whispering to themselves after hearing the news. Shock and disbelief seemed to be the dominant feelings among the two teams.

"Sir, we've got something. Not sure if it's what you're looking for, but here it is," the pilot interrupted as he transferred the feed to the cargo hold.

The video showed a feed of the square at UNGA headquarters. The council had just begun approaching the center of the square. Everyone in the cabin watched as Minister Gantley spoke and Barnes was sentenced to death. They watched as the chamber was brought out and as she got in. The team felt a wave of nervousness wash over them as she climbed into the chamber. Even though she had lied to them, it still felt wrong that she was about to die. They couldn't turn away though, they had to watch for the signal, and not knowing what it was, meant they had to keep an eye on everything. All of the sudden, a flash blinded the feed. When it returned, the screen flickered and rolled just for a few seconds.

"Was that the signal?" the commander asked.

Almost as soon as he asked, the team heard a familiar voice.

"Commander, it's time to move," Barnes' voice said.

"Let's move, tell all forces it's a go," the commander said without hesitation

"Yes sir," the pilot said as he engaged the SDD.

"You won't have long. You need to be quick and precise. As I said I would, I will take care of Admiral Vincere," Barnes' voice continued to speak as the SDD engaged.

"How is this possible? We saw you die," the commander asked once they entered the distortion.

"Yes, my body is no longer with you. My mother always taught me to play the long game. I figured it was only a matter of time before I would die whether from natural causes or because of my own actions. I knew that I couldn't atone for all of my wrongs in my lifetime, so I had to find another way. I now exist within the UNGA quantum intelligence system. I have access to every UNGA system including planetary defenses, the entire UNIC fleet, and all communications. They didn't know it but when they sentenced me to death, they gave me access to far more than I would have when I was alive," Barnes said.

"It was something I started working on a long time ago. When I first joined the group, before the UNGA was founded, the research into quantum computing was so far ahead of what the government had. Once Jonathan and I realized the possibility of transferring consciousness, I began to work on it in secret. Unfortunately, we weren't able to solve some of the equations before Jonathan died, but it was his work and his memory that gave me the motivation to finish. I can go into specifics of how it works, but no time for that now," she continued.

"Commander, we've arrived. Disengaging SDD," the pilot said.

As the falcon came out of the space distortion above Earth, there were hundreds of resistance ships also entering the space. It would've been hard for the UNIC to engage them all even if so many of the ships didn't have UNIC transponders. The chaos on the bridge of the UNSS Spirit was almost total. As Admiral Capetolli deployed fighters to counter the assault, the UNIC ships couldn't tell the difference between friendly ships and the hundreds of resistance ships that appeared as UNIC.

"Beginning our approach sir," the pilot chimed in again.

The falcon made its way through the confusion, dodging and weaving between both friendly and enemy fire. The goal was to get the falcon in low Earth orbit to drop the TITAN team and then join the attack on the headquarters once the team was inside. Once they made it to low Earth orbit, they made their move.

"Open the door, this is our stop," the commander said.

The team engaged their mag-grav boots as the lieutenant, Sierra team, and Kilo team put on the oxygen masks behind them. As the door opened and sucked all of the air in the cargo bay into space, the rush of air pulled Sierra and Kilo teams to their harnesses. The lieutenant, fully strapped in, was jolted around in her seat. The TITAN team approached the edge of the door.

"Let's go!" the commander shouted as they jumped.

As they hurtled toward the Earth, they had to dodge other ships flying by between them and the Earth. They narrowly avoided ship after ship, almost colliding with a Condor as it maneuvered to deploy resistance forces on the ground. As they entered the Earth's atmosphere, the glow of the planet's natural defenses enveloped them. The team and the commander descended toward the surface, witnessing aircraft flying up to the battle happening above.

As they approached the surface, they could see Renata, it appeared small at first but still was visible against the landscape from this height. Throughout the descent, more and more detail became apparent. They began to make out armies of soldiers preparing to defend the headquarters against an assault. They deployed the braking panels and reverse thrusters as they got within range of the surface, slowing them down just before they landed, again landing with enough force to crack the concrete leaving a crater. As soon as they landed, gunfire erupts from almost every direction. Hundreds of soldiers descend upon them with overwhelming numbers.

The team moved with a purpose, faster than most could lead, the bullets were just seconds too late. The commander drew his AAR-10 and began firing as soon as he landed. His precision was lethal, dispatching soldier after soldier, as he moved to cover. The team did exactly the same, when they pulled the trigger, there was no need to second guess impact. They continued their assault with ruthless efficiency as Toa let rockets fly from the arrow. The team managed to make it to cover and ducked behind a retaining wall.

"Commander," the lieutenant's voice was heard over the comms.

"Lieutenant, what's your status?" the commander asked.

"Inbound," she replied as the sound of the falcon above drew their attention.

The lieutenant fired everything she had into the horde of soldiers. Rockets and gunfire exploded from the falcon, decimating entire squads of soldiers. All of the sudden, an explosion rocked the falcon, sending the ship crashing to the ground behind the team.

"Lieutenant!" the commander shouted.

There was no response. The team continued to lay down fire as the commander waited for a response. The commander started to break off and head toward the downed falcon.

"Commander, we need to focus on the mission. The lieutenant can handle herself," Jossen said as he motioned toward the army that stood in front of them.

"Go ahead, I'll catch up in a minute," he said as he turned towards the downed falcon.

The team continued with their mission, making their way through the seemingly endless sea of soldiers. They saw the building just up ahead about two klicks, but between them and the building, were still more than a hundred soldiers. A low rumbling began as they picked off soldier by soldier. The team knew that sound all too well.

"I'm almost out of ammo," Toa said.

"I think we all are, we need to get some more before that rhino gets here," Jossen responded.

"There!" Jossen said as he spotted a group of downed soldiers behind a short concrete wall.

The team continued to fire as they moved, shots ricocheting off of their armor. They slid behind cover, reaching for the rifles that laid on the ground.

"We need to find something we can use to take out that rhino, guess I should've held on to those rockets," Toa said as he reloaded.

The noise that started as a low rumbling had grown to a thunderous sound, causing the vibration of the ground beneath their feet.

"Too late," Coughlin commented as she peeked over the edge of the wall.

The rhino had made its way to the same landing pad that Barnes had occupied shortly before their arrival. It positioned itself between them and the entry.

"We need a plan, and we need one now," Taylor said as she saw the turrets being aimed their way.

"Ok. Harden, think you and Coughlin can get around to the side of that thing? If you can get a shot with SR, hit one of the cores on the back, that should be enough. We'll draw their fire," Jossen said.

"Whoa, I'm drawing what?" Toa said jokingly.

"Yeah, I only have five rounds left though. It would take at least that many to pop the core," Harden replied.

"Don't worry, I'm used to covering people's asses, I do hang out with Toa a lot," Coughlin remarked.

"Ouch that hurt," Toa replied.

Coughlin laid down fire as she moved to flank the rhino with Harden. The rest of the team attempted to draw fire, dispersing from cover as the turret tried to decide which target to follow. The team was fast, it was hard for the turret to track them. The soldiers in the tank must have grown impatient and began firing while the turret was tracking. The jolt hit the ground with incredible impact, even the nanite armor wouldn't stand up to that. The DELaW fired shortly after the railgun, while a more precise weapon, it didn't have the same conclusive impact. It hit the ground, leaving a scorched impression about a foot deep. The nanite armor was no match for these weapons, the only advantage they had was speed.

Harden and Coughlin arrived at a point where they were able to get a clean shot. Harden lined it up, firing the first round straight into one of the cores. He fired another into the core before soldiers in the area realized where the shot came from. The soldiers returned fire with Coughlin as Harden tried to line up the next shot. He fired, striking the core for the third time. The core began to smoke.

"How much longer?" Jossen asked as they continued running between cover.

"Almost there, just a couple more shots," Harden responded as he lined up the next.

Harden pulled the trigger once more, but this time a soldier got in the way. He paused as he took a breath, knowing he only had one shot left.

"One shot left," he said as he stood up, sighted in on the target, and fired.

"Nice hit," Coughlin said.

"It's not down yet though," Harden responded.

Smoke billowed from one of the cores on the rhino. The team knew that while it was close to critical, it wasn't going to blow itself.

"Looks like we'll have to do this the hard way. Ok team, let's all flank the Rhino, both," Jossen said as he was interrupted.

"Sierra team, you got that Rhino right?" the lieutenant asked over the comms.

"Affirmative," Jennings responded.

Just then, a rocket fired from the direction of the downed falcon. The rocket hit the tank, causing an explosion that was amplified by the ruptured core, almost splitting the Rhino in two.

"Nice!" Toa exclaimed.

"We still have a job to do," the commander reminded the team.

"Sierra, Kilo, let's lay down some suppressing fire so they can get to that building," the lieutenant said as she joined the team.

"Will do," Santos said as both Sierra and Kilo teams fired everything they had.

"You heard the lieutenant, let's move," Jossen instructed the team.

Harden and Coughlin made their way through the soldiers, on their way to join the team. They joined up in front of the wreckage of the rhino, taking cover before forging ahead to the entrance. Sierra and Kilo teams continued to push back the remaining soldiers.

"Ok, we need to get to the entrance. It's straight up ahead, about a half a klick away," Jossen said as he formulated a plan.

"Harden, take these," the commander said as he handed him a cartridge of SR ammo.

"Don't worry Toa, I brought you something too," he said as he removed the arrow launcher off his back.

"Is it my birthday?" Toa asked as he cradled the launcher in his arms.

"On three, we move to the entrance one, two, three," Jossen said as they ran toward the entrance.

As they did, two mounted guns opened fire on the team. Harden grabbed his SR-10 and lined up the shot while running for cover. The first shot hit the target just before he slid behind cover.

"One down," Harden said.

"Ok, how about the other? Coughlin, Toa, I want you on those guns," Jossen said.

"Moving now," Coughlin replied.

"On it," Toa responded.

Harden peeked from cover to line up the next shot. The mounted gun let loose as soon as he saw him. Unfortunately, for the soldier on the mounted gun, it was just a second too late. Harden already had a beat on his location. He jumped to his feet and let the shot fly, as the round hit its target he was also struck.

"Harden!" Taylor screamed as she watched him hit the ground.

"Two down," Harden moaned as he recovered.

The shot had grazed his armor, leaving a streaking gouge on the left side of his chest. He got to his feet as the sound of the mounted guns firing filled the air. This time the guns weren't firing at the team. Coughlin and Toa focused the firepower on the remaining troops as Sierra and Kilo teams advanced to their position. The rest of the team moved forward to the main entrance. Toa and Coughlin kept additional troops at bay while staying on the mounted guns.

"We got this, you guys go ahead," Coughlin said as UNIC reinforcements arrived.

"We may not be TITANs, but there's no way we're letting you get all the action," Jennings said.

Sierra and Kilo teams unloaded a case, setting up the portable miniguns that they brought. They formed a staggered perimeter around the entrance to the headquarters. The steady stream of bullets seemed to be working, keeping the UNIC reinforcements from advancing.

"That's right!" Santos exclaimed.

The rest of the team ran into the headquarters. Upon entering, it became obvious that it was going to be tiresome to get to the 100th floor. There were UNIC soldiers everywhere in the building.

"Commander, it looks like Vincere has arrived with the Forge," a resistance officer's voice said over the comms.

"What?! I thought Barnes said she was going to take care of him. Our ships won't last long with two starships up there," the commander replied between gunshots.

"He's here for a reason," Barnes said.

"Ok," the commander replied, he seemed confused by the answer.

"Sir, something's happening. He's activating the ship's offensive weapons," the voice again came over the comms.

"Barnes, can you please tell me how this is beneficial for us?" the commander asked.

"Sir, the Forge has just started to engage UNIC forces," the voice said.

"The Forge, they're not quite in control of their systems at the moment," Barnes said.

The team continued to the elevator, clearing forces as they moved. As they finished off the last of the soldiers in the lobby, they pressed the button, assuming they could bypass having to fight their way up the stairs. The elevator didn't respond as the building was on lockdown.

"A little help?" the commander asked.

"Oh, so I'm the elevator attendant now?" Barnes asked snidely.

The elevator system activated, and the door opened.

"Well there's no way we're all fitting in there," Taylor said as she peeked in.

"Ok, Taylor see if you can find a terminal on another

floor. We'll head up and deal with the council. I'm sure Toa and Coughlin wouldn't mind your help once you upload the videos," Jossen said as he stepped into the elevator.

As the commander hit the button for the 99th floor, the doors closed, and the elevator began to moan as it struggled to function.

"Is it supposed to take this long?" Jossen asked.

"You realize these things have a weight limit right? This elevator was designed for humans, not like the lifts on the Forge," Barnes responded.

As the elevator slowly departed, Taylor began searching for a terminal. She was able to locate one, but it was badly damaged by the firefight inside the lobby.

"There is a terminal on the 2nd floor. Stairs are just down the hall," Barnes replied.

"Watch your back guys, there's bound to be all kinds of obstacles up there," Taylor said as she headed for the stairs.

Back in the elevator, the slow pace of the ascent allowed Jossen, Harden, and the commander a moment of reprieve. The silence of the moment proved to be too much for the commander, recognizing an opportunity to lighten the mood.

"So, Taylor huh," the commander said as he turned to Harden.

"You don't get to ask," Harden responded.

"I'll take that as a yes," the commander shot back.

Jossen patted Harden's shoulder sympathetically. There was another brief moment of silence as the elevator came to a grinding halt. The doors opened slowly and revealed a long empty hallway. There were at least fifteen doors down the length of the corridor, but not one soldier to be seen.

"Let's take this slow, there are a lot of doors and anything could be behind any one of them," Jossen said.

The three of them moved slowly down the hall, training on each door as they moved. As they got within fifty feet of the last door at the end of the hall, two doors opened behind them. Several TITAN operators poured into the hallway.

"Contact," Harden said as Jossen and the commander turned around.

Jossen and Harden felt as though they were looking into a mirror through time, the standard-issue operator nanite suit stared back at them. Tension began to build as each operator stood motionless, turning fractions of a second into lifetimes.

TEN
PROTOCOL

AS THE UNSS Forge emerged from the spatial distortion, a chaotic battle was already underway. Hundreds of ships engaged each other above the Earth as the ground assault on the UNGA headquarter began. Vincere seemed surprised as the UNSS Spirit appeared to be having trouble fending off the attack.

"Launch the fighters and the swarms. Target every ship as an enemy," Admiral Vincere ordered upon seeing the mayhem.

"Sir, we would be targeting actual UNIC ships as well, we would be killing our own people," a voice responded.

"Target every ship. We will not allow the resistance to gain the advantage. That's an order and get me Admiral Capetolli, he needs to know we intend to target every ship," the Admiral commanded.

"Sir, we can't launch the fighters," a voice responded.

"Sir, we can't reach Admiral Capetolli," another voice said.

"Admiral, our weapons systems have begun to target

UNIC forces on the surface. We have no control over the weapons system!" another voice yelled.

"Understood. I want all systems manually shutdown. When we restart them, we will need to take manual control of all systems," Vincere instructed.

"That's going to take some time sir," Captain Rahni mentioned in a low tone as he stood beside the Admiral.

"We don't have a choice, without control, we are worse than sitting ducks. We will do more harm than good if we waste time trying to find out why these systems don't work," Vincere replied.

While the Admiral appeared annoyed on the outside, on the inside he was overjoyed. He couldn't have thought of a better position to be in than this. Instead of having to pretend as though he was trying to save the council, he could just as easily remain still and let the power struggle play out. *All that will be left is to clean up and assume power*, he thought to himself.

Meanwhile, in the hallway on the 99th floor of the UNGA headquarters, the tension between operators and former operators peaked. The momentary silence between former brothers broke as shots began to ring out. There was little room to maneuver but the standard ammunition barely stopped the TITANs forward movement.

"Nanite armor against nanite armor...this isn't going to end well," Jossen said as the operators advanced toward the team.

"What about nanite armor versus none?" the commander asked.

He pulled his mag-launcher and hit each of the operators. The projectiles hit their target and brought them to a sudden halt. They stood there frozen while Jossen and Harden remembered how it felt to be stuck in that magnetic field.

"Ummm, they still have their armor," Jossen noted.

"Do they?" the commander asked as he fired a shot from his pistol at each of the operators.

The rounds struck the nanite and their armor retreated back into the housing. The look of surprise on the operator's faces was all too familiar for Jossen and Harden. The operators stood there, completely exposed.

"Jones? What are you," Harden asked, recognizing him without the armor.

Before Harden could finish his question, the commander fired his rifle and hit each of the operators in the chest. They dropped immediately to the ground, no longer able to fight the magnetic force that had stopped their movement. Harden and Jossen stood there, attempting to process the fact they had just helped kill two of their own.

"Must be a shock, but I told you that these would be people you know and that we would need to stop them. You may think you can convince them there is another way, that what we are doing is right and they're on the wrong side of this, but this is not that time. If you hesitate like that again, you may be the one lying in a heap on the floor. They won't hesitate to kill you if they could, their mission is to stop you," the commander said as he slung his rifle.

"We know, but watching a TITAN die is not something we are used to. We just need to make sure the council pays for every fallen TITAN," Jossen responded.

"Listen, I've killed on both sides, and let me tell you that it never gets better, I remember every face, every single one. I may be good at what I do, you can say I was made for it but that doesn't change the fact that there is a consequence for each and every life I've taken," the commander said.

Jossen and Harden realized they couldn't afford to second guess themselves like that again. If they had done that on any other mission or even during a training exercise, they would've been killed. Everything seemed different now though, almost like they were watching the events in the hallway unfold in a movie.

The team continued through the door at the end of the hall. They found themselves in a large open room devoid of any people or furnishings, an eerie feeling began to creep up on them as they thought this would've been the perfect place for an ambush. They explored the area and found a singular large staircase that led to the 100th floor. They slowly made their way up the stairs, only to find more empty space, although this area seemed more like a lobby. There was a large circular UNGA seal on the floor and the wall in front of them curved with the seal. The wall had the letters UNGA in large print scrolled across it. As they took another step forward, doors opened in the wall and the council along with a team of guardians stepped out.

"This is finally over, we know everything, and we have evidence of what you've done," the commander said confidently.

"Over? You think this is over? We've obviously given you more credit than you deserve. You know nothing and you've accomplished nothing," Minister Yamato said.

"You think you have the upper hand? You think what you're doing will somehow bring peace? Your misguided thinking will do nothing but get people killed," Minister Sarapong added.

"Everyone will find out what you really are. The time of the council is over," Harden said defiantly.

"Not from where we stand," Minister Halin said.

The guardian team moved forward. They took up positions in front of the council, providing a living barrier. They didn't say a word as they stood there like statues. Their armor was exactly like an operator's, the only distinguishing feature was the deep blood red color.

"Don't make us do this. This isn't what we want," Jossen said to the guardians.

"If it's not what you wanted then you wouldn't be here," Minister Gantley replied.

The guardians ran toward the team. Jossen engaged one of the guardians up close, their movements were fast, and their hits were hard. Harden and the commander engaged two operators each. As Harden fought both off he reached for his pistol. He tried to fire on them but wasn't able to get a shot. The commander was in the same situation, trying to get a shot off with the pistol but not getting a clear shot.

"This can go on for quite some time," Minister Sarpong said to the other ministers while he watched the melee.

"The files have been uploaded," Taylor's voice came over the comms.

Her voice was enough to distract Harden for a split second, just enough to allow himself to be kicked in the chest, stumbling back as he regained his balance. This stumble gave him a momentary advantage to line up a shot. Harden fired the pistol, the guardian didn't attempt to dodge the bullet, thinking his armor provided more than enough protection. Once the shot struck the guardian, his armor began to deactivate. The rest of the guardians stood there stunned, watching as the defenseless TITAN stood there. The commander fired two shots in rapid succession, hitting the two guardians he was fighting. The other two guardians immediately rushed Jossen and Harden, knowing they had to move quickly to disarm the team. The commander fired twice in rapid succession, hitting them both and neutralizing the threat.

"I told you we didn't want this," Jossen said.

"Leave now, the council is no longer yours to protect.

They have lied to us all and will pay for what they've done. You've been deceived just as we were, nothing was what they claimed it to be," Harden said as he lowered his weapon.

The TITANs stood there for a moment, no longer guardians but weakened TITANs. They looked at the council and looked back at Jossen, Harden, and the commander.

"You TITANs should know better than anyone why we can't leave. We have a job to do and while it's not always easy or convenient, we have dedicated our lives to it," one of the TITANs replied.

"I understand completely," Jossen said with sadness.

Jossen turned to Harden and the commander then turned to look at the council. He reached for his rifle and turned to the TITANS. It only took two seconds for Jossen to put a bullet in all five of them. Jossen knew they wouldn't give up, that they would lay down their lives to protect the council, whether they had their nanites or not. The commander and Harden immediately focused their weapons on the council members.

"Just so you know, their deaths are on your hands, after all, you are the ones who made them that loyal right? Loyal to a fault, willing to lay down their lives to protect your lies," Jossen said.

"Ok, what's one more life, or five? So what now? We stand trial or you just execute us here, then what? Who takes our place? Someone has to ensure that humanity can continue to exist," Minister Gantley asked.

"It doesn't matter who takes your place. I'm here for justice, not just for me but for every life the council has destroyed," Harden said as he took a step forward.

"And what of the billions of lives that have been saved? Is there justice for the billions we've helped? You look at the lives destroyed but not the lives saved, seems a bit short sighted if you ask me," Minister Guerrero asked.

"I don't care about the good you think you've done. I've seen the devastation brought about by the UNGA, more specifically the council. The good that you think you've done is an illusion, nothing more than misdirection," the commander replied.

"You and your new recruits must not think too highly of us. I'm sure Barnes informed you of what we have built, what we have done, and what we are willing to do to ensure humanity's survival," Minister Gantley said.

"At this point, I'm honestly tired of the back and forth," the commander aimed his rifle at Gantley.

"You've seen the files from Barnes' data card I assume? You have probably even seen what she had hidden on that ancient USB drive of hers, although I doubt you know the whole story or you wouldn't be standing in front of us right now," Minister Gantley asked.

"We've seen the data on Project Olympus and that's exactly why we're here. We're not going to let you tighten your grip on humanity by unleashing those monsters on your own people," Jossen said sternly.

"Then I assumed correctly, you weren't able to decrypt all of the files. Either that or you aren't intelligent enough to put all of the pieces together," the minister responded.

"You know what, I agree with Harden, we aren't getting anywhere. Let's just finish this now," Jossen said as he took aim with his rifle.

"Wait!" Barnes' voice was heard in the room.

"I thought that might draw you out. You have access to all of our files I assume," Minister Gantley said.

"Yes," she responded bluntly.

"Why don't you take a look at the files under the

Encounter Protocol? It has several layers of the best encryption money can buy, so even with your new form, it should still take a moment" he said as he stared at the team.

"Hey guys, the videos have been uploaded. Barnes, can you help get these out to everyone?" Taylor's voice cut through the tension.

"Nice work Taylor," Harden remarked, happy to hear her voice.

"Did you find anything else on that treaty we were discussing earlier?" Harden asked Taylor.

"No, I was going to upload them to the system to see if Barnes could," Taylor was interrupted.

"How could you?" Barnes' voice felt like a kick to the gut.

"Well there's no point in being subtle now, why don't you tell your people what you found?" Minister Gantley asked.

"This is...I don't understand. How is this?" Barnes had a hard time finding the words.

"Barnes, you better start making some sense soon or we're going to just call it a day here and finish this up," the commander said.

"The treaty they signed. They used me, they used us all," Barnes said.

"Allow me to enlighten you as it seems Barnes can't find the words. In the year 1947, a ship crash-landed in a desert in the United States. Many assumed that the crash was the result of an accident, but we later found out that it was no accident. The ship was piloted by an extraterrestrial being, sent on a mission to bring humanity a means of salvation... technology that would allow the human race to protect itself against a threat that had been moving across the galaxy for hundreds of millions of years. These technological advancements did not come without a cost though," Minister Guerrero said.

"This being informed the government of the time that there were several races of intelligent beings in the cosmos. Each of these races had previously visited Earth, each also having different purposes and agendas. One race, in particular, was interested in the human race as slaves and test subjects. They would come to Earth and abduct humans periodically, as there wasn't much the governments could do to protect their people at the time, they were called harvesters. Another race was interested in saving the species of the Earth, in their mind, all living things had a place in the universe, we called this species, advisors. While they had already developed defenses against the more hostile race, they noticed that we were ill-equipped to handle any type of attack. They offered the nanites and the cores as a way to develop the defenses required to repel any attack by these creatures but did not provide the necessary knowledge to utilize either one. They knew we weren't ready, but once we were able to unlock their secrets, then and only then would we have a chance," Minister Halin continued.

"For the longest time, we heard nothing from any other species. We continued to research the nanites and the core that was provided during that first interaction. It took almost 80 years to understand the technology in any meaningful way. Our organizations had been working on these technologies feverishly, trying to develop them to ensure that if these hostile species did come back, that we would be able to defend ourselves, save our own species. It wasn't until after the climate crisis and the great war that we were really able to make significant advances. Someone must have been paying attention, as the first time we utilized the SDD, the species we had been warned about made contact," Minister Sarpong said.

"Their demands were simple. They required a set

amount of humans, approximately 100,000 per year, to be sent to predetermined coordinates. If we were to provide them these humans, they would have no need to show up at our doorstep. It became difficult to *lose* that many humans every year though, especially after the war ended and we had our own work to do. We needed to come up with a new way. We found a useful scapegoat in the resistance. They provided us cover for the abductions while allowing us to focus almost unlimited resources toward the war effort, toward developing the TITANs," Minister Yamato said as he was cut off.

"The colony, the outpost, that was?" Barnes asked.

"That's right. We've had to do this ever since we became a spacefaring species. At this point, we've sent them millions. Still, it is nothing compared to what would happen if we did not," Minister Gantley said.

"So the TITAN program was developed to defend humanity from these beings? What of Project Olympus then, just a better defense for when they come for us all?" Harden asked.

"Project Olympus was created after we received a communication from the harvesters. It took years to decode, although we didn't have you working on it Barnes, if we did, it might've been decoded sooner. The communication referenced stopping the human race from injecting the nanites into a living human weapon, that if it were to occur, humanity would be able to destroy the harvesters," Minister Gantley replied.

"We did what we needed to do to keep humanity safe. What is a million when compared to a billion? What is billion compared to ten billion? You think you know what's right and what's wrong, but I assure you, you have absolutely no idea," Minister Gantley continued.

"So we are supposed to let five people decide the fate of

humanity? Let the puppet masters pull the strings, deciding who lives and who dies, who is taken from their families, who gets experimented on. This has to end," the commander said.

"If not us then who? If we hadn't acted when we did, sacrificed what we have, all of this may not exist. While we may have lost our humanity, it was always to ensure the survival of the species, to ensure others didn't have to lose theirs. Without the UNGA, the world would still be in chaos, we would have fallen victim to these harvesters long ago. Our entire species would be dead or enslaved," Minister Halin interjected.

"You may think you've saved humanity, but in reality, you've simply traded our freedom for existence, one form of slavery for another. I would like to believe that if given a choice, people would rather fight to the death than turn over their fellow man to these things. Humanity has always waged war on each other, I know that suffering has always been a part of our history. The good news is our history is also full of perseverance, kindness, unity, and victory in the face of insurmountable odds. You never gave us a chance, you decided from the beginning which path we would take. Well, that ends now," Harden said.

"Indeed it does. The weapons developed in Project Olympus were created based on the communication from the harvesters. It seems, however, we were wrong in assuming that what Project Olympus created would be able to stop the harvesters. What the director didn't and more than likely still doesn't know is that there was a second batch of subjects at a secondary site. This facility housed one million test subjects and were farther along than the tests being conducted on the Forge. We needed the director to believe that the test subjects she was working on were the only ones. When she told us about the subjects, we already knew the results. In fact, the harvesters had already infiltrated the secondary facility, somehow converting the subjects to do their bidding. These harvesters then used the test subjects to abduct the colonists. It seems we were fooled, we now believe the message was meant to encourage us to perform these tests, we provided the harvesters with a new weapon," Minister Gantley said.

Harden was done listening to the council, with Jossen and the commander following his lead, they backed the council against the wall. They always knew this day might come, the day when they were outplayed. As the council backed against the wall, Jossen moved to grab Minister Sarpong. Jossen's hand slid through the minister's holographic arm.

"What?" Jossen asked.

"What, do you honestly think we would stay in this building knowing that you were planning an assault? Do you think we would wait around for another attack from the harvesters? You still don't understand, this is the long game. We plan for every eventual outcome. Our goal has always been to ensure humanity's survival and today is no different. We have taken an arc of sorts, loading some of humanity's best and brightest to ensure that whatever happens, our species survives," Minister Sarpong said.

"Commander, I'm detecting a spatial distortion above Earth. The energy signature is not one that is recognized in any system," Barnes said.

"Uh, I'm going to need more information than that," the commander responded.

"We truly hope that you survive them. Regardless of what you think of us, we were and will always be on the side of humanity," Minister Gantley remarked as the projections faded.

Warnings began to sound throughout the building. The

team moved to the window and looked up at the sky. From their vantage point, they couldn't see anything other than the ships still engaged in battle.

"You all need to get out there now. The energy signature is from one of *their* ships, it has already launched fighters, and they are targeting all human ships. I've activated the Spirit's defenses, but the Forge is under manual control. I'm working on reactivating the planetary defenses, but it will take some time before they are operational," Barnes said.

Jossen, Harden, and the commander raced back to the elevator. As they reached the ground floor, they headed straight through the lobby to the entrance. Toa, Coughlin, and Taylor were outside along with Sierra and Kilo teams. As they all gathered in front of the building, they witnessed hundreds of alien ships engaging both UNIC and resistance fighters in the skies. The UNIC and resistance soldiers that had been focused on battling each other stood there, gawking in complete shock at what they were seeing.

"What the hell is all that?" Toa asked.

"I would guess those are the harvesters," the commander said as he watched larger ships descend to the surface.

"We need to move!" the commander said.

The commander noticed that the larger ships appeared to be positioning to unload troops. As they got closer to the surface, they were able to see the ships in more detail. The exterior of the ship appeared to be made entirely of nanites, a deep grey in color. It was about the size of a UNIC Condor but looked more like an elongated egg turned on its side. The nanites retreated from the sides creating an opening, through the opening, the team could see that the troops being carried were the same creatures they saw in the footage from the outpost. The creatures began jumping off the ships, landing with a noticeable impact on the ground below.

"We can't let these things get the upper hand. Sierra, Kilo, gather these UNIC soldiers and set up defensive positions. Delta, Lieutenant, you're with me. Let's go welcome our new visitors," the commander said as he spotted the closest of the dropships.

"You heard the commander, let's move! Who's in charge here?" Santos asked as his team approached a group of UNIC soldiers.

"Corporal Briggs," the corporal said.

"Ok corporal, we need to set up defensive positions. Let's start with the heavy weaponry in the back, get these soldiers up to the front. We need barriers in place asap and where are the rhinos and badgers?" Santos directed as he laid out the defense.

"You heard the man!" the corporal shouted at his soldiers.

The UNIC soldiers began to move with a purpose. They began deploying the heavy weapons while moving cases of munitions to the front lines. It seemed like too little too late, but they had no other choice, the enemy was already advancing.

"I need rhinos and badgers out here asap!" the corporal shouted into his comms.

Back on the Forge, UNIC personnel were scrambling to identify the unknown ship. The fact that the ship was put under manual control made everyone's jobs much more difficult. Admiral Vincere had immediately ordered defensive actions upon seeing the large unidentified ship appear from the distortion. Admiral Vincere had been caught completely off guard by this turn of events, trying desperately to find a way to turn this in his favor.

"I want to know what that thing is right now!" he

demanded as his crew had little capability to provide him with answers.

"Do we have any ability to communicate? We need to reach the council," he asked.

"Sir, we have tried multiple attempts, but we can't reach the council. We have been monitoring the UNGA feeds and it seems that someone has uploaded videos of the council members executing a wounded UNIC soldier and one that appeared to show them, growing people. The video is saying that the UNGA isn't what we think it is, that they have fabricated this war to remain in power. It is suggesting that the council is to blame for the missing colonists," the soldier said with uncertainty.

"So the council is either dead or in hiding. I need to get to the surface as soon as possible. Without the council, without the proper leadership, we don't stand a chance. Ready my ship, I'm going down there," Vincere commanded.

"Yes sir!" Captain Rahni replied as he made the preparations.

At the same time, Admiral Capetolli tried desperately to get control of the Spirit. His crew was working diligently to determine what was causing the systems to act seemingly on their own. A captain came running up to the Admiral, stopping for just a moment to catch his breath.

"Sir, we have identified that Admiral Vincere is headed to Earth's surface. We believe that he is attempting to establish order given the unknown status of the Council," Captain Wetyzak said.

"If the council is dead, Admiral Vincere will want to gain control of the UNGA as soon as he can. With this new threat, I'm not quite sure which is worse," Admiral Capetolli remarked.

"I understand your hesitation to trust Vincere," Barnes' voice was heard throughout the bridge of the Spirit.

"Director Barnes?" the Admiral asked confused.

"Yes Admiral," she responded

"How is this possible?" he asked.

"I'll explain later, we don't have time for that now. I will be turning the Spirit's systems back over to you. We need your help to take out this new threat," she said as systems began coming back online.

"What exactly is this new threat?" he asked

"We are not completely sure. We know that they are an advanced species and are responsible for all of the missing colonists. I will be bringing the Forge's systems back up as well, but I have to wait for Admiral Vincere to depart," Barnes said.

"Understood. What about this capital ship, should we be focusing all firepower on that?" Capetolli asked.

"I will handle the capital ship," Barnes said.

On the Forge, preparations for the Admiral's departure were finalized.

"Admiral Vincere, your ship is ready," Captain Rahni said.

"Good, I will depart immediately. You have the con," Admiral Vincere said as he exited the bridge.

He made his way to a heavily fortified falcon. He entered the ship with a team of operators. He had every intention to take charge of the UNGA, although many onboard the Forge had no idea.

"We need to get to UNGA headquarters immediately," he instructed the pilot.

"Yes sir," the pilot responded as he plotted the course.

The falcon took off, the space around the Forge was littered with enemy ships. They did their best to engage enemy ships while performing evasive maneuvers. After a brief detour, they began to head toward Earth.

"I'm sorry Admiral but I can't allow you to reach the surface," Barnes' voice was heard over the comms in the falcon.

The Admiral quickly disengaged the harness and moved to the cockpit. He watched through the display as the falcon began to course correct, lining up directly with the capital ship. The Admiral was a smart man, he recognized what was happening immediately.

"Sir, the controls aren't responding. Navigation is locking in a new course. I have no control!" the pilot said as he frantically attempted to override the controls.

Back on the ground, a harvester drop ship hovered over the ground just about a klick and a half away from the commander. Creatures began dropping out of the ship, impacting the ground with tremendous force as they seemed completely unfazed by the drop. It was hard to make out what they looked like from the distance, but they appeared to be large dark distorted figures.

"Barnes, we could really use those planetary defenses," the commander said as he and the team tried to close the gap between them and the harvesters as quickly as possible.

"I'm working on it. It shouldn't be too much longer," Barnes replied.

"I count ten of them," Jossen said as the creatures lumbered toward them.

"Toa, Coughlin, take out the ones on the left. Harden, Taylor, take out the right. The commander, lieutenant, and I will go up the middle," Jossen continued.

The team split up, not sure exactly what to expect as they closed the gap. The team began to open fire as they approached. While the bullets hit their intended targets, they didn't seem to have much effect. The harvesters continued toward them, not returning fire, as they did not appear to have any projectile weapons.

"These rifles aren't doing much damage, any suggestions?" the commander asked the team.

"I think we need to get closer, try to find a weakness," Taylor suggested.

"Maybe we just go at them hand to hand," Toa said sarcastically.

"She's right, we need to find a weak spot. Let's try to divide and conquer," Harden said.

The closer they got, the clearer they could see their enemy. They had already seen the humanoid figures from the video, the long legs and arms, but other features became distinguishable as well. The dark nanite skin was a rough texture, similar to a porous rock. Their heads were elongated and had what looked like thick plates from the forehead stretching back behind the head. They had two sets of eyes, spaced further apart than a normal human's, with one set on top of the other. The same thick plating that was present on the forehead also extended down a thin strip where the nose would be on a typical human face. This strip of plating mushroomed at the bottom, extending beyond the face.

The same plates that protected the creature's head also protected other areas as well. Plates seemed most prominent around vital human organs. The chest was covered with plates and extended down the midsection. The creature's back had plating from the base of the skull down to the small of the back, seemingly protecting the spine.

Jossen approached one of the harvesters, shooting him point-blank with the AAR, as the bullets hit the creature, Jossen witnessed why the bullets had little effect. As the bullet struck the plate and left a small indent, it began repairing itself.

"The plates are pure nanites," he said as the others began to engage their targets.

Toa came face to face with one of the harvesters. As the harvester swung his arm, Toa was able to dodge it, while landing a blow to the creature's chest. The harvester looked down slightly at him, unfazed, as if Toa were an insect. The creature swatted Toa and this time landed a blow that sent Toa into the air.

"Toa!" Coughlin said as she rushed the harvester, firing repeated shots from her TSG.

Toa struggled to get back to his feet, it took him a moment, but he realized Coughlin needed him. As the harvester turned toward Coughlin though, Toa noticed something.

"The side of their head. There's a spot near where I guess an ear would be, it doesn't have the plating," he said as he grabbed the carbon fiber knife and lunged at it.

The harvester turned quickly, grabbing Toa in midair with its long rough fingers, and slammed him to the ground. The harvester stepped on Toa's chest, the weight of the harvester not only pinned Toa but created fractures in his armor. As the harvester pulled back his arm to deliver a devastating blow to Toa, Coughlin pressed the TSG between the plates against the side of the harvester's head and pulled the trigger. Even the nanite skin wasn't able to protect against that kind of point-blank carnage, the harvester dropped in a lifeless heap on the ground.

"Nice shot girl!" Toa exclaimed as the harvester landed next to him.

"Yeah, well it's not over yet. Plenty of time for you to make it up to me, except this time, try not to get pinned,"

Coughlin responded as she continued to engage the remaining harvesters.

The rest of the team were dealing with their own encounters. The commander rushed one of the harvesters, letting rounds fly as though he had unlimited ammo. As the commander reloaded, the harvester came within feet. The clip clicked into place as the commander fired round after round into the creature's face, eventually hitting it in the eyes. The creature let out a horrific howl as the commander continued his assault, emptying the clip into its face until the creature fell.

"Another down, their eyes don't have plating either," the commander said.

As the team identified the weak spots on the harvesters, they relayed them to the rest of the UNIC. Unfortunately, more dropships kept coming, dropping harvesters as they passed above. The team finished off the remaining group of harvesters in a chaotic but coordinated effort. Dozens of rhino tanks finally mobilized and took aim at the dropships, hitting them with DELaWs and railguns. Some of the dropships crashed to the ground while others returned fire, shooting small but powerful green blobs. The blobs themselves were the size of a soda can but upon impact, devastated their target, causing an explosion that left several tanks in smoldering twisted craters.

"We need to take out their flagship. If we don't, these things will keep coming and tear us apart," the commander said.

"Jossen!" the lieutenant screamed.

Everyone turned to see a recently dropped harvester holding Jossen up off the ground by his neck. In the chaos and confusion, it seemed that a harvester had gotten behind him. Jossen struggled to aim his rifle behind him, firing one-handed as the bullets struck the harvester's armor. Harden lined up a shot, letting a round fly. The round hit the plating, damaging it enough that one more might be enough to drop it. He pulled the trigger a second time but not before the harvester ran his hand through Jossen's midsection, cracking through the TITAN's armor. The round ripped through the weakened plate of the harvester, dropping it as both Jossen and the harvester fell to the ground. The team rushed over, knowing they were already too late. Jossen gasped for air as the team stood around him in shock.

"Jossen," Taylor said as she grabbed his hand.

Jossen struggled to breathe while the team tried to comfort him. He choked his final breath as his arm went limp. The team was silent, still processing the loss when a laser fired just over their heads. A dropship that was headed right for them was struck, blasting a hole clean through it. The ship began to fall from the sky, heading right toward the team. Harden grabbed Jossen's lifeless body as the team ran for cover.

"Planetary defenses active," Barnes came over the comms.

DELaW turrets throughout Renata became active, firing on the enemy ships in rapid succession. UNIC and resistance fighters watched as the dropships and enemy fighters came crashing to the ground. Above the Earth, satellites launched their assault, targeting the enemy's energy signature. The capital ship started to maneuver, appearing to ready a weapon of some kind.

Back on the falcon, the Admiral already knew his fate. He had been outplayed, no different than a game of chess. He thought he had the pieces in place, but it was Barnes that controlled the board. Even at a time like this, Admiral Vincere had to admire Barnes, while being beaten was bad, he took comfort knowing that he was beaten by one of the best.

"Well played Barnes. I have always admired your determination, the sheer force of will that allowed you to always succeed, even when we believed you failed," Admiral Vincere conceded.

"Admiral, your sacrifice will not be in vain. Your contribution will be remembered by humanity as one of selflessness after today. Just so you know, I never wanted it to end this way, but you made your play," Barnes said.

"Indeed I did, and I wouldn't change a thing. They were on to you for a while, I had no choice but to play the hand I was dealt," Vincere replied.

"That's always been humanity's problem. *Playing the hand you're dealt*, instead of changing the game to suit your hand," Barnes said.

"Sir the SDD is activating. The coordinates are set for," the pilot said.

"How fitting, you even managed to throw a little icing on the cake huh?" Vincere asked.

"Seemed like the least I could do, to send these creatures to the same inescapable fate as the first TITANs, except this time there will be no way out," Barnes replied.

As the falcon approached the capital ship, a distortion began to appear ahead of it. Enemy fighters turned to engage the falcon, but by then, it was already too late. The distortion moved with the falcon and encompassed a third of the enemy ship as the falcon creened toward the capital ship. Just at the moment of impact, the distortion dissipated, and a third of the capital ship was transported to the coordinates set by Barnes. Admiral Capetolli watched as the remnants of the destroyed capital ship spewed light and gas. It hung there, suspended in space, completely disabled.

"I want everything we have launched at what's left of that ship, I don't want to see a piece larger than my boot floating around," Admiral Capetolli ordered. The Spirit immediately began firing relentlessly on the mostly destroyed ship, breaking the debris into smaller and smaller pieces.

While all of this was happening, humanity's forces were still battling the harvesters on the ground. Harden and the team got behind cover, the dropship billowed smoke as it came closer and closer to the ground. The edges of the gaping hole that the laser created still glowed red hot, sending sparks and molted materials raining down on the Earth below. Several harvesters jumped from the ship before it crashed. As the ship gouged a long rut in the ground, it came to a stop in front of the barrier the team was behind. The harvesters not far behind the ship came charging at the team.

"Here they come!" the Lieutenant shouted.

The team sprang into action, Harden being the first to engage. He stood up, SR in hand, and began firing on every open target. He focused on the weak points identified in the earlier encounter, firing a shot through the eye of one harvester while tearing through the side of another's head. The rest of the team engaged as well, running out to meet their enemy face to face. Toa and Coughlin attempted to tag team one of the harvesters, Toa distracting while Coughlin positioned for the kill. Taylor and the commander did the same, dodging attacks while taking every opportunity to strike the vital points. Harden continued supporting the team, picking off harvester after harvester with well-placed shots from his sniper rifle. It wasn't long before he ran out of ammo.

"I'm out," Harden said as he threw down the rifle.

The lieutenant remained behind cover with Jossen's body, firing everything she had to distract the harvesters as much as possible. She knew she wouldn't be able to defend herself in an up-close encounter, choosing to support the team from a distance. Toa was taking a beating for Coughlin as they dispatched as many harvesters as they could.

"They just seem to keep coming. So we took out the dropships but it's not helping with the harvesters already on the ground," Toa exclaimed as he engaged another harvester.

"Lieutenant, we need some heavier firepower," the commander said.

"On it," the lieutenant replied, leaving Jossen's body behind as she retreated.

"Commander!" Harden yelled as he noticed three harvesters charging him.

Taylor turned to look as the harvesters approached the commander. He stood his ground as they encircled him. The commander kept his eyes on all three, pivoting to ensure they didn't surprise him. The first harvester lunged at the commander as he moved to the side, dodging the attack. The second grabbed him, lifting him into the air and slamming him to the ground. The third approached, threatening a debilitating blow. Taylor launched herself into the middle of the melee, knocking one of the harvesters to the ground, allowing the commander to get to his feet.

"Taylor!" Harden yelled as he ran up behind one of the harvesters.

Harden plunged his carbon-fiber knife into a razor-thin space between nanite plating at the base of the harvester's neck. The harvester let out a blood-curdling screech as it turned to face Harden, the knife still in the base of its neck. As the harvester faced him, harden threw a punch, the harvester grabbed his fist. Harden attempted to break free, but the harvester grabbed his other hand. It lifted him up, seemingly trying to rip his arms off. Harden's deep groan became louder as the force became almost unbearable, the sound of cracking armor foreshadowed what was about to happen. All of the sudden, the harvester let go, dropping Harden to the ground. Harden looked up as the harvester stood there, staggering before falling to the ground. Taylor stood behind it, holding out her hand, and pulled Harden to his feet.

"Just needed a little more force," she said, referring to the knife that he left in the harvester's neck.

They looked at each other for just a second before Taylor saw the reflection in Harden's visor. The commander was still surrounded by harvesters. Taylor and Harden quickly turned to face the situation, just in time to witness the commander raising up what looked like a small canister.

"Don't do it!" Harden yelled as he took a step forward.

The blast that emanated from the canister was enough to send both Taylor and Harden catapulting backward. The heat and force from the blast stripped away layers of the nanite armor, leaving most of it compromised. They both laid on their backs as they realized what had happened. The sky seemed to be alive; swarms of ships moving like flocks of birds, debris streaking across the sky as it burned up in the atmosphere, and starships appearing as small moons in the heavens. They both sat up, surveying the devastation the thermogrenade caused. The charred crater that was left told the story of the ultimate sacrifice.

"No!" the lieutenant screamed as she came running to the scene.

She had gotten back just in time to witness the blast. She dropped to her knees, crying hysterically as her face was in her hands. Harden and Taylor got to their feet, their armor still charred and smoking. They took a quick look around, noticing there weren't many harvesters left. A couple of harvesters were making their way toward the group as Toa and Coughlin joined Taylor and Harden. They were silent, prepared to defend the grieving lieutenant as the harvesters approached.

"You monsters! You took him from me!" she screamed as she jumped to her feet.

The lieutenant looked over her shoulder as the rhino she was waiting on rolled over the hill. She ran over to it while the team fell back, still ready to defend her and themselves. The lieutenant jumped into the rhino, unleashing everything the rhino had on the approaching harvesters. The first harvester was struck by a laser to the chest, while the other two scattered. The lieutenant was used to the movements of the harvesters, having witnessed and engaged TITANs in the past. She led the first with the railgun, firing once she had a beat on it. The projectile struck the harvester in the stomach, nearly tearing it in half. The other harvester had made its way closer to the rhino, as the team prepared to engage.

"Don't you dare, this one is mine," the lieutenant said as the team moved.

The harvester jumped onto the rhino, prepared to open it like a tin can. It began peeling the armor plating off, looking for the human inside. The harvester finally peeled back the inner layer, revealing the lieutenant inside. As the two locked eyes, the harvester's head disappeared in a bright red flash. The lieutenant had been slowly positioning a laser directly at the harvester's head. The lifeless body slid off of the rhino, falling to the ground. The lieutenant then proceeded to continuously drive over the body, crushing it with each back and forth. Once she was satisfied, she exited the rhino. The team stood by, not sure what mental state the lieutenant was in.

The battle was wrapping up above Earth, the Forge

targeting all remaining enemy fighters. It wasn't long before they were all destroyed. The remaining UNIC and resistance ships made their way to the surface to assist the ground forces with the cleanup. Soon the skies above Earth were crowded with falcons, Ospreys, and Condors chasing down any and all enemy forces.

As the team carried Jossen's body back to UNGA headquarters, they witnessed the destruction all around them. The landscape was scarred with wreckage, human and harvester bodies lay scattered. As the team approached, Jennings and Santos stood silent. Harden gently placed Jossen's body on the ground, as both UNIC and resistance soldiers gather around.

"He sacrificed himself for us, for all of us just like he always said he would," Harden lamented.

"And we will not follow the mistakes of the past, his sacrifice and Commander Hanlon's is not for the foolish pursuits of the past. Their sacrifice is for everything humanity stands for, everything it could be," the lieutenant remarked.

The team stood there for a moment, looking at all of the soldiers who had gathered around them. They saw the same soldiers that only a day ago would be killing each other, standing side by side, fighting side by side. They stood there in victory, each one of them covered in dirt and blood, now bearing the scars of war. A war that would span humanity's differences, a war for survival of the species.

Several soldiers stepped forward, lifting up Jossen's body. They held him high and carried him to the entrance of the UNGA. They placed him on top of the concrete monument to humanity's fallen. All of the hundreds of soldiers who gathered stood at attention; the UNIC, the resistance, all saluted the ones who sacrificed themselves today. The lieutenant stepped forward, laying a destroyed AAR-10 at the bottom of the monument. She then turned to address the crowd.

"The human race faces its greatest challenge. One that will require us to set aside our differences, our petty squabbles, and face this new future with a renewed unity. We have attacked each other for long enough. Today we found that it doesn't matter what we call ourselves, how we define our affiliations, or what side we're on. The only thing that matters is our survival. We are up against a new enemy, one that doesn't distinguish between UNIC or resistance, one that doesn't care about civilians or combatants, one that has no regard for human life. We must unite, we must come together as a species if we have any chance of victory," she said as she paused, holding back the tears that began to well up.

"We must honor the sacrifices that have been made today, sacrifices that have been made on both sides. We can, no we will come together to face this unprecedented threat. We will come together, and we will be victorious. Losing this war is not an option, failing is not an option. Our friends and families will be counting on us, we must be prepared to do everything we can to confront this new enemy. I know that we can, I believe that if we stand united, we can face this new threat and free humanity from the struggles that have plagued us for far too long!" the lieutenant said.

The crowd cheered, knowing that things were indeed different now. The lies of the past were now diminished, everything that had torn humanity apart seemed insignificant. Humanity would have to look to a new leader, one who could pick up the pieces and reshape existence into what it was meant to be. Once the cheers died down a bit, a voice was heard from the crowd.

"Who will take the place of the council? Who is going to be in charge?" the crowd asked.

"That's not up to any one person, that will fall to each and every one of us. We the people must decide who will lead humanity now. Our destiny is now within our grasp but seizing it is no easy task. Just know that we will keep fighting to ensure we protect what matters most, regardless of what the future holds," she said.

The team stepped up to support the lieutenant, saluting her, while the rest of the crowd followed their lead. As the team stepped back the crowd cheered once again, lifting the lieutenant in celebration. As they watched, they couldn't help but remain somber, knowing that this new enemy may have been pushed back but they weren't defeated.

"Harden, Taylor, Toa, Coughlin," Barnes' voice came across the comms.

"I am truly sorry about Jossen and the commander. This is a devastating loss, but you must not lose heart. You will be needed now more than ever. This isn't over, it is only beginning. I have gone over the information in the council's files and there is much to tell. I am sending a falcon to bring you back to the Forge. We have a lot to catch up on," Barnes said as a falcon approached.

Harden turned to the team, cocking his head to the side as Jossen used to. The rest of the team nodded in agreement before boarding the falcon. As the falcon lifted off, the crowds on the ground could be seen celebrating the victory. Harden knew this celebration would be short-lived as an important question remained, who had sent the harvesters in the first place?

Visit www.michaellanebooks.com for information on additional books in the Humanity Remade Series